First Sunday in October

A Novel

Wanda B. Campbell

MICAH 6:8
BOOKS

Author's Note

First Sunday in October is the "baby" that paved the way for my literary career. When I picked up a pen and writing pad on December 13, 2005, I had no idea eight years later I would have eight "babies" in print –all bestsellers. **TO GOD BE THE GLORY!**

Those of you who have read the original version will notice a few changes that enhance the storyline, and you will see my growth as a writer. Many of you have followed me from the beginning. "Thank You" is not enough to express my appreciation. Without readers the journey would be very lonely an unfulfilling.

If this is your first Wanda B. Campbell novel, welcome. Thank you for investing your time and resources. I hope you enjoy the Simones as much as I do.

I enjoy hearing from readers. Feel free to email me at: **wbcampbell@prodigy.net.** You may also join my Facebook group: **Wanda B. Campbell Readers and Supporters.**

Enjoy!

Other books in the Simone Series:
Book 2 – Games, Coming 2014
Book 3 – Liberation (2012)
Book 4 – Unresolved Issues (2012)

Chapter 1

"No, not now," Julia groaned as the alarm clock went off. She stretched her arms above her head and squinted at the big red bold numbers. It couldn't be 6:00 a.m. already, but the early morning October sunlight coming through her window confirmed it. Julia sat on the side of her bed and looked around her spacious bedroom while she warmed her feet in the soft fibers of the plush carpet. As with the two previous days, thoughts assessing her life flooded her mind.

Julia Renee Simone had everything a woman, or anyone else for that matter, could possibly want—materialistically. Life was good. She could buy whatever she wanted, whenever she wanted and could go wherever she wanted. She was the fifth of Carey and Ana Simone's eight children. With two older brothers, two older sisters, two younger brothers and a younger sister, there was always someone looking out for her and she was always looking out for someone. The Simones were a close-knit family. A day rarely passed without some form of communication from a family member. Their family motto was: "People come and people go, but your family will always be here." Sure they disagreed as children and even as adults, but they never allowed a difference of opinion to divide them. Carey and Ana wouldn't allow it.

In the early years, the family had struggled just to keep food on the table while Carey worked day and night trying to start his architectural and construction business. His faith in God, hard work and perseverance paid off. Today, The Simone Company was highly respected in the industry. Currently, four of Julia's siblings ran the company, with Carey Sr. serving as CEO. Julia's remaining siblings worked in the area of law enforcement and medicine.

Julia inherited her father's business sense. She started her own real estate development company, Pinnacle Developments, when she was only twenty-three years old, after the untimely and tragic death of her first husband, Sean. For her, it was love at first sight. At least that's what she thought. She later realized she was in love with the idea of being in love.

She'd met Sean Hampton on campus at UC Berkeley during the second semester of her freshman year. Julia was flattered when the upperclassman took an interest in her. They dated for three years and were married one month after she graduated. They were ecstatic when, after only six months, Julia became pregnant. Unfortunately, Sean was struck and killed by a drunk driver while he was changing a flat tire on Interstate 80, when Julia was eight months pregnant. The birth of her only child should have been a happy event, but for Julia it was bittersweet. LaShay Hampton was born exactly thirty days after her father's death. Her resemblance to her father was daunting. Sean Hampton, being a successful stockbroker, planned well for his young family's future. He made sure that neither Julia nor his unborn child would ever want for anything in the event of his untimely departure. Julia used some of the insurance money to start her company. God had blessed her business and now she was a multi-millionaire with millions in assets from one tip of California to the other.

Now, at age forty, life was good, or so she thought. It had not always been easy for her, but life was still good. With God's help, she survived the death of one husband, a loveless and abusive second marriage, a devastating miscarriage and all the ups and downs of being a single parent, as well as numerous failed relationships. LaShay was now eighteen and a college freshman at Stanford University and Julia still looked youthful. She was a perfect size ten. She worked out every morning in order to keep her body fit, which was the reason her alarm clock was going off at 6:00 a.m. on a Sunday morning. Even on Sundays she'd have her meditation time and ride her treadmill and StairMaster before going to church.

People often mistook Julia and LaShay for sisters. They both were five-foot-seven, and had the same smooth cappuccino skin and shared the same size clothing. LaShay mirrored her father's face, but her long legs and curvy hips came straight from her mother. Julia's French and African-American heritage gave her long thick curly black hair, while LaShay enjoyed shoulder-length silky hair. The two were more than mother and daughter; they were best friends. They'd cried together, laughed together, and had grown up together. Julia couldn't be happier now that LaShay was away at college, even if Palo Alto was only one hour away from her secluded Blackhawk estate. She loved her daughter unconditionally, but recently came to realize that she'd put so much energy into her daughter that she had somehow lost sight of the things that made her happy. Julia realized that outside of Shay, as she fondly referred to her daughter, work and church on Sunday, there really wasn't much to her life. When Shay moved into the dorms two months ago, she realized how alone and incomplete she was.

Sure she had her family, but her siblings were spread throughout California, except for her older brother Jonathan, who practiced law in Arizona. They each had families of their own. She and the youngest, Andre, were the only unmarried members in the family. Now was the time for her to find out what made her happy.

Julia had always enjoyed running her business and was very proud of its success, but lately she didn't find it fulfilling anymore. She enjoyed going to church on Sundays, but felt that there was more she should be doing with the ministry; she just didn't know what. She'd rededicated her life to Christ six years prior and was growing closer to Him every day. Today she would start to find out where God wanted her and what he wanted from her.

Julia slipped from the bed and fell to her knees. With adoration and thanksgiving, she opened her mouth and poured out her emotions. Julia felt God leading her to Proverbs Chapter 3. She opened her Bible and began reading at the first verse. She stopped at the fifth verse.

Trust in the LORD with all thine heart; and lean not unto thine own understanding.

"God, I don't understand why I'm so uncomfortable with my life right now. Show me how to trust you with my whole heart," Julia whispered from her heart, then continued reading the next verse.

In all thy ways acknowledge him, and he shall direct thy path.

Julia closed the Bible and talked to God. "Heavenly Father, I acknowledge you as all-knowing and everlasting. You are a great and merciful God whom I love with my whole heart. My desire is to accept your will for my life. Heavenly Father, show me what your perfect will is for my life and what path I should take."

Chapter 2

R eggie slowly applied the brakes as he approached the stop-
light. Having had the black Mercedes S500 for less than a
month, he was still cautious how he handled her. Not that
the fine machinery couldn't handle anything his six-foot-three-inch
frame could give, Reggie was just a careful kind of man. From his
many past mistakes, he'd learned that it was best to take all things
slow. He had made numerous mistakes by moving too fast and he'd
paid a high price.

"God, what do you want me to say today?" Reggie asked audi-
bly. He had spent half the night studying, but he still didn't feel confident about this morning's message. Reginald Lamont Pennington
was the pastor of True Worship Ministries Church. Following the
leading of God, he left his job of twelve years as an electrical engineer
and founded the church five years ago, right in the heart of Oakland
where outreach was most needed.

At first there was resistance from neighboring businesses and local residents. There was even a petition presented to the City Council
to stop the purchase of the 25,000-square-foot abandoned retail store.
Five years prior, the building had been vacated when a major retailer
closed. For five years no one wanted the building, not even the rats
and roaches that frequented the premises. Reggie wasn't discouraged
when the neighbors said they preferred the drug addicts in their

neighborhood over a church. Reggie had heard from God. He knew that no matter the obstacles, the Lord would work it out. And He did.

Reggie believed so much in what God had spoken to him that he sold two of the six duplexes that his parents had left him as an inheritance. Since the properties were free and clear, Reggie was able to take one hundred percent of the proceeds for a down payment on the church. He kept his parents' hillside home to live in and the remaining four duplexes as a means of monthly income. Without a mortgage or rent to pay, he could devote himself to the ministry full-time and still have a monthly income exclusive of the church. Reggie never wanted to be a financial burden on his church, so he made sure he lived within his means. Thanks to the real estate boom in northern California, the income from his rental property was enough to cover his living expenses. The salary he received from the church was usually placed in his savings account. He didn't believe in splurging on himself when so much was needed for the ministry. In fact, the only reason he was driving a new Mercedes was because the church purchased it for him as a fifth anniversary gift.

Reggie loved doing God's work. In the five years since its inception, True Worship had grown from five members to well over five hundred. Many of his early protestors were now his parishioners. True Worship was a diamond in the rough and a safe haven for all walks of life. At True Worship there was something for everyone. The most popular ministries included Singles Ministry, Couples Ministry, Men of Stature, Ladies of Excellence, Youth in Action, Kingdom Praisers, Bread of Life Ministries, Prayer Clinic, and his favorite, Street Evangelism. Reggie was extremely grateful to God for turning his vision into reality. Reggie cherished each member, and prayed daily on how he could best serve God's people. He desired not to give them recycled messages or riddles, but rather practical lessons that they could relate to and apply to their everyday life. Which is why he was perplexed over this morning's message. After intense meditation, he still didn't have clear direction.

The car horn from behind reminded him that he was at a stop-light. Reggie waved his hand to the driver behind him as a form of apology as he crossed International Blvd. "Well, God, I'm just going to have to trust you on this one," Reggie said out loud as he drove into the church's parking lot.

"Good morning, Pastor," Brother Tyrone expectantly greeted his pastor as he entered the building through the side door leading to his office.

"How are you doing this fine Sunday morning?" Reggie responded.

"Blessed of the Lord. I'm looking forward to a powerful word today, Pastor."

Reggie couldn't help but smile. He was so proud of Tyrone. He had come such a long way in five short years. Standing behind his desk, Reggie recalled their first meeting as if it were yesterday.

Tyrone was one of the homeless drug users who used to call the old abandoned building home. One day while clearing out debris, Reggie spotted Tyrone curled up in a corner, shaking, with a crack pipe nearby. Reggie was more grieved than afraid when he looked upon the frail man with no shoes. It was obvious Tyrone hadn't had a bath in weeks. His clothes were dirty with holes everywhere. His hair was matted and he was missing a few teeth. Reggie took him to one of his empty rental units and allowed him to shower. While Tyrone showered, Reggie searched the trunk of his car for his gym bag. Inside he found the sweat suit he kept for after his workout sessions. He even had a change of underwear. Once Tyrone was clean and dressed complete with a pair of Nikes that were a half-size too big, Reggie took him to a popular local restaurant known for its fabulous southern-style cooking. Reggie instructed Tyrone to order whatever he liked. That's exactly what Tyrone did. He ordered everything he thought he wanted. He started with the smothered pork chops along with rice, cabbage, candied yams and cornbread. Then he realized that he also had a taste for fried catfish, collard greens, macaroni and cheese and peach cobbler for dessert. He washed it down with ice-cold lemonade. Reggie sat there in amazement at how much food Tyrone consumed. Reggie was a hearty eater himself, but he couldn't hold a finger up against Tyrone.

For over an hour Reggie witnessed to Tyrone about God and His love for him. Reggie learned Tyrone had been raised by loving, God-fearing parents. He was the oldest of three children. His parents had worked very hard to provide for him and his siblings. Reggie also learned that Tyrone was a very intelligent young man. He'd earned a full scholarship to the University of San Francisco. Tyrone had been unable to keep up with the pressures of being a college freshman and trying to hold down a job. He'd started doing drugs as a way to "keep up." It all went downhill from there. Now, twelve years later, Tyrone was a homeless college dropout, hooked on crack. Reggie ministered to Tyrone and offered to help in any way he could. He gave Tyrone his number and told him to call him anytime. Tyrone verbalized his gratitude and stated he was genuinely touched by Reggie's generosity.

As the cleanup of the building continued Reggie would see Tyrone hanging around, trying to help out. Tyrone wouldn't show up every day at first. Maybe once a week, then twice a week, until eventually he was there every day, looking for his new friend. Some days he wouldn't talk at all, just work. Other days, he'd talk non-stop and end by asking for prayer. Finally, one day as they filled the last dumpster, Tyrone suddenly stopped and grabbed Reggie by both arms. With water-filled pleading eyes and trembling voice, he looked Reggie directly in the face, and said, "Just like the prodigal son, I realize that it's time for me to come home. Please help me get back home."

Reggie led Tyrone to salvation right there on the spot. Tyrone had been home ever since. In fact, Tyrone Davis was the most faithful deacon at True Worship.

"Well, Brother Tyrone," Reggie said looking at Tyrone now, "as long as I've got you praying for me I know everything is going to be all right."

Chapter 3

J ulia stepped from her car and scanned the parking lot for her best friend. She spotted Nikki waving from across the crowded parking lot.

"I'm so happy you agreed to join me for church today," Nikki exclaimed as she and Julia walked through the double glass doors. "Girlfriend, you are really going to enjoy yourself. We know how to get our praise on here at True Worship."

"I'm sure I'll enjoy myself," Julia responded, with anticipation.

Julia and Nikki Thompson had been friends since sharing a dorm room at UC Berkeley. Nikki had moved back to the Bay Area from Chicago five years ago. Since her return the two of them vowed to dedicate one day a month as "girlfriend day." On this first Sunday in October, Julia decided they would spend their time praising God at Nikki's church and then drive out to the Berkeley Marina for an early dinner at their favorite restaurant, Skates.

Julia was genuinely happy for the joy and peace her friend had found at True Worship. Nikki talked nonstop about her new church. Nikki had given her life to Christ a little over a year ago. Julia was delighted her friend had finally found a church home that she loved. Nikki's eyes lit up whenever she spoke of Pastor Pennington and his powerful messages. Nikki would even take notes on his sermons and share them with Julia during the week. Nothing Nikki had shared could have prepared Julia for what she saw and felt once she walked inside the doors of True Worship Ministries.

Julia had been around church all of her life, but she had never experienced the presence of God like she felt it that day. True Worship felt like home. From the ushers at the door she felt nothing but genuine love as they greeted her. The Praise and Worship service was so powerful, she actually felt like she was sitting at the feet of Jesus. She praised, worshipped, cried and danced like there was no one else in the building but her. Several members stood, swaying from side to side while clapping their hands to the music.

Julia's eyes were closed during Praise and Worship and while she listened to the choir, so she didn't notice when Pastor Pennington entered the sanctuary. When the choir finished singing, she remained standing, but still kept her eyes closed and silently gave thanks to God.

"It's time to hear a word from the Lord. Let's all stand and receive our pastor at this time. God bless you, Pastor Pennington." The young minister smiled as Pastor Pennington stepped to the podium.

Julia's eyes fluttered open and in slow motion her vision came into focus. She was not prepared for what she saw next. Nikki had raved so much about how much she loved Pastor Pennington and how much she'd learned from him, that Julia assumed he was a much older man. Nikki respected him as being a wise father figure who knew how to relate to his members in the areas they needed most. Pastor Pennington may have been all of those things to Nikki, but to Julia he was the finest man she'd ever laid eyes on.

From her seat in the fifth row, she estimated him to be six-three or six-four and about 250 pounds—all muscle. His smooth, dark-chocolate skin matched perfectly with his dark-brown eyes. His neatly trimmed goatee outlined a perfect pair of full lips that when parted revealed the sweetest smile she'd ever seen. His teeth were perfectly straight. She wondered if they'd naturally grown that way or if he'd worn braces. His ministerial cassock couldn't hide his perfectly chiseled body. By the cuts in his massive upper body, she could tell he worked out on a regular basis. Looking at him was like looking at Wesley Snipes and Morris Chestnut all rolled up into one. His voice was deep and melodious. When he spoke he reminded her of a young Billy D. Williams in *Lady Sings the Blues*.

Nikki tapped her on the arm. "Are you okay?"

Julia didn't notice that the rest of the congregation was already seated and she was the only one still standing. Her cheeks burned and Julia quickly sat down.

"Today I'm going to talk to you about something most of us have a hard time doing," Pastor Pennington began. "It's a simple thing, but we make it a hard thing. We know that we are supposed to do it, we talk about doing it, but the truth is the majority of us really don't do it. That simple thing is simply trusting in God. Please turn with me to a very familiar passage of scripture, Proverbs chapter three, verses five and six."

Julia gasped when she heard the scripture reference. She couldn't believe he was going to preach from the same scripture she'd just read this morning. Julia listened attentively as Pastor Pennington explained the word trust and what it really meant to have trust in God.

"Trusting in God means that we have to act in faith," Pastor Pennington continued. "Oftentimes, God doesn't show us the whole picture, because He knows that we wouldn't do what He wants us to do. So He shows us one step at a time to see if we are willing to take that step without knowing where it will lead us. We have to believe that God loves us and that He knows what's best for us. He doesn't want us to lean on our own understanding or knowledge. He doesn't want us to depend on our abilities, but on His guidance. God wants us to be able to trust Him and not trace Him."

Pastor Pennington continued for another twenty minutes. Afterward, he asked the congregation to stand. He then ministered prayer to the congregation.

"Girl, I know you enjoyed the service," Nikki said as she and Julia walked through the vestibule after the benediction.

"I sure did."

"But what was going on inside your head when Pastor Pennington took the podium? Girl, you were standing and staring like you'd seen a ghost," Nikki exclaimed.

Julia shrugged her shoulders. "I was just surprised that your pastor is so young."

"He's not that young. He's a year old than we are," Nikki responded.

"Oh," was the only response Julia could think of as they walked through the parking lot.

After a brief moment, when no one was within in earshot, Nikki stopped and turned and looked Julia directly in the eyes.

"What you meant to say was that you were surprised at how fine he is. Don't even try and deny it," Nikki said as Julia made a sorry attempt to contradict her. "Girl, this is me you're talking to. It's all right. I know he's fine and so does the rest of the female population at True Worship."

"Is that the reason you attend so faithfully?" Julia joked.

"I don't look at him in that way. I mean Stevie Wonder could see that he's a good- looking man, but I'm not attracted to him in that way. Although he's only a year older, I truly respect him as my spiritual father. To look at him in any other manner would be incest. Now if you were to ask one of these little hot mamas running around here, you might get a different story."

The two shared a laugh and continued walking toward their cars.

"How are you doing today, Sister Nikki?" Julia turned when she heard the male's voice.

"I'm fine, Brother Tyrone. How are you?" Nikki replied.

"I'm fine. You have a good week, Sister Nikki, and I'll see you at Bible Class on Wednesday."

"See you Wednesday." Nikki smiled at Tyrone, then turned and looked at Julia with a look that said, *DON'T GO THERE.*

Julia couldn't help but laugh at her friend. Having the attention of a God-fearing man was good for her friend. At least one of them could be happy. She waved her hand at Nikki, and said, "Whatever, girl, I'll meet you at the restaurant," then headed toward her Jaguar.

Chapter 4

"I'm ready whenever you are, Pastor," Minister Johnson said, as he stuck his head inside Pastor Pennington's door.

"I'll be right out, Minister Johnson," Reggie replied. He couldn't believe it was time to leave for his very important meeting at Pinnacle Developments. He had spent the early part of the morning reviewing the proposal with his administrative assistant, but for the last hour, he just sat at his desk reflecting on yesterday's worship service.

He wondered who the young lady was sitting next to Sister Nikki Thompson. He remembered her well for several reasons. He enjoyed the sincerity and the energy she displayed during Praise and Worship service. She appeared to have blocked everyone and everything, except God, out of her mind. It didn't seem to matter that she had on a designer suit or that her hair was flowing everywhere. When her hair hung in her face, she simply pulled out a clip and pulled her hair into a ponytail. She'd done it with such ease; he could tell that wasn't the first time her hair got in the way of her worship. For a moment there, he thought she might have forgotten that she was in a sanctuary filled with people when she stood there gawking at him. She looked so scared, like she was suspended in space.

The second reason he remembered her was because of her beauty. At first he wondered if she was related to Sister Nikki, but figured not because even from where he stood her mixed heritage was noticeable. Her cappuccino skin, full lips and curvy figure told of her African-American ancestry, but he was at a loss as to where the long, thick, curly black hair came from.

"What am I doing?" he asked himself out loud. "Why am I sitting here thinking about a woman I'll probably never see again?" He stood, grabbed his briefcase and headed out of the office.

* * *

"Your one o'clock appointment is here, Ms. Simone."

"Thanks, Michelle," Julia responded to her assistant.

"Give me five minutes and then send Mr...." Julia paused and glanced down at her schedule. "...Johnson in. And, Michelle, you've been with me for two years now. It's okay to call me 'Julia'."

"I know, Ms. Simone," Michelle replied, in her no-nonsense professional tone.

Julia rushed into her office bathroom to relieve herself. She'd been testing her bladder for the last hour while she daydreamed. Having her own private bathroom was the thing she loved most about her spacious office on the twenty-fifth floor of the commercial building she owned. She'd chosen the top floor because of the name of her business, Pinnacle Developments. From her office window she enjoyed great views of the Bay Bridge, Golden Gate Bridge and the San Francisco skyline.

As Julia straightened her clothes and tightened her ponytail, she remembered the words Pastor Pennington had spoken the day before. "Trust in the Lord. When you hear the Lord speak, just trust what he says." That's exactly what Julia had done ten years ago when she purchased the depressed land at Emery Bay. The land was undeveloped and the people in the area were underserved. None of the major developers wanted to have anything to do with it because of the cost involved in cleaning up and developing the fifty acres. Julia took a giant leap of faith and contracted with the city to develop the land. From the beginning, there were three strikes against her. She was young, a female and a minority. She felt like the little shepherd boy, David, going up against Goliath. When more established developers laughed at her ideas, she felt like giving up. When things were really rough she'd call her dad and he'd guide her over the hurdle.

Emery Bay turned out to be the best investment she'd ever made. Today, ten years later, Emery Bay was the most sought-out commercial space in the Bay Area. What was once a deserted, blighted area now was home to two nationwide home improvement stores, ten major hotels, over fifty restaurants, over three acres of prime retail stores, luxury apartments, condos, three major pharmaceutical companies and numerous businesses. She was so proud of her accomplishments that she decided to keep her offices there. God had taken both Emery Bay and her business from the bottom to the top. "Thank you, Lord," she said out loud as she exited the bathroom.

"Come in," Julia said as she stood and walked around to the front of her desk at the sound of the knock. She smiled and prepared to extend her hand to greet her visitor.

"Good afternoon, Ms. Simone. I'm Minister Russell Johnson form True Worship Ministries in Oakland where I serve as Administrative Assistant." The gentleman made a gesture to his right. "This is our pastor, Reverend Reginald Pennington."

Julia felt like peaches suspended in Jell-O. Nothing on her body could move. Not her hand, legs, or eyes. Even her smile was stuck in place. She couldn't believe that the man who consumed most of her thoughts that morning was standing right in front of her, looking more gorgeous than he had the day before. This time instead of a cassock he was wearing a double-breasted black suit that fit like it was sewn onto his body. He was just as fine close up as he was from afar. She was glad that she had just used the bathroom; otherwise, she was sure she would have peed on herself.

Focus, Focus, she told her brain, as she fought to gain control of her thoughts. Finally, she shook Minister Johnson's hand. "It's nice to meet you, Minister Johnson." She then willed herself to look Reginald Pennington directly in the eyes and extended her hand to him.

17

You can do this. He's just a man, she told herself before she said, "Welcome to my office, Reverend Pennington, I've heard a lot about you." As he shook her hand she noted how strong and big his hands were. Just having her hand in his gave her a sense of security.

"I hope it was all good," he responded in that rich voice that captivated her the day before.

"As a matter of fact, it was all good. My friend, Nikki Thompson, attends your church and she speaks very highly of you."

"So, Nikki is a friend of yours. That explains your presence at service on yesterday. I was wondering who that crazy woman was who didn't know how to sit down after she danced all over the church," Reggie teased.

"I wasn't that bad, was I?" Julia tried to keep from blushing. She wasn't even aware that he'd noticed her.

"No. You weren't bad at all," Reggie said and flashed a half-smile.

Minister Johnson cleared his throat.

"I'm sorry. Gentlemen, please have a seat." Julia gestured toward the two leather chairs in front of her desk. While they settled into the chairs, she walked back around her desk and sat in her executive chair. Remembering that she was a business professional, she made eye contact with Reverend Pennington, and asked, "What can I do for you today?"

Reggie shook his head as if to clear it, then after a prolonged pause, he began, "Pinnacle Developments owns the piece of property adjacent to our church." He cited the address. "We would like to purchase this property, for a fair price, of course."

"Of course." Julia nodded, trying to keep her eyes away from his massive chest. His pectorals took up more space than she thought necessary.

"After doing extensive research and a very thorough market analysis, my administrative assistant and I have prepared this offer, which we feel is fair and reasonable." Reggie handed her the offer. "Please understand, Ms. Simone, that True Worship Ministries has become a vital organism in the East Oakland area. We feel that we could serve our community more effectively if we acquire the additional property."

Julia leaned back in her chair. "And exactly what do you plan to use the space for?"

"We have a two-year plan to open a community center; complete with a gym and recreation facilities for the neighboring youth, a state of the art job training center, and a daycare center for low-income residents. We also want to expand our food pantry."

"That's very impressive, Reverend Pennington," she said as she silently admired his left dimple.

Julia picked up the offer and attempted to study its contents. She was very familiar with the property and knew the property was worth at least twice what they were offering. It really didn't matter because the way Julia was feeling at that moment, Reginald Pennington could have bought both her and the building for a dime.

Julia moved her eyes across the documents to give the impression that she was reading them. In actuality, she couldn't focus on the words. She was too busy trying to figure out why this man made her feel so nervous. Her legs shook uncontrollably underneath the desk. It had been six years since she gave up her last relationship and re-dedicated her life to God. She was not looking to start a relationship with anyone but Jesus and certainly not with Pastor Reginald Pennington. Yet she had to admit that she was attracted to him. She decided to end the façade.

"Reverend Pennington, Minister Johnson, I can't give you an answer today. I will look over your offer in more detail and do some research of my own. I promise I will get back to you by the end of the week."

Reggie stood and placed his left hand in his front pants pocket. "Ms. Simone, I believe the Lord is going to give True Worship this property just like he gave us the building we're in now."

His deep voice sent chills through her. She had to regain control. "Let me guess, Reverend Pennington, the Lord told you in a vision?"

"Something like that," he said without flinching.

"Well, Reverend Pennington, I serve the same God you do. Let me see what kind of vision he gives me." With that said, Julia stood and walked around to the front of her desk. Minister Johnson stood and she escorted them both to the door.

Before leaving, Reggie turned and asked, "Will you be joining us for church on Sunday?"

"No, I won't, I think—I know I had better attend my own church this week."

"Well, maybe you could join us for Wednesday night Bible Study? I think the more time you spend at True Worship, the more you'll want to part with that building."

"We'll see about that, Reverend Pennington. Have a good day, gentlemen." Julia gave him a dismissive smile, then turned and walked back to her desk.

* * *

"What is the matter with you?" Reggie said out loud once he was in the confines of his vehicle. "You were practically telling her, no begging to see her again. What about Sunday or Wednesday?" He couldn't explain why his stomach did a flip-flop when he saw her either. Sure he was surprised to see her there. He had no idea that the woman who had been on his mind all morning was *the* Julia Simone. He had done his homework and was aware of her reputation in the real estate world, but he didn't know she was a Christian and so beautiful. In his day, he had seen and had his share of attractive women, but none compared to the natural beauty he saw in her.

Physically, in his eyes, she was the perfect woman: the perfect height, size, color and curves in all the right places. And her hair, he loved her hair. Her soft-brown almond-shaped eyes and smile just made him melt. The hand he shook was so soft, that he had to fight the urge to stroke her cheek to see if it was equally soft.

For the past eight years he devoted his life to the ministry. Although he knew he was an attractive man and that some of the ladies in his church were attracted to him, the fact that he was single and celibate didn't bother him. He was content with serving the church. "Well, Lord, I'm not looking for a wife and I certainly can't have a girlfriend, so whatever this thing is with Julia Simone, it will just have to pass. Besides Julia Simone is not my type. She's too independent for a man like me. When I do settle down, I want to be the main provider of my household. I want to be able to give my wife everything she needs. Ms. Simone already has everything she needs and wants. But, Lord, I have to admit I am attracted to her," he made the declaration as he inserted his favorite CD.

Chapter 5

It had been three days since Julia received the offer from True Worship. She'd promised to have an answer before the end of the week. Today during her prayer time, as she'd done the two days prior, she asked God for direction. She always invited God into her decision-making process. So far, He had never let her down. She'd received the same answer every day. The answer didn't make logical sense to her. It also didn't make good business sense. As she wrestled with the decision in her head, she heard the words of Isaiah 55:8.

For my thoughts are not your thoughts, neither are your ways my ways.

Julia acknowledged that even if she followed what she felt in her heart, it wouldn't hurt Pinnacle's bottom line at all. She looked at the clock. If she was going to beat the morning commute, she had better shower and get dressed in under thirty minutes.

Just as Julia merged her dark-green Jaguar with soft-gold interior onto Interstate 680, her personal cell phone rang.

"Hi, Mom." It was Shay.

"Hey, baby girl. How are you?"

"I'm fine, Mama. Just wanted to let you know that I'll be home this weekend."

"Oh really," Julia said with suspicion. "What's on your agenda?"

"Not much, I just want to hang out and do laundry. Oh yeah, maybe do a little shopping in your closet." Julia and her daughter shared a laugh. The only thing that Julia didn't like about having a daughter the same size as she was sharing her clothes. Julia also knew that Shay's idea of doing laundry was leaving her dirty clothes for the housekeeper to take care of.

"In that case, I'll see you and your dirty laundry tomorrow. Drive safely."

"I will. Love you, Mom."

"I love you, too, baby girl."

Julia grinned the remainder of the way. Now that her baby was coming for a visit, the commute didn't seem as bad. She had something to look forward to.

"Michelle, could you please contact the gentlemen from True Worship and schedule an appointment for tomorrow morning after my tour? If not tomorrow, then the next available," she asked her assistant upon entering the office.

"Sure thing, Ms. Simone," Michelle replied.

Julia sat at her desk and sorted through her phone messages. She spent the next hour returning phone calls and emails, then checking the status of her latest major development—the Point Richmond Project. Tomorrow, she would tour the waterfront property. Although the construction was on schedule and within budget, she still personally toured the site every Friday and got a weekly progress report from the Project Manager.

"Ms. Simone, Reverend Pennington is on line one," Michelle sounded over the intercom.

"Were you able to schedule his appointment?"

"Yes. He'll be here at eleven o'clock tomorrow," Michelle paused, "but he asked to speak with you."

"Thank you, Michelle," Julia said and wondered why Reverend Pennington needed to speak to her now. She would have preferred to communicate with Minister Johnson, that way she'd at least be able to focus.

She pressed the blinking line. "Good morning, Reverend Pennington," Julia said in her professional voice.

"Good morning, Ms. Simone."

This man is even fine over the phone, Julia thought, but voiced, "What can I do for you today, Reverend Pennington? I understand you have an appointment for tomorrow."

"That's correct. I just wanted to thank you for getting back to me, I mean to us, in a timely manner."

"I'm a woman of my word, Reverend Pennington."

"You've proven that." He paused. "I look forward to doing business with you."

"I'll see you tomorrow, Reverend Pennington. Have a good day."

What was that about? Julia wondered. Surely the good reverend could have waited twenty-four hours to say that. "Who knows?" she said out loud and continued working.

* * *

Reggie nervously sat in Julia's office, waiting for her. He could've kicked himself for asking to speak to her yesterday. For a reason he couldn't explain, he had an urge to hear her voice and now he was anxious to see her. He looked down at his watch. She was already fifteen minutes late. He didn't know if that was a good sign or not.

As he surveyed the room, he couldn't help but admire her good taste. He loved the huge mahogany desk and the plush cream carpet. The desk was one which he would have chosen, but would have never splurged on. One wall was covered with original paintings from various African-American artists. The opposite wall displayed Julia's degrees and awards of recognition from various civic and social organizations. There was even a picture of her, along with the mayor of Emeryville, City Council members and the governor, at the groundbreaking ceremony of Emery Bay.

In the corner, behind her desk, stood a six-foot mahogany cabinet. On the center shelf was a cherry wood framed picture of an older couple—a Caucasian man who could stand in for Sean Connery and a creamy dark-chocolate woman, that Reggie assumed were Julia's parents. Next to the photo, in a matching frame, was a group of about fifty people of various ages, colors and sizes. On the top shelf was a picture of a young girl wearing a cap and gown; he wondered who she was. His thoughts were interrupted by Julia's voice.

"Reverend Pennington, I'm so sorry to have kept you waiting," she said as she rushed in. "On Friday mornings I tour my construction sites. The tour lasted longer than expected. Give me a minute to print the documents and we'll get started," Julia said in an apologetic tone.

"No problem," Reggie responded as he examined her. He'd expected to see her in a power business suit; instead, she sported Levi jeans, a hooded sweatshirt and Timberland boots. Her hair was pulled back into a ponytail, making the gold hoop earrings visible. Even dressed casually, she was beautiful. His eyes lingered on her hands, as he was reminded of their softness. He quickly had to remind himself of why he was at her place of business.

"All right, Reverend Pennington, let's begin," Julia said, as she removed the documents from the laser printer. "I have carefully reviewed your offer as well as your market analysis. I cannot in good conscience sell you the property for what you are proposing."

"But—" Reggie interjected.

"Please let me finish, Reverend Pennington. My analysis of the property and the surrounding area would require me to sell it for twice as much as your church is capable of paying."

"But—" Reggie interjected again.

"Please, let me finish."

Reggie felt his temper rise and unloosened his tie. He brought his emotions under control and gestured for her to continue.

"To be perfectly honest with you, Reverend Pennington, I like what you want to do with the building. I believe in the vision you have and I would like to support that vision," Julia paused, "if you will allow me."

Reggie sat back in the chair. "I'm listening, Ms. Simone."

"If I were to sell you the building under your terms, I would do so at a considerable loss. However, if Pinnacle Developments were to deed the property over to True Worship Ministries as a charitable contribution, it would help both of us. True Worship would own the building and Pinnacle would have a huge tax write-off." She leaned back in her executive chair and smiled.

Reggie couldn't believe what he'd just heard. "Ms. Simone, are you saying that instead of selling us the property, you would rather give it to us?"

"That's exactly what I'm saying, Reverend Pennington. True Worship would have to pay the title and transfer fees. Does this sound like something your church would be interested in?" Julia asked.

"We gladly accept your offer, Ms. Simone." Reggie paused. "May I ask why you are being so generous?"

She raised an eyebrow. "Reverend Pennington, before you left here on Monday, I told you I would pray about my decision. I wasn't joking. I prayed, Reverend Pennington, and this is the answer God gave me. You told me before you left that the Lord would *give* you this building. That's exactly what He told me to do, to give it to you. I do ask one thing of you."

"What's that, Ms. Simone?" he asked cautiously.

"I ask that no special recognition be made in regards to this transaction. I'm not doing this for accolades or recognition. I'm doing this because this is what God has told me to do. Is that understood, Reverend Pennington?"

"I understand. But that won't stop me from doing my victory dance on Sunday morning. I'm so excited, if you were to drop a tambourine right this minute, I'd ask you to hold my mule." They shared both smiles and laughs. "You think that I'm playing, don't you?" Reggie said as he raised his hand in a wave of praise.

"Reverend Pennington, I have no doubt that you know how to get your praise on." She placed the documents into an envelope. "Take these documents and have your staff look them over. I'm sure you'll find everything in order," she said, handing it to him.

"When you are done you can bring them back to my assistant. We'll handle everything from there."

"Ms. Simone, I'm stunned. You don't know how much you've just helped True Worship. By not having to pay for the building we can move up our plans for construction."

"I'm glad I could be of help to you," Julia said as she stood.

Not quite ready to leave her presence, Reggie asked, "I know you don't want any recognition, but how about lunch as a way to say thank you?"

"That sounds wonderful, considering I haven't eaten this morning. Where did you have in mind?"

"There's a Chinese place down the street, *PF Changs*. Have you heard of it?"

"Yes, it's one of my favorites. Just give me a minute to make a quick phone call." Julia quickly made her phone call while Reggie resumed looking at the photos in her cabinet.

"Are these your parents?" Reggie asked when she finished. He pointed at the framed photo.

"They sure are and these are my brothers and sisters. She pointed to the picture of her siblings along with their families.

"Wow, you come from a big family," Reggie commented.

"My parents had eight children. I am number five," she said proudly.

"And who's this young lady?" He pointed to the picture on the top shelf.

"This here is my baby, my one and only child: LaShay Hampton. She's a freshman at Stanford."

He studied her face for a moment. "You surprise me. I never would have thought you were old enough to have a grown daughter. You look so good—I mean you look so young."

Julia blushed. "Why, thank you, Reverend Pennington. I'm forty; I had my baby when I was twenty-two."

"Sounds like the two of you are very close," Reggie said with a hint of sadness in his voice. "We are, Reverend—"

"Please call me 'Reggie'," he interrupted.

"Only if you call me 'Julia'."

"Okay, Julia. Are you also close to her father?" Reggie asked cautiously.

"No, he's deceased."

"I'm sorry, I didn't mean to pry."

"Sure you did, you wanted to know if I'm attached," Julia mumbled.

"Excuse me?"

This time Julia spoke clearly. "That's all right, but we better get going before the lunch crowd."

Standing inches from him inside the elevator, Julia grew anxious. What was she doing and how was she supposed to eat in front of this black Adonis? *I should have said 'no' and instead popped popcorn in the microwave.*

When they reached the main floor, Reggie suggested they walk the two blocks to the restaurant, since the weather was nice. Relieved, Julia quickly agreed. She didn't think being in an enclosed space with him was a good idea, considering she couldn't keep her eyes off his protruding pectorals.

The two of them walked leisurely through the plaza, enjoying the fresh breeze from the Bay. The plaza streets were lined with dozens of prime retail shops and specialty stores. The smell of fresh-cut flowers caught Julia's attention. She stopped at the sidewalk flower shop and admired the beautiful roses. "These are so beautiful and they smell heavenly," Julia said, as she inhaled the soft petals again.

"I see you like roses," Reggie commented.

"I enjoy roses, but carnations are my favorites."

"Really? I figured a woman like you would prefer calla lilies or something rare and exotic."

She shrugged and continued walking. Moments later they were seated at a booth inside PF Changs. After giving their orders, they handed the waitress their menus and sat quietly and stared out the window. Both looked around the restaurant and then at each other as if they were unsure of what to say next. Both let out an audible sigh when the waitress delivered their drinks.

Reggie figured he would try a safe subject. He didn't want her to get the impression that he was interested in her personally.

"So, Julia, what church do you attend?" he asked.

"House of Prayer Community Church. My pastor is Reverend Robert Leonard."

"Really? Reverend Leonard is one of my spiritual fathers. He was a great help to me when True Worship was only a vision."

"Is that so?" Julia asked.

"Yes. Reverend Leonard is a true man of God. He was the only local senior pastor that encouraged me to hang in there while City Hall and the residents of the area protested. 'Son, God gave you a vision and my God don't lie. So you hang in there because it's going to happen'." He imitated the senior gentleman's voice. "I respect him for pushing me to move forward, instead of fighting me because I was young."

"That's my pastor, always trying to help somebody," Julia replied.

"We have a fifth Sunday fellowship with House of Prayer this month. Maybe I'll see you there?"

She took a sip of water. "Maybe. Now tell me a little about yourself."

"What would you like to know?"

"For starters, where are you from?"

"I grew up in Oakland and graduated from Bishop O'Dowd High School. I graduated Cal State Hayward, which is now Cal State East Bay, with an engineering degree. Later on I went to seminary at Patton College and American Baptist Seminary of the West."

"No wonder you have a heart for the community. It's your home and part of who you are." Julia unfolded the napkin on her lap. "What about your family? Do you have a large family?"

"No. I'm an only child. My father was a nuclear scientist at the lab in Livermore and my mother was a local schoolteacher." Knowing what the next question would be, he added, "They both died in an automobile accident, seven years ago."

"I'm sorry to hear that. You must miss them a lot."

The empathy mirrored in her eyes soothed Reggie's hidden pain. "More than you know," Reggie replied, after taking a sip of water.

The food arrived and Reggie said grace. They ate in silence, except for an occasional comment about how good the food was. Reggie had never tried the lettuce wraps, so Julia offered him some. He did the same with his spicy shrimp. By the end of the meal they were completely stuffed.

"That was delicious. This is going to cost me an extra thirty minutes on the StairMaster," Julia commented as she placed the soiled napkin on the plate.

"You work out?" Reggie asked.

"Every day."

"So that's how you do it," Reggie stated.

"Do what?"

"Eat like you just did and still maintain a nice figure." As soon as he said the words, he wanted to take them back.

"So you think I have a nice figure. Why, Reverend Pennington, I'm flattered," Julia mused. "You're pretty easy on the eyes yourself. The way I see it, you must exercise regularly or have a very high metabolism," she said as she gestured at the empty dishes in front of him.

"You're right; I'll pay for it later at the gym."

They sat for a few more moments before Reggie asked for the check and Julia left to use the ladies' room. When she returned he was waiting for her near the exit.

"Thank you for lunch, Reggie," Julia said.

"No, thank you. I wish there was more I could do to show my sincere appreciation for what you've done for True Worship."

"Lunch is appreciation enough," is what she voiced, then mumbled, "Keep smiling like that and I'll remodel the building for you." Reggie was distracted by a street vendor and didn't hear the comment.

They walked quietly back to Julia's office building.

"I'll have the signed documents back to you one day next week," Reggie announced when they neared the building entrance. "Maybe we could have lunch again. There's a great Thai place about a half-mile down Ashby. Or maybe dinner on the marina?"

"Are you asking me out on a date?" Julia inquired. She had a smile on her face, but his face grew hard and serious.

In a firm tone, he stated, "Julia, I don't causally date. When and if I ever do decide to date it will be for the sole purpose of leading to marriage." She narrowed her eyes. "Don't worry; you have nothing to worry about. I would never date a woman like you."

Julia stopped abruptly and didn't make any attempt to hide the agitation in her voice "That's the second time today you've used the term, *a woman like you*. Exactly what do you mean by that?"

Reggie turned to face her. "I mean, independent women like you, who have it all and don't need a man for anything. You know the type, I-got-my-own-stuff kind of woman. One who would rather take care of herself than to allow a man to provide for her. You can have anything you want without the assistance of a man and you would have a hard time respecting a man that doesn't have as much as you do."

Julia just stared at him. She was shocked at his off-base perception of her. He may have been wise when it came to spiritual matters, but when it came to her, he didn't have a clue.

"Well, Mr. Pennington, you seem to have everything figured out. And you're absolutely right." She pointed at Reggie. "I don't need the assistance of this man, to help me find my way back to *my* office. That's something I can do all by myself. Have a good day, Mr. Pennington." She turned and left him standing there wondering what had just happened.

What was that all about? Reggie thought as he walked slowly to his car. He didn't understand what had just transpired between him and Julia. One minute they were sharing each other's food, the next minute he was being dismissed. Maybe what he said had been harsh to her, but in his mind it was the truth. He'd been around plenty of women and in the past his summation had proven correct. He hadn't meant to respond that way, but he was thrown off balance when she said the word *date*. Sure he enjoyed her company and he was grateful to her for being a blessing to True Worship, but he told himself that he was not interested in dating her or anyone else.

For the past five years he had devoted his life to True Worship and would not allow anything or anyone to distract him from the ministry. If he wanted to date someone, there were plenty of available and willing females in his own congregation. Each week there was at least one sister offering to cook his meals or clean his house. He discouraged his admirers by openly stating his mother had taught him how to both cook and clean, and what he couldn't handle, a cleaning service would.

Maybe I gave her the wrong impression by asking her about her daughter's father. Why did I ask her to have dinner with me anyway? I should have just left when we finished the business. Maybe I was unfair to her, he thought to himself. Merging his Mercedes onto Powell Street, he made a mental note to apologize to her for any offense his words caused, when he brought the documents back. In the back of his mind he wondered what a date with Julia Simone would be like.

* * *

"Who does that narrow-minded jerk think he is?" Julia said out loud as she slammed her office door. "The nerve of him. He doesn't even know me and yet he has the audacity to categorize and stereotype me after he spent two hours flirting with me. Mr. I-Don't-Date." She walked around and sat behind her desk. She took a deep breath in an effort to calm herself.

She was extremely disappointed that Reggie turned out to be so antiquated in his thinking and so off base with his analogy of who she was. She would have expected that from her older counterparts, but not from the innovative Reverend Reginald Pennington.

Whereas most pastors didn't recognize female ministers, True Worship had three ordained female ministers on staff, in leadership roles. Nikki had conveyed to her on numerous occasions how Reverend Pennington would discuss issues that traditionally the "church" would shy away from. Issues like homosexuality, pornography, teenage pregnancy and physical abuse in the church.

"If we want different results, we have to change our way of thinking and our way of doing things." Nikki had repeated her pastor's words on many occasions.

Julia sighed. "Well, I guess it's true what they say about most preachers. They may sound wise and profound when the anointing is on them, but try to hold a conversation with them when the anointing is gone and you'll find that most of them are ten cents short of a dime." Julia made a mental note not to be available when he returned the signed documents.

Chapter 6

Julia couldn't believe it. She'd been up for four hours with her devotion time and daily workout, and had gone to the supermarket while Shay remained in a coma-like sleep. She'd come home to rest. Shay carried a full load at Stanford and so far she had adjusted well to her heavy schedule and the hours of endless studying. Julia knew her baby was tired and probably hadn't had a balanced meal since her last visit, four weeks ago. She decided to make her a hearty breakfast of bacon, sausage, grits, eggs, and buttermilk biscuits, along with freshly squeezed orange juice.

She moved around the gourmet kitchen with ease. The kitchen was the main selling point in the decision to purchase the home. She liked the fact that the ten-thousand-square-foot two-story, Mediterranean-style home sat on a whole acre of land, but she fell in love with the kitchen. She loved to cook. Everything in the kitchen was perfect, from the double oven to the pecan solid oak cabinets and hunter-green granite countertops.

Just as she placed the biscuits on the center island, Shay glided into the kitchen and sat in her favorite chair at the table.

Shay rubbed her hands together. "You sure do know how to wake a girl up."

"Well, what do you know, the dead has been resurrected. I hope you are hungry, I made your favorites."

"Thanks, Mom, you know my favorite part of being at home is enjoying your cooking."

"Yeah, that and wearing my clothes." Julia retrieved a plate from the cabinet. "Before I forget, have you seen my black leather jacket and matching skirt?"

"Sure have. It's hanging in my closet," Shay giggled, then added, "in my dorm room."

Julia rolled her eyes as she set the plate on the counter.

"Don't worry, Mom, they are in good hands."

"I would much rather have them in *my* hands." Julia smirked.

While Shay ate, she gave her mother an update on school. This month she decided she would major in Psychology. Last month it was Political Science. It was a good thing she wouldn't have to make a solid decision until her junior year.

Once Shay finished eating, cleared her dishes and placed them in the dishwasher, she turned and gave her mother an unsure look. "Mom, can I ask you a question?"

"Sure, baby girl, what is it?"

"Mom," she hesitated, "don't you think it's about time you started dating?"

Julia drained the juice from her glass. Where was Shay going with this? "Why would you say that?"

"Well, Mom, technically I'm an adult now. I'm in no rush, but eventually I'll be leaving home for good and you'll be alone. I know you love your business, but don't you want to have a loving relationship with someone special? Maybe marry again?"

Julia's hands fidgeted as she analyzed her daughter's words. She'd given herself the exact same speech numerous times in the past two months and still didn't have a solid answer. "I would love to have someone to spend the rest of my life with, but that hasn't happened as of yet," she finally answered.

Shay stilled her hands with her own. "Mom, I know there's someone special out there for you. I've been praying for you to find your soul mate. I believe the two of you are going to find each other real soon," Shay stated with confidence.

"Thank you, baby." While mother and daughter embraced, images of Reginald Pennington flashed before Julia and left a sour taste in her mouth. If she were to marry again, it certainly wouldn't be to someone as arrogant and self-centered as the good reverend. She'd done that before and had the scars to prove it.

Chapter 7

J ulia stood outside and greeted the visitors as they entered House of Prayer while waiting for Nikki to arrive. Today was the Fifth Sunday Fellowship service with True Worship and as usual, Nikki was running late. How she managed to hold down a teaching job at the community college was a mystery to Julia. She imagined that her students probably spent half of the class waiting on Professor Thompson.

"Hey, girlfriend, I hope you saved me a seat," Nikki said, trying to catch her breath after rushing toward the entrance.

"You know I saved your always-running-behind self a seat." The two friends hugged.

"I love you, too, girl," Nikki responded.

"What's your excuse today?"

"I wouldn't exactly call it an excuse, but morning service ran a bit over. Oh, girl, Pastor Pennington preached today. I'll have to tell you about it later. Anyway, I had to wait for Tyrone to lock the church up," she said matter of factly.

"You had to wait for Tyrone? And just why did you have to wait for Tyrone?" Julia asked with a sly grin.

"We rode over together; thought that would save on parking." Nikki smiled.

"Hmm, I bet you did. I knew there was something going on between you two."

Before Nikki could offer a rebuttal, Reverend Pennington approached the entrance along with Brother Tyrone.

Nikki made introductions. "Brother Tyrone, this is my best friend, Julia Simone."

Tyrone extended his hand to Julia. "It's a pleasure to meet you. Sister Nikki has told me a lot about you."

She shook his hand, and replied, "It's nice to finally meet you. I wish I could say that I've heard a lot about you," Julia sneered at her friend, "but my dear friend has withheld that piece of information from me."

"Anyway," Nikki snapped at Julia. "You've already met my pastor, Reverend Pennington."

Julia casually, but respectfully greeted Reggie. She was well aware of the fact that they were in a public place and there were eyes glued to them as he shook her hand, for what she thought was just a little too long.

"It's good to see you again, Reverend Pennington. I look forward to hearing you bring the Word this afternoon." With that, Julia excused herself and went inside the sanctuary.

Julia knew she would see Reggie today, but his presence still had an unnerving affect on her. She hadn't seen or spoken to him since she literally ran into him at her office three weeks ago. She was running to make the elevator when she rounded the corner and ran smack into the *Rock of Pennington*.

"Are you all right?" he asked, as his strong arms steadied her.

"I'm fine. I didn't see you coming." In a flat tone she added, "What can I do for you, Reverend?"

"I'm here to drop off the signed documents." He pointed to the envelope on the floor, which had fallen upon impact. He bent to retrieve them.

"You can leave those with my assistant. She'll forward everything over to the Title department." Julia turned to leave, but Reggie touched her arm.

"Julia, if I can still call you that, can I speak to you for just a moment?"

Julia moved her arm out of his grip. She couldn't allow his touch to wear her defenses down. After all, he was still rude and arrogant, but gorgeous nonetheless. "Outside of business, what could you possibly have to say to a 'woman like me'?" she snapped.

Reggie sighed and looked directly into her eyes. "I want to apologize for my actions the other day. I now realize that I may have given you the wrong impression as to what my intentions were."

"And exactly what impression was that? The impression that you are a stereotypical jerk, or that you are so stuck on yourself that you think every woman wants you? Tell me something, do you always assume that just because a woman shares a meal with you, she wants to date you?" She placed her hand on her hip. "Did it ever occur to you that *you* are not my type?"

He didn't answer.

"Just because you are a handsome man, doesn't give you the right to prejudge a person's character."

Reggie looked bewildered. "So you think I'm handsome?"

"Did you hear anything else I said?"

"Yes, I did and seriously, I'm sorry. In the future I'll be sure to watch my conversation. Please accept my sincere apology. It's important for me to have your forgiveness." Julia looked puzzled. "How else will I be able to preach every Sunday, knowing I've offended my brother, or in this case, my sister?" he said, flashing his breathtaking smile.

Julia smiled and shook her head. She was weakening. "All right, I'll accept your pathetic apology."

Feeling a little awkward, the two exchanged a quick, friendly handshake.

"You really think I'm handsome, huh?" Reggie repeated.

"Let it go, Reggie, just let it go." Julia rolled her eyes and headed for the elevator.

Now, as she prepared for service to begin, she wondered if she would be able to concentrate on the service. She found the two seats she reserved for her and Nikki and began to pray. Just the memory of being in close contact with his chiseled body had taken her on an express ride from spirituality to carnality.

* * *

Reggie sat in Reverend Leonard's office, waiting for the fellowship service to begin. He studied his sermon notes one final time, then decided to change into his ministerial cassock. He and Reverend Leonard decided it was a good idea for the visiting minister to preach the sermon during the fellowship services.

As he changed, Reggie's mind drifted to Julia Simone. Today she was just as beautiful as ever in that navy blue suit with rhinestones. How did she know blue was his favorite color? He didn't recall mentioning it. Maybe Sister Nikki told her, but how would she know? And those soft hands—he wondered what those would feel like roaming his body. "Lord, have mercy," he cried out loud when he realized where his thoughts were headed. He wasn't interested in her, yet she managed to awaken desires he hadn't had in years.

After changing into his ministry attire, Reggie sat at Reverend Leonard's desk with his head bowed in prayer. That's how Pastor Leonard found him.

"God bless you, son. It's so good to see you. I know you got a word for us today," the elderly man said, as he patted Reggie on the shoulder. Reverend Leonard genuinely loved Reggie. He couldn't have been more proud of Reggie had Reggie been one of his biological sons and had told him as much on several occasions.

Reggie stood and gave Reverend Leonard a hug that expressed his appreciation for the faith he'd always had in him. "Thanks for inviting True Worship. I'm sure this will be an edifying service."

"Son, I'm not going to distract you. I know how important it is to hear from the Lord before you mount the pulpit. I hope you work up a good appetite, because the Hospitality Committee has prepared a feast fit for a king in the dining hall." With that, Reverend Leonard left the office. Moments later Reggie heard the organ prelude, indicating the start of service.

Praise and Worship at House of Prayer reminded Reggie of his home church. Reggie nodded his approval as he observed how the two congregations praised the Lord together like one big, happy family, even though the sanctuary was so full, chairs had to be added in the aisles.

House of Prayer and True Worship were similar in many ways. They both were mixed congregations of well over five-hundred members. Both churches provided outreach services to the community. Most importantly, both churches had leaders who believed in praising the Lord by any means necessary. On any given Sunday, you could find people from the pulpit to the back door, going forth in a holy dance, shouting at the top of their voices, or even being slain in the Spirit. It was a common scene to see Reggie and Reverend Leonard leading the praise party.

The crowd finally settled down after the combined church choirs rendered two foot-stomping numbers. After Reverend Leonard's third dance and fifth hallelujah, he quickly raised the offering and now stood at the podium.

"Saints of the Most High God, it's time for the Word of God."

Shouts of, "Amen," "Hallelujah," "Bless his name," and "Speak, Lord," were heard throughout the sanctuary.

"But before we bring this anointed Man of God in the person of Reverend Reginald Pennington," Reverend Leonard paused to wipe sweat from his forehead, "I'm going to ask Sister Julia to grace us with a sermonic hymn."

Julia walked to the podium as shouts of, "Sing Sister, Julia" and "Let the Lord use you," rang through the sanctuary. After receiving the microphone from her pastor, she nodded at the musicians, closed her eyes and with what appeared to be little effort, delivered a soul-stirring version of "We Shall Behold Him."

Reggie sat in his seat with his eyes and ears glued to Julia. He had no idea she could sing, let alone had such a beautiful voice. She was singing unto the Lord, but she mesmerized him. She sang with such emotion, it brought tears to his eyes. When Reverend Leonard asked the audience to stand and receive the Man of God, it took Reggie a minute to get his bearings.

When he finally mounted the podium, he fought the urge to look in the direction of where Julia sat. He firmly gripped the sides of the podium and willed his legs not to carry him to where she was. He finally cleared his throat, and said, "Let us pray."

An hour later, the congregation had moved from the sanctuary into the dining hall. Inside the elegantly purple and gold decorated room, that could comfortably seat 300 people, the hospitality committee had prepared a buffet that would give the Golden Corral some serious competition.

Reggie and Reverend Leonard were seated at the table reserved for the ministers and their spouses. Reggie didn't notice that he was the only minister, male or female, without a spouse.

However, several of the young single ladies did. On a few occasions, when he looked up from eating, he noticed some smiles and even a couple of winks. One sister was bold enough to hand him a note with her telephone number on it. He, in turn, passed the note to Reverend Leonard who gave the sister a stern look of disapproval.

Reverend Leonard was a very observant man. Reggie's enthrallment with Julia wasn't lost on him. The look in Reggie's eyes revealed more than a superficial appreciation of music. Reggie had shared with him the details of their business transaction, so he knew Julia had been a blessing to True Worship, but he wondered if Reggie really understood that God was up to something.

"Reggie, how old are you now?" Reverend Leonard began.

"I'm forty-one, sir."

"Son, have you thought about settling down?"

"No, sir," Reggie said after a swig of lemonade. "At this point in my life, I'm completely devoted to the ministry. I don't have time for a wife."

"That's wonderful, son, but even God said it was not good for man to be alone," Reverend Leonard replied.

"You are right, sir, but the Bible also says there's a time and a season for all things. I just don't feel it's the right time. Besides, I haven't found anyone that special yet. You know it takes a very special woman to be a pastor's wife."

"You're right about that, son," was what Reverend Leonard said with his mouth, but in his mind he said, *This poor boy doesn't have a clue.*

"Excuse me, Pastor, would you like some more lemonade?"

Reggie dropped his fork when he heard her sweet voice. He was hoping he would have a chance to speak to her before he left. He wanted to tell her how much he enjoyed her singing. He had been scanning the room without any success. When he turned around, he understood why. She had traded in her navy blue and rhinestone suit with matching heels, for a long black skirt, white blouse and flats. Her long tresses were now pulled back into a ponytail.

"Sure, daughter." Reverend Leonard acknowledged Julia, then grinned at Reggie.

Julia's hands shook slightly as she filled Reverend Leonard's glass. Julia then slowly turned to Reggie, and asked, "How about you Reverend Pennington? What would you like for me to do to you?" She cleared her throat. "I mean, would you like for me to refill your glass?"

"Yes, please and thank you." He never took his eyes off her face.

"This poor boy doesn't have a clue. He can't even spell clue," Reverend Leonard grumbled. He then decided he'd have a little fun with them. "Sister Julia, I know you must be tired. Why don't you take a break for a moment?"

"I don't think that's a good idea with all these hungry and thirsty people in here," she replied.

"Baby, these people aren't handicapped, they know how to serve themselves. You see Sister Jenkins has already pulled her foil from her purse." The three of them shared a laugh.

"I guess it won't hurt if I take a quick break." She walked around the table and sat in the chair opposite Reggie. "I enjoyed your sermon today, Reverend Pennington. You are a very powerful preacher. I see why Nikki's always raving about you. The two times I've heard you, have been very moving," Julia said sincerely.

"Thank you. I appreciate that, but you could raise the dead with that voice of yours. Why didn't you tell me you could sing like that?"

"You never asked."

Reggie's thumb and forefinger brushed his chin. "Julia Simone, you are full of surprises."

They made small talk for a few more minutes, about nothing in particular, before Julia went back to serving. Neither of them noticed they had left Reverend Leonard completely out of the conversation.

He didn't mind at all.

Chapter 8

J ulia hated Monday morning traffic. On a good day it usually took her an hour to commute to her office. Today was not a good day. The three-car pile-up that occurred an hour prior had traffic backed up for miles. The rain only added to the problem. It amazed her that in bad weather conditions people drove carelessly. When Julia finally entered the parking garage, she was frustrated and irritated. She politely greeted Michelle, retrieved her messages and checked her email.

Trying to find solace from the early morning mayhem, she looked out her office window in search of the tranquility the Bay usually afforded her. But today the rain and fog not only cast a gray haze over the Bay, but also obscured her view of the San Francisco skyline and the Golden Gate Bridge. She put in her favorite CD and reviewed the building inspector's report on the high-rise condos at Point Richmond. Halfway through the report, her personal cell phone rang. She recognized Nikki's number from the caller ID.

"Hey, you."

"Did I catch you at a bad time?" Nikki asked.

"No, not at all."

"Good, because I have one question to ask you."

"Go ahead."

"*Girl*, what did you do to my pastor? Pastor was stuck in his seat like someone had put crazy glue in his chair." Nikki laughed.

"I don't know what you are talking about," Julia replied innocently.

"Don't tell me you didn't see how he was looking at you while you sang, "We Shall Behold Him." He looked like he wanted to jump up and hold *you!* You know I saw you sitting down at the table talking to him when you should have been pouring lemonade."

After all these years, it still amazed Julia how much Nikki knew about everyone else's business and how very little she knew about her own.

"I don't know what you're talking about. Reverend Leonard asked me to sing and that's what I did."

Nikki smacked her lips. "And sing you did. I know you can sing, but girl you sounded like you were about to cut a CD or trying to get the winning votes on *American Idol.*"

"Well, I'll take that as a compliment." Julia thought for a moment. "Was he really watching me?"

"Girl, yes, he was." Nikki turned serious. "You know he asks about you a lot and I saw how he looked at you when we were outside. I think he likes you."

"I doubt that; I'm not his type." The dryness in her throat was projected in her voice.

"And how would you know that?" Nikki asked.

"He told me so."

"Well, his mouth may have said those words, but the look he had in his eyes sent a totally different message."

Feeling the need to change the conversation, Julia said, "Now, may I ask you a question?"

"Sure."

"What's going on with you and Brother Tyrone?"

"I don't know what you're talking about." Nikki laughed, this time nervously.

"Girl, don't try to play me," Julia warned.

"Seriously, at this moment we're just good friends."

"Is that all?"

"For now it is. We are attracted to each other, but we've decided to take things slow and see what happens."

"I hope things work out for you." Julia really wanted her friend to find someone special, even if she couldn't.

"Me, too, and I hope things work out for you and Pastor."

"I wouldn't waste any energy on something that's not going to happen," Julia said with finality.

"Girl, I got to go," Nikki rushed off the phone. "The students for my next class are arriving."

"Talk to you later."

Julia sat at her desk and thought about Nikki's words. If Reggie was interested in her, he sure had a funny way of showing it. In her opinion, the only things Reginald Pennington was interested in were True Worship and himself.

She looked at the caller ID when her cell phone chimed again. "Hi, Mommy," she said cheerfully.

"Hi, sweetie, how are you doing today?" Ana Simone asked.

"Mommy, I'm fine now that I hear your voice." Julia really meant those words. No one could soothe her like her mother. No one knew her like her mother, either. Ana Simone had a built-in radar that could detect when each of her eight children needed her assistance, were in trouble, or just plain lying. Julia had never been able to hide anything from her mother. When she and her siblings were younger, Ana would warn each of them by saying, "You better not do anything you are not supposed to, because I'll find out about it. If I don't catch you with my own eyes, God will show me in a vision." Of course, Julia and her siblings did many things they weren't supposed to, and true to her word, Ana Simone found out every time. It may have taken awhile, but eventually, she'd find out.

"Are you and Papa doing all right?"

"Honey, we're fine. Your father's taking care of business with Chantel and Stephan." Chantel and Stephan were Julia's older sister and younger brother. Carey Simone was grooming the two of them to take control of The Simone Company by the end of next year.

"Is Daddy really going to retire?"

"That's what he says, baby. Sweetheart, I didn't call to talk about your father. I called to talk about you." Ana's tone was serious.

"What is it, Mommy?"

Never being one to tiptoe around an issue, Ana Simone directly asked, "Baby, aren't you ready to settle down with someone?"

Julia's jaw fell.

When Julia didn't respond, she continued, "I was just looking at the picture you sent me of you and Shay at her graduation. The average person looking at this picture would assume that you are happy, but you know I'm not the average person. I'm your mother and I can see the sadness in your eyes. Baby, you are alone and you are tired of being alone."

Julia remained quiet.

"Baby, I've watched you suffer a devastating loss and I also watched you give yourself to someone that didn't deserve you. I know you are afraid to love someone, but you have so much love inside of you that you have to give it to someone. You chose to give that love to Shay because it was safe, but she's a young adult now and soon she'll be moving on with her life. Baby, deep down inside, you want and need to love someone and have him love you back. Baby, I know God has someone for you. I'm praying God will open his eyes soon."

Except for the sniffles, Julia was quiet. Ana Simone was something else. How her mother had managed to sit in her San Fernando Valley estate and read her mail four hundred miles away was a mystery to her.

"I love you, Mommy," was all she could say.

* * *

On Tuesday, Reggie attended noonday prayer at True Worship. His church mother, Mother Elsie, usually conducted the prayer. Mother Elsie was an elderly woman, believed to be in her early seventies, and an anointed prayer warrior. Mother Elsie didn't play when it came to the things of God. If you were wrong, she'd tell you.

If you were right, she'd encourage you to continue. But under no circumstances would she beat around the bush. "It is what it is," seemed to be her slogan.

Mother Elsie claimed that God talked to her. The congregation believed this to be true, because when Mother Elsie told you something was going to happen, you could write it on the calendar with the exact time of arrival. She didn't play with the young women either. She made sure the single available sisters understood that her pastor was not available. If she saw a sister flaunting herself, trying to catch his attention, she'd pull her short-skirted tail, and say, "Baby, go sit yourself down somewhere and while you're at it lower your skirt. Pastor doesn't want you. If he did he would've told you by now. You make sure he sees all of you every Sunday. If he hasn't approached you after you've left nothing for the imagination, that means he's not interested." Some of the sisters resented her for her directness, but Reggie appreciated her for having his back.

"God bless you, Mother Elsie. That was some powerful prayer. Mother, if you keep praying like that, things are going to change around here quickly. You know what we believe: Prayer changes things."

"I know that's right, Pastor." She paused. A few months ago, God told her some things were going to change at True Worship and at the Fifth Sunday Fellowship, God told her exactly what those changes were.

"So, Pastor, are you ready for things to change around here?" Mother Elsie asked.

"Mother, I'm so excited I can barely contain myself. I've been praying and waiting for this to happen since the doors of True Worship opened," Reggie said with a wide grin.

"Pastor, I'm happy for you, too. A First Lady is just what True Worship needs."

Reggie's grin disappeared. "Mother, what are you talking about? I'm not getting married nowhere in the near future. I was referring to the remodeling of our new building."

"I'm happy about that, too, but I'm overjoyed about the new lady in your life," Mother answered, unfazed by his denial.

"Mother, the only lady in my life right now is you. I'm not looking for a wife. All of my attention is on True Worship and how I can better serve God's people." Reggie smiled and placed his arm around her shoulders.

Mother Elsie turned and walked away, mumbling, "That's the problem. You're so busy looking out for the church, huh; you need to look out for yourself. Your wife is dancing and singing right in your face and all you can see is the ministry. You need to try and get some ministry for yourself. You're right, prayer changes things, but God changes people. I know what to do for you, huh; I'm going to put some prayer on you."

Later, seated at his desk, Reggie smiled as he read the grant deed to the newly acquired building. Minister Johnson had picked up the final documents from the title company earlier that morning. Reggie was so excited about the blessing that he wanted to celebrate. Without thinking, he picked up the headset and punched in the numbers.

Reggie whistled the notes to the old Kool and the Gang song, "Celebration," while he waited.

"Pinnacle Developments, how may I direct your call?"

"This is Reggie Pennington, is Ms. Simone available?"

"Just a moment."

"Hello, Reggie, how can I help you?" Julia asked, when she answered the line.

"I have the answer to your question," he stated.

"Excuse me?"

"On Sunday, you asked me, what would I like you to do for me."

"Oh, so now, two days later, you know?" she smirked.

"I'd like something to drink."

"Sorry, but I'm all out of lemonade and if that's all you called for, I suggest you try the corner store."

"Actually, I'd like some prime rib, tiger prawns and a view of the Bay to go along with the lemonade," he added.

"Reggie, you like a lot of things, don't you?"

"I'm excited. I just got the new deed and I feel like celebrating."

"Let me guess," she said sarcastically, "there's no one in your church you can celebrate with."

"There is, but I'd like to show you some appreciation for what you've done," he answered.

"The last time you tried that, it ended in a disaster," she reminded him.

"I promise, I'll behave myself."

After a prolonged silence, she responded, "I don't have anything on my agenda for the evening and a little company would be nice, even if it is you. What did you have in mind?"

"Skates."

"Nikki must have told you that's one of my favorite places."

"No, she didn't, but I love the food. So, for what time should I make reservations?" He was confident she'd accept.

"It might be a better idea if I have Michelle make them. I guarantee you we'll get the best table. Shall we say six o'clock?"

"Sure." He paused. "Julia, I apologize in advance if this offends you, but you do understand that this is not a date?"

"Of course, Reggie, I understand. You would never date a woman like me. Just make sure you pick up the check. I'll meet you at six o'clock." With that, she hung up the phone.

That went well. He looked at the clock, he had four hours to check on his rental property, get a haircut, shower and drive across town for dinner. As he locked away the deed and gathered his briefcase, it never occurred to him that, when he thought about someone to celebrate with, Julia was the only person that came to mind.

Chapter 9

J ulia pulled into the Skates parking lot at exactly six o'clock. She quickly straightened her clothes and removed her hair clip. As she walked through the lot, she was glad she'd worn her black wool pantsuit and long wool coat. The November air was dry and cold. The strong, steady wind from the Bay added to the chill factor.

As she neared the restaurant entrance, she spotted Reggie standing out front wearing dress slacks, a pullover sweater and leather jacket. Everything was black except for the small gold cross that hung around his neck. His hair and goatee appeared to be freshly trimmed. This was the first time observing him in casual clothing, stubbornness prevented her from admitting she liked what she saw.

"Good evening, Julia," he said with that sweet deceiving smile of his. "I'm glad you decided to accept my invitation."

"How could I pass up a free meal at one of my favorite places?" was her dry response.

"It's cold out here, let's go inside." He held the door open for her.

Skates literally sat on the Berkeley Marina. The place was known for its dynamic views of San Francisco, and the Bay and Golden Gate Bridges. At night the Bay Bridge was beautifully draped with a coat of lights. Skates had a very diverse clientele. On any given day, you would find business executives in tailored suits dining alongside couples in jeans and T-shirts. No matter the time of day, Skates was always packed and tonight was no exception. Without a reservation, people usually waited up to an hour to be seated. Sometimes with a reservation, people still had to wait for a table to become available.

As soon as Julia walked through the door, the restaurant manager greeted her.

"Good evening, Mr. Pennington and Ms. Julia. Your table is ready. Please follow me."

Julia ignored Reggie's puzzled expression. "Thank you, Henry."

They followed Henry while the patrons who'd been waiting to be seated stared. Henry led them to the best table in the house. He then assisted Julia with her coat and chair.

"Ms. Julia, I'll have Cindy bring you some strawberry lemonade. Mr. Pennington, what can I get for you?" Henry asked, turning to Reggie.

"I'll have the same," Reggie responded, but he was still confused.

Henry signaled the waitress. "Will you be having your usual tonight?" he then asked Julia.

"Yes, but instead of a Caesar salad, I'll have the clam chowder."

He turned to Reggie. "And you, Mr. Pennington?"

"I'll have the prime rib, medium well, with tiger prawns. I think I'll try the clam chowder also."

"Sit back, relax and enjoy your evening."

"Thank you," Julia and Reggie said in unison as Henry turned and left.

"I don't believe this," were the first words out of Reggie's mouth. "I've been here on several occasions and not one time has anyone waited for me at the door or called me by my name. How is it that the manager knows your name and what you like to eat?"

The waitress placed their drinks on the table along with warm bread.

Julia acknowledged her. "Thanks, Cindy."

"You're welcome, Ms. Julia." The waitress smiled and walked away.

Julia addressed Reggie's question. "You know what they say, money talks. If you spent as much money in here as Pinnacle does on a regular basis, Henry would greet you at the front door, too. I like the treatment, but I don't put value in it because I know the motive behind it."

"Just how much does Pinnacle pay for this royal treatment?" he asked.

She raised her eyebrows. "Let's just say I know the entire staff by name."

Reggie rested his elbows on the table. "Julia, can I ask you a personal question?"

"Sure, you're free to ask me whatever you like." She paused to sip lemonade. "Now, will I give you an answer? That depends on the question."

He leaned in closer. "Just how successful is Pinnacle?"

"Don't beat around the bush, Reverend. This is not Sunday worship service where you need to pace your sermon. What you really want to know is how much money do I have?"

He raised his hands and leaned back. "All right, you got me on that one," he admitted.

"Well, I can't give you an exact figure, but at the present time Pinnacle has over seven figures in real estate assets, which provides us with a very liquid cash flow. Over half of our real estate assets are right here in Emery Bay. Of course our numbers will increase once Point Richmond is completed."

"Wow," was all Reggie could say. He took a sip of his lemonade. "What made you choose a profession predominately controlled by males?"

"If you ask my father, he'd say it was his DNA. He's probably right, but I've ways liked to design and create things. While my sisters played house, I daydreamed about turning our backyard into great places like New York City or Las Vegas, anything with lights." She smiled.

"When I was older, my father taught me how to read his drawings. I would study the drawings and then ride around town trying to find the perfect place to put his creations." She sipped her lemonade and continued, "After my husband's death, I just took the chance and started my own company with the insurance money, which is not very much in the real estate world. Thanks to God's guidance and my father's help, Pinnacle has been a phenomenal success.

"How far do you want to go with Pinnacle?" Reggie asked before he sipped his lemonade.

"I really don't know. I've accomplished everything I'd set out to. After the Point Richmond project is completed, I'm thinking about taking a break for a while. I've made enough money that I could live on the residuals for the rest of my life."

The soup arrived and Reggie gently touched Julia's hand and said grace. "Tell me about Point Richmond," he said once he finished.

With pride, Julia explained the waterfront development while they ate clam chowder.

"Sounds fabulous, I would like to take a tour."

"Sure, just let me know when you have an available Friday morning."

They finished the soup in silence until Reggie brought up an earlier statement. "How long were you married?"

"Fourteen months," Julia said with a hint of sadness. "Sean was killed in an automobile accident when I was eight months pregnant."

"That explains why you and your daughter are so close."

"Dinner is served," Cindy announced, as she cleared the dishes and set the entrée on the table.

Reggie appeared surprised when he noticed they had ordered the exact same meal. "Great minds think alike," he commented.

"They sure do and sometimes average guys like you get lucky," Julia mused.

"Very funny," he smirked.

They continued talking while they enjoyed the food and the view. They laughed and talked through the entire meal. They caught the attention of fellow patrons when they laughed uncontrollably about how Mother Clark's dentures fell out of her mouth and into the aisle, while she danced in the spirit at the Fifth Sunday Fellowship service.

It was evident neither one of them wanted to end the evening when Julia said, "I thought this was a celebration," and ordered a bottle of non-alcoholic champagne, without an objection from Reggie. They toasted and spent the next hour sipping champagne while Reggie shared, in more detail, his future plans for True Worship.

"Oh, my goodness, it's after ten o'clock," Julia said when she looked at her watch. "I had better get going. I have a busy day tomorrow."

"Do you live near here?" he asked.

"No, I'm about an hour away." She paused. "I live in Blackhawk."

"Of course, where else would a woman like you live?"

Julia rolled her eyes as she stood and reached for her coat. "And where does a man like you live?"

"I live in Oakland on Campus Drive," he answered as he assisted her with her coat.

She was familiar with the area. "I bet you have a great view of the city from there."

"It's nice," he said nonchalantly as he laid the bills on the table. He then put on his jacket.

They walked side by side into the cold night air.

"On second thought, I think I'll stay here tonight," Julia said when she saw how foggy it had become.

"You have a house here also?" he questioned.

"I keep a furnished condo in Emery Bay for late nights when I don't feel like driving. I usually spend a couple of nights out of the week here, but I always drive home on Fridays," she explained.

"Where did you park?"

"I'm right over there."

Not sure of where she meant, he asked, "Where?"

"I'm in the Jag over there next to the black Mercedes."

"Thank you for making it easy for me," he said.

"What do you mean?"

"After I walk you to your car, I won't have far to go. That's me in the Mercedes."

Julia thought about how in sync they'd been the whole evening without trying to be. They had chosen the same color clothing, ordered the same meal, and without realizing it, Julia had parked her car right next to his.

"Nice, not quite what I expected for a man like you," she teased.

"I'll follow you to your condo," he told her.

"You don't have to do that; it's not like we're on a date," was her response, but she was really flattered.

"I know that, but it's dangerous out here. I don't want to come in, I just want to make sure you make it home safely."

"Suit yourself." She appreciated his concern, but didn't think it was necessary to tell him.

Once she was inside of her car, he handed her his card with his cell number on the back. "Once you're inside your unit, call me and let me know you made it inside safely," he instructed.

She took the card and placed it on the console without objecting.

"Julia, I have really enjoyed your company tonight. Thank you for giving me a chance to redeem myself. Maybe we could do this again sometime, you know, just hang out."

"Sure," she said, and without thinking, wrote her personal cell number on the back of her business card and handed it to him. He took the card and told her to lock her doors. He then went around and got in his car.

While driving down University Avenue, Julia suddenly realized she'd just given Reginald Pennington access to her twenty-four/seven.

Chapter 10

"Do you have any plans for Thanksgiving?" Reggie asked. It was during the holiday season that he really missed not having his parents around anymore.

Over the last two weeks he and Julia had spoken to each other every day and hung out for lunch a few times. Sometimes they'd talk for a few minutes. Other times, they would spend hours talking about everything from local sports to the Bible. He learned that they both shared a love for baseball, and through their conversations, he realized Julia's commitment to God was real. She'd shared with him she recently had accepted her call to the ministry and was in training. "If there's anything I can do, please let me know," he told her. He was genuinely happy for her.

He found himself looking forward to their daily chats and sometimes debates. Despite the fact that they had more commonalities than differences, he still didn't see her as his type and worth pursuing. He convinced himself that she was just a fun person to talk to, a buddy. She made him laugh with her sarcastic sense of humor and when he was excited about something, she was excited with him. Without her knowing it, she'd made him feel less lonely during this holiday season.

"Shay and I are going to help feed the homeless at the church in the morning. Then, we're driving up to Napa for dinner at my brother's house," Julia answered.

Reggie didn't understand why he felt disappointed he wouldn't see her. It wasn't like he didn't have anything to do. Every year he went out with the evangelism team. True Worship would be delivering hot meals and ministering to the homeless all day. Afterward, he'd go and visit with his aunt and uncle in Stockton. He had more than enough to occupy his time, but he would have loved to hang out with her.

"How about you?" she asked.

Reggie went over his plans, wished her a happy holiday, and after he told her to drive safely, said good-bye. It was Tuesday and she probably wouldn't be available to talk to him until Saturday.

Suddenly, he was starting to feel lonely again. He sat on his couch and looked around his expansive living room. Not much had changed since he had moved in seven years ago, after the death of his parents. That's the way he wanted it. It made him feel close to them in some sort of way. He'd kept most of the furniture his parents left also. They had just bought it a year before the accident. He remembered how happy his mother was when she finally got her French set. She'd talked about it for as long as he could remember. She did a holy dance right there in the living room, while Reggie and his father laughed.

John and Mary Pennington had given him a strong foundation. His parents didn't attend church regularly until his teenage years, but they instilled in him good values and morals. Unable to have any more children, they poured all of their attention into Reggie. They worked hard to make sure he didn't want for anything. It wasn't until Reggie attended college that they realized they'd made a mistake. His mother was the first to see it.

Reggie was a selfish, spoiled brat. He expected the young women on campus, and anywhere else, to cater to him and him alone. It didn't matter to him that the young ladies were in school to receive an education. Reggie wanted their undivided attention. He wanted them to be available to him whenever he wanted and for however long he wanted. He didn't consider their feelings at all. If one didn't do what he wanted, he would simply drop that one and find someone else. No matter how attentive a female was, he would never commit.

"Son, what is wrong with you? It's not right how you treat these women. You change women like you change clothes. You are not the center of the world. You can't have everything your way," his mother would tell him constantly.

"If you don't love these women, then stop sleeping with them. How many women you sleep with is not the measuring stick for a man. One day you are going to hurt someone and yourself," his father warned.

He looked at the wall portrait of his parents above the fireplace. "I wish I had listened to you," he said as he wiped a tear from his cheek. He cried regularly in the confines of his home.

He got up and walked over to the bay window. "God," he prayed as he looked out over the city, "please fix what I have messed up."

Chapter 11

Julia checked her cell phone. She was surprised when she didn't have any messages from Reggie. The last time she'd spoken to him was two days before Thanksgiving. That was four days ago. She'd gotten used to hearing his voice on a regular basis and she missed the conversations. She decided to give him a call just to let him know she was back in town. She became concerned on the fifth ring, because he usually answered her calls by the second ring.

She was about to hang up when a groggy, congested voice answered, "Wello."

"I know you are not still in bed, it's almost noon," she said.

"Wes, I am. I dink I caught de flu. I got fever and chills and my body aches all wover."

"You poor baby," she teased. "Do you need me to bring you anything?"

"Weah, a new body."

Julia laughed at his response. "You'll have to wait until Jesus comes back for that, but I'll see what I can do to help you feel better in the interim."

"Dank you," the two words sounded labored coming from Reggie.

"That is, if you don't mind taking help from a woman like me." Julia threw the jab, then hung up before he could throw a comeback. She phoned Nikki.

"Hey, girl, your pastor has the flu and I'm going to check on him. Do you think Tyrone could meet me at his house? I know he has a key and I'll feel more comfortable having a third person around?" she explained.

"Hold on a minute, I'll ask him." A moment later Nikki returned to the phone. "He'll meet you there in one hour."

"Make it an hour and a half; I have a quick stop to make."

"All right, but can you clear up something for me?" Nikki baited.

By the smirk in Nikki's voice, Julia knew what was coming next.

"I thought you weren't going to spend any of your energy on my pastor."

"Nikki, we are friends, that's all. I'm just going to check on him just like I would check on you if you were sick," Julia explained, although she wondered if that was all there was to it.

"Whatever you say, girlfriend, whatever you say."

Tyrone was standing on the porch when Julia pulled into the driveway ninety minutes later.

"Thanks for meeting me, Tyrone. I hope I didn't mess up your plans too much." She gave Tyrone a knowing smile. She hadn't missed the fact that he was with Nikki when she phoned.

"It's all right, Sister Julia. I'm always available to help my pastor out," he said as he helped Julia with the bags. Tyrone unlocked the door and she followed in behind him. He led her to the kitchen and placed the bags on the center island. "I'll go find him and see if he's awake."

"Go ahead, I can handle everything in here," Julia replied.

Tyrone disappeared and Julia surveyed her surroundings. The kitchen wasn't as large as hers, but it contained everything she needed. The yellow and white décor gave the kitchen a bright and airy feeling. She searched the wood cabinets until she found a stockpot. She used the double sink to fill it with water as she prepared to make her famous homemade chicken noodle soup. After the soup was started, she finished putting away the juice and bottled water.

She left the cough syrup, decongestant, Vapor Rub, and Tylenol on the kitchen counter near the sink.

A few minutes later Tyrone returned.

"Pastor was in bed, burning up. I'm going to help him get washed up and then I'll bring him into the den, so I can change his bed linens." He pointed to the room adjacent to the kitchen.

"Take your time. I'll wait for you in there," she said as Tyrone disappeared again. She stirred the stockpot, added some seasonings and replaced the lid, then decided to take a tour of the ranch-style home.

She walked into the living room and admired the breathtaking view of the city that the bay window freely offered. Above the fireplace was a portrait of who she assumed were Reggie's parents. She thought Reggie resembled his mother more than his father. Her dark- chocolate skin mirrored his. On the mantle was a picture of a handsome baby boy wearing the cutest little sailor suit. "It doesn't make any sense, you were even fine as a baby," she stated to the photo. On the opposite end was a picture of Reggie at his college graduation. Julia wondered if he was the same egotistical jerk back then as he was today.

She walked down a hallway lined with African-American artwork. She wondered how much of the décor was Reggie's idea. She had a feeling it hadn't changed much since the death of his parents. Next to the bathroom she found the linen closet. She looked inside and removed a sheet, blanket and a pillow. She took them into the den and arranged them on the brown couch.

Inside the den was a wall-to-wall oak entertainment center complete with a 60-inch television. She inspected his DVD collection. He had a large selection of old Sidney Poitier films. "Impressive." She loved Sidney Poitier. He also had many of her favorite comedies. The shelves on the right side housed a huge selection of tapes from renowned preachers and Christian teachers.

"Sister Julia, you've got it smelling real good in here."

Julia turned around to see Tyrone helping Reggie to the sofa.

Reggie was wearing black and green checkered flannel cotton pajamas covered by a black robe. His skin looked flushed and his eyes were sunken. He was weak and could only take small steps. She quickly moved to help Tyrone remove his robe and lay him on the couch.

"I wish I could smell it," Reggie managed to say.

"At least you'll be able to taste it in a little while," Julia said as she removed his slippers and covered him with the blanket. Once he was comfortable on the couch, Tyrone left and went to change his bedding. Julia left and returned with the medicine and bottled water she'd brought. She set the tray she'd found in the kitchen cabinet on the wooden table in the den.

"You need to take this," she said pouring the decongestant. He opened his mouth and swallowed without protesting. "Now take two of these, they'll help bring your fever down and should help with the body aches also." She handed him the Tylenol and some water.

He slowly obeyed then lay back down. "Dank you," he said in a raspy voice.

She reached for the Vapor Rub, then hesitated. "I need to rub this on your chest. If you're uncomfortable, I'll have Tyrone do it." Julia waited for him to respond.

"Go ahead," he answered and pulled the cover back.

Julia unbuttoned the first two buttons of his pajamas. She opened the jar and placed a small amount of the ointment into her hands. Being careful, she gently massaged the cream into his chest. She stopped when a soft moan escaped from his lips, more for her benefit than his. She fastened his pajamas and covered him with the blanket. As he lay there with his eyes closed, she thought, *If you weren't so wrong for me, I could really get into you.*

* * *

Ninety minutes later, Reggie awoke to the sound of Julia and Tyrone's laughter. Reggie looked around to see Tyrone seated in the chair opposite him and Julia sitting Indian-style on the floor in front of him only inches from the couch. The two were enjoying the play, *Madea Goes to Jail*. He lay there quietly watching Julia.

"I didn't know you were awake," she said when she turned her head to him. She placed the back of her hand on his forehead. "Your fever seems to be subsiding. I think you should try to eat something."

"Whatever you say, doc."

Tyrone helped him sit up while Julia went into the kitchen. She returned with some more water and a bowl of soup. She surprised both Reggie and Tyrone when she sat on her knees in front of Reggie and fed him the soup. When he finished, Tyrone helped him to the bathroom, while Julia cleared the dishes. When she returned to the den, she noticed he was moving steadier and his color was better.

When the DVD ended, Julia announced it was time for her to leave. She gave Reggie instructions on how much medicine to take and when to take it. "Make sure you drink plenty of fluids. There's more water and juice in the refrigerator. Take it slow and easy, Reggie. Don't try to do too much too fast," she warned. "You're not Superman. I'll call and check on you later," she added before walking out the door.

Reggie asked Tyrone to hand him the phone, so he could call and give instructions to Minister Johnson for tomorrow's service.

"Pastor, I hope you don't mind me saying this, but I really like Sister Julia. I think she's a good person. You made a good choice."

"You're right, Tyrone, she is a good person, but we are just friends. Neither one of us is interested in the other beyond that."

"You're sicker than I thought," Tyrone said.

Chapter 12

"How sweet," Julia whispered, inhaling the fragrance. Reggie had sent her a dozen red carnations to thank her for tending to him over the weekend. She had called him on Sunday, after church, and twice a day since, to check on him. Last night he sounded like his old self. They even had a short debate about the national healthcare initiative. Julia sighed and read the card.

A friend loveth at all times…

Thanks for being my friend,

Reggie

"What are you trying to say?" she wondered out loud.

Reggie was starting to touch her in places she knew were not safe. She was treading on thin ice when it came to her feelings toward him. Julia warned herself to be careful, because the attraction was not mutual. He had made that clear on several occasions.

She had dinner plans scheduled with him later that evening, but now wondered if she should cancel. "I should put some space between us before I regret it." The ringing of her cell phone interrupted her thoughts. It was Reggie.

"Hello, sweetheart."

The sound of his voice calling her "sweetheart" unglued her. "Hey," was the only response she could manage.

"Did I catch you at a bad time?"

She swallowed. "No, I was just reading your card. Thanks for the flowers."

"Are we still on for tonight?"

Her mind told her to say no, but she decided she would listen to it another time. "Sure."

"What do you have a taste for?"

She thought for a moment and tried to think of some place that was not cozy. "How about Zachary's?"

"If that's what you want, but I can afford to take you somewhere nice."

"Zachary's will be fine. I'll see you at six."

Zachary's was crowded as usual. They made the best stuffed pizza in the Bay Area. Julia thought it had the perfect casual atmosphere. They placed their orders and found a table in the front, facing the street.

Reggie thanked her again for nursing him back to health and Julia teased him about how pitiful he looked.

"You were such a baby. Oh, by the way, you were a handsome baby."

"How would you know?" he asked.

"The other day, at your house, I saw your picture."

He looked puzzled.

"You know, the one on your mantle of you in your little sailor suit," she clarified.

"Oh, that picture," he said, then changed the subject. "So, Julia, tell me why you never remarried. Based on how well you nursed me, you'd make someone a good wife." His face twisted. "Oops, that could be considered a sexist statement."

"It is, but I wouldn't expect anything less from you."

The sound of his laughter warmed her.

"I think I would make a good—correction, I'd make an outstanding wife. Unfortunately, my second husband didn't agree."

"You've actually been married twice?" he asked, with a hint of condemnation.

"Yes, and it was the worst four years of my life."

"You don't have to tell me about it."

"I know I don't have to tell you anything, but I know you want to know. Besides, I really don't mind sharing the dark spots in my life. God healed me of those old wounds years ago and I've moved on."

"You got me again. An inquiring mind wants to know," he admitted.

"I'll start at the beginning. I met David White when Shay was four years old. He was a new developer like me. We were married after only five months of dating. Things appeared to be fine in the beginning. I use the word 'appeared' because my parents tried to warn me about him. 'He's a wolf in sheep's clothing,' was what my mother said. Of course I didn't listen. I was too busy enjoying the attention he showered on me. After we married the attention stopped. Instead of loving me, he competed with me. He grew jealous and bitter when my business grew and his didn't. When I refused to close my business and work with him, he became abusive. At first he started calling me nasty names, but eventually he started hitting me."

Reggie took a sip of his lemonade, but his eyes remained glued on her as if the thought of some lowlife putting his hands on her left a nasty taste in his mouth.

"In the midst of this, I got pregnant. At first, I thought having a baby would help David settle down because he had always been good with Shay. My hopes soon disappeared when he told me to have an abortion. Of course, I didn't and that only made matters worse. One night when I was four months pregnant, he came home and told me he was leaving me for his girlfriend. He marched upstairs to our bedroom to get some of his things and I followed behind him, crying."

Reggie placed his hand on top of hers.

"I begged him not to leave, but he wouldn't listen. I grabbed him and he knocked me to the floor, called me a female dog and left the room. Still not ready to give up, I got up and followed him. I met him just as he started down the stairs. I grabbed his arm and this time he threw me down the stairs. I stayed there until Shay, who was eight at the time, found me the next morning lying in a pool of blood and called nine-one-one. After that I was done. He didn't contest the divorce and I never saw him after that." She took a bite of her pizza.

Reggie sat there, speechless. He didn't appear hungry anymore; he seemed angry, hurt and amazed.

"I'm amazed. After all you've been through, you don't sound bitter."

"It took a *long* time and a lot of prayer, but I was able to forgive him. It didn't happen until I really dedicated my life to God. I had to take responsibility for my part and accept that I made the bad choice of marrying David White. I refused to heed the many warnings. Only after I was able to forgive myself, was I able to forgive him and move on. Trust me; I could not have done it without God."

"Julia, you are an amazing woman. I really mean it. I feel blessed to have you in my life." Sitting in front of him was a living example of what he preached to his congregation, true forgiveness. If David White could be forgiven, maybe there was hope for his situation.

"Now it's your turn. Tell me why you never married."

Reggie appeared to think for a moment about how much he wanted to disclose. "I was engaged once, but things didn't work out," he finally said.

"What happened? Did you suddenly decide she wasn't your type?"

"Actually, it turned out that I wasn't right for her."

"And since then?"

"Before I dedicated my life to God, I had my share of let's just say, 'fun,' but nothing serious."

"Do you think you will ever get married?"

"I honestly don't know. I do know that marriage is not a priority in my life right now. I'm not blind, I know there are several women who are positive they would make the perfect wife for me, but I'm not interested in none of them. I'm completely devoted to the well-being of True Worship. I don't have the time or the desire to work on a relationship that would lead to marriage. Maybe in a few years, but right now, I'm not interested."

Julia changed the subject by commenting on the weather.

Chapter 13

"Y ou can't control God with a time clock. God moves in His own time. He knows what's best for us even when we don't and He knows the right time to give it to us."

Julia listened attentively to Pastor Leonard.

"He knows that if He gives us things prematurely, we won't appreciate them and we will abuse them. We have to learn how to patiently go through the process. It's through the process that we learn who we really are and who God is. The process is where He removes the crutches and takes us out of our comfort zone. He does this so He can teach us to completely rely on Him, not on our ability. Trust God through the process. Trust that He knows what's best for you. Hold on to every word God has given you. God is not a man and He doesn't lie. God is God enough to make every promise good."

Shouts of "Amen" echoed through the sanctuary.

"I enjoyed your sermon today," Julia told Pastor Leonard, when she greeted him after service.

"Thank you, Sister Julia." A big grin creased his face. "How are things going with you and my son?"

"Your son?" She was confused because both of Reverend Leonard's sons were married.

Reverend Leonard looked around as to make sure no one was in earshot, and for the benefit of the professional lip readers, covered his mouth, and whispered in her ear, "Reverend Pennington."

"Oh, there's nothing going on between us. We're just friends." She shook her head vigorously.

"Does that mean you are not interested in him?"

"He's not interested in me—outside of friendship," Julia explained.

"What makes you think that?" Reverend Leonard had a puzzled expression.

"He's told me so. Repeatedly," she added.

"That boy doesn't have a lick of sense. If I could afford it, I'd buy him some. On second thought I don't think anybody has that much money," Reverend Leonard mumbled, then said out loud, "Remember what I said this morning, God knows what's best for us, even when we don't.""

* * *

Julia watched the rain beat against the windshield of her Jaguar as she waited for Nikki. Today was the first Sunday in December, and Girlfriend's Day. They agreed to meet after church to get a jump on Christmas shopping, since both had missed the Black Friday pandemonium due to spending time with family. As she watched the rain collect and slide down the window, she was glad she had changed into her Levi's and a sweatshirt.

The longer she waited, the more thoughts of Reggie cluttered her mind and clouded her thinking. After Zachary's the other night, she'd decided she would stop communicating with him so much. Her emotions had traveled to a place that were guaranteed to bring her nothing but heartache.

Nikki tapped the passenger side window. Julia hadn't seen her drive up. She unlocked the door and Nikki jumped inside.

"Hey, I see you decided to get comfortable also," Nikki said in reference to Julia's attire.

"I didn't feel like walking around a crowded mall in my Sunday go-to-meeting suit and heels," Julia answered.

"I feel you on that one. I went into the bathroom after church and put this sweat suit on."

As they rode, they each gave the highlights of their respective worship services. Julia pulled into a parking spot at Stoneridge Mall after being stuck in bumper-to-bumper traffic on Interstate 680. Just as she was about to open her car door, Nikki grabbed her arm.

"Julia, I need to talk to you for a minute."

Her tone concerned Julia. "What's going on with you?"

"It's not me, Julia. The question should be, 'What's wrong with you'?"

"What are you talking about?"

Nikki sighed. "Julia, you and I go way back. You know things about me that my own mother doesn't even know. I trust you with my life and I thought you felt the same."

Julia shrugged her shoulders. "What's this all about? You know you're my girl."

"Then why didn't you tell me that you and Pastor are serious?"

Julia was becoming frustrated with the constant references to her and Reggie's non-existent relationship. She slapped the steering wheel. "How many times do I have to tell you, we are just friends?"

"That's what your mouth keeps telling me, but your heart is saying something completely different."

Julia huffed and looked away.

"Tyrone told me how Pastor refused to get out of bed, until Tyrone told him that you were there. He said Pastor acted like a teenager preparing for his first date, trying to coordinate his pajamas and robe.

Julia's dry chuckle stuck in her throat. "You've got to be kidding."

"No, I'm not. And what about how you wouldn't leave his side? Tyrone said you sat on the *floor* next to him the entire time, *and* you spoon-fed him. That doesn't sound like friends to me." Nikki used her fingers to emphasize quotation marks. "That sounds like a woman taking care of her man. If you're dating, just say so, but please don't lie about it, especially not to me."

Julia rubbed her forehead. "Nikki, to be totally honest with you and myself, I am starting to have feelings for him. Serious feelings. But, girl," she paused, "he doesn't want me," she said just above a whisper. "Sometimes I think he's sending a different message by his actions. Like the other day when he called me 'sweetheart.' But then he constantly reminds me that he's not interested in me outside of friendship. It's hard for me to accept because he calls me every day, sometimes twice a day. He sent me flowers and on a few occasions, held my hand. I honestly don't know what to think. One thing I do know is that, if I'm not careful, I'll end up with a broken heart."

Except for the rain beating against the window and Julia's sniffles, the car remained silent.

After a couple of minutes Nikki placed her arm around Julia's shoulder. "Girl, I don't think he really knows what's happening to him. I think he's been alone for so long that he doesn't recognize that he needs someone. I think he has substituted True Worship for companionship. I also think he used your financial status as an excuse not to get close to you. Now let me tell you what I do know. I know I've never seen him smile as much as he has these last two months. I know his face lights up every time he mentions you to me, which is quite often. I know, from Tyrone, that you are the only woman he's allowed into his home for any reason." Nikki squeezed her shoulder. "Listen to his words. But watch his actions even closer. He's falling for you just as hard as you are for him, if not harder."

"Do you really think so?"

"Yes, I do. You'll see, it's all a part of the process."

"That's why I love your unorganized butt; you always know what to say." Julia laughed and returned the embrace.

Chapter 14

Christmas was exactly two weeks away and Julia had completed her shopping list, right down to Shay's new iPhone. She was ready to give herself and her employees a much-needed break. She closed Pinnacle every year during the holiday season for two weeks to give her employees time with their families. With the cold weather and off-and-on rain, there wasn't much more work the contractors could do anyway.

This morning she made the last worksite tour of the year. Reggie had met her there and she gave him the grand tour of the Point Richmond Project. She had decided to take Nikki's advice and continued to spend time with him. The relationship status was the same, except now Reggie addressed her as "sweetheart" on a regular basis and made a habit of holding her hand. On a few occasions, his arm rested on her shoulder. Over the last two weeks, they'd been together eight out of the fourteen days. They had gone to dinner and taken in a couple of movies. Reggie and Tyrone went fishing in the lake alongside her Blackhawk estate. After the men cleaned the fish, she and Nikki fried it up with French fries and coleslaw served on the side.

Reggie waited in her office, while she met with her staff in the conference room to give out holiday bonuses. They were going to spend the afternoon ice skating. Julia hadn't ice skated in years, so when Reggie suggested they go, she gladly accepted.

"I'm all done. Shall we take your car or mine?" she cheerfully asked, upon entering her office.

"I'll drive, that way I know we'll get there in one piece."

"I know you're not making fun of my driving?"

"Julia, you are a beautiful and intelligent woman, but sweetheart, you have a speed demon that needs to be cast out."

"Forget you," she said and playfully slapped him on the arm, pausing long enough to squeeze his biceps. She stuffed her photo ID and keys into her front jean pocket, clipped on her cell phone and headed out the door with Reggie in tow.

For the next hour and a half they played liked they were kids again. Both were more than a little rusty on the ice. Reggie tried to play it cool by creeping along the side rail.

"Oh no, you're not. You said we were going ice skating, not ice creeping." With that said, she pushed him away from the rail. He took two steps and landed on his butt. They spent most of the time helping each other off the ice. When they finally found their groove, it was almost time to leave.

"I haven't had this much fun in a long time. My body will pay for this fun tomorrow," Reggie announced while changing into his shoes.

"I believe you. I didn't know you could laugh so much," she replied.

"I can't believe you pushed me and made me fall like that."

"Why not? You made me fall for you a long time ago," Julia said without thinking. Fortunately for her, it went right over his head.

"Hey, let's go get some ice cream," he suggested. "It's only sixty degrees out, but I'm game if you are."

"Sure," she quickly accepted. "Cold Stone's just a block over, we can walk."

Inside Cold Stone they shared a banana split, with banana, chocolate, and strawberry ice cream. They were so involved in their debate on who was the better football team, the Oakland Raiders or San

Francisco 49ers, that they didn't see Reverend Leonard and First Lady Leonard approach the table.

"Well, this certainly is a wonderful sight to see," Reverend Leonard started.

"Hello, Pastor and First Lady," they said almost in unison.

"I'm so glad the two of you are getting along so well. I could tell on my way over here that the two of you are really enjoying each other," First Lady Leonard said with a smile.

Julia covered her mouth to keep from giggling. First Lady Leonard's dentures shifted when she spoke.

Reggie appeared not to notice. "What brings the two of you here?" he asked.

"The same thing that brought you here. My sweetheart had a taste for some ice cream," Reverend Leonard answered. "I'm glad she did because seeing the two of you together has made my day. We don't want to interrupt, we just wanted to say hello. Y'all have a nice day," Reverend Leonard said with a smile.

"Yes, Lord, make sure you have fun," First Lady added, as her teeth shifted back into the original position.

"If I didn't know any better, I'd think they're trying to marry us off," Reggie said after they walked away.

"No!" Julia said sarcastically and continued eating ice cream.

On the walk back to Reggie's car they held hands and laughed at each other's jokes. He unlocked the car and opened the door to the trunk to place his jacket inside. Before Julia got inside, she noticed her cell phone on the passenger seat. She didn't realize it had fallen off her clip. The second Julia picked up her cell phone she knew something was wrong. She had ten missed calls.

"Oh God," was all she could say as she checked the call log. Eight of the ten calls were from the 650 area code where Shay was.

"What's wrong?" Reggie asked as she tried to call the number.

The line was busy. "Please, God, let everything be all right," she whispered.

"What's wrong?" Reggie asked again, with urgency.

Her phone rang and her hands trembled when the 650 area code appeared again. "Hello!" she yelled into the phone.

"I'm trying to reach Julia Simone," the flat voice stated.

Julia's breathing accelerated, and she struggled to get out, "This is she."

"Is your daughter LaShay Hampton?" the voice asked.

Her stomach began to quiver. "What's happened to Shay?"

"I'm calling from Stanford Medical Center." Julia gasped and felt her knees buckle. The caller continued, "I'm sorry to inform you, but your daughter was in an automobile accident."

If it weren't for Reggie, Julia would have fallen to the ground. She hadn't noticed, but he'd walked around the car and stood behind her when he heard her mention Shay's name. The phone fell from her hands, as she bent over, gripped her stomach, and cried out, "God, please, not my baby."

Reggie held her in one arm as he picked up the phone with his free hand and got the caller's location. He then reclined the passenger seat and laid Julia inside the car. He didn't have any tissue, so he grabbed a clean towel from his gym bag. After handing the towel to Julia, he fastened both seat belts and sped toward the interstate.

He prayed hard as he weaved through traffic. Occasionally, he glanced over at Julia, who sobbed uncontrollably. In between prayers, he stroked her head and assured her. "Sweetheart, it's going to be all right."

Reggie made the hour drive in forty-five minutes. He parked near the emergency room entrance. Her body shook as he helped her out of the car and led her inside. He went directly to the information desk, still holding Julia as he talked with the attendant.

"We're here to see LaShay Hampton. She was brought here by ambulance from a car accident."

The young man checked his log.

"Are you a relative?" the young man asked.

"She's her mother," Reggie answered as he pressed Julia closer to him.

"I'll let the nurse know you're here."

Reggie guided her to the nearest vacant seat. "Baby, everything's going to be fine," he assured her again, but this time he kissed her forehead.

Moments later a nurse came and escorted them to the room where Shay was being treated. Julia became frantic when she saw that the bed was empty.

"Where's my baby?" she demanded from the nurse.

"Your baby is going to be all right. She's downstairs in Radiology having an X-ray done." A female dressed in jeans and a Stanford sweatshirt entered the room behind the nurse. She was the same complexion as Julia and they shared the same almond-shaped eyes. Julia's lips were slightly fuller than the woman's and Julia was about an inch taller. She had the same black curly hair, but she wore it short like Jada Pinkett Smith. She stepped forward and hugged Julia.

"Angie, is she really okay? What happened?" Julia asked.

"The other driver ran a stop sign and slammed into her."

Julia gasped.

"Thanks to God and her seatbelt, she doesn't appear to have any major injuries. She does have a concussion, which is common. She banged her head against the airbag. We're waiting for her blood work and Mike's downstairs reading her films, just to make sure there aren't any internal injuries."

"Have you been with her the whole time? Did you see her?" Julia questioned.

"Yes, I did. I got here about forty-five minutes ago. Shay has me listed as an emergency contact in her wallet, since I'm close by. When the hospital saw my name, they paged me immediately."

"I'm so glad you were here." Julia hugged her and started crying again.

"You are such a cry baby," Angie teased, rubbing her back.

Julia looked over at Reggie and noticed his confused expression. She released her embrace.

"I'm sorry, Reggie. This is my oldest sister, Angelique. Angie, this is a friend of mine, Reverend Reginald Pennington."

Angie gave Julia a girl-we-need-to-talk look before addressing him. "It's good to meet you, Reverend Pennington."

"Please call me 'Reggie'."

"Only if you call me, 'Angie.' The only person that calls me Angelique is my mother, and that's only when she's mad at me."

"Dr. Sorenson, your niece's blood work is back," the nurse called from the doorway.

"Excuse me a minute," Angie said and followed the nurse outside.

"So, your sister is a doctor?" Reggie asked.

"She's an internal medicine doctor and her husband, Mike, is a radiologist. They are both on staff here."

"Just as I thought, her blood work is fine," Angie said when she returned.

"And so are her X-rays." A dark-haired Caucasian male added, from behind Angie.

"Hey, Mike." Julia hugged her brother-in-law.

"Have you calmed down yet? I know how you can get about your grown baby," he teased.

"I'm doing fine, now. Does this mean she can come home?" Julia asked.

"Yes, it does, but not tonight. She has suffered a concussion and she has a nasty knot on her head, so we are going to keep her overnight for observation. You can take your baby home tomorrow," Angie explained.

"Thanks, guys." She turned to Reggie. "Mike, this is my friend, Reggie."

Mike and Angie shared a quick glance. "It's good to finally meet a friend of Julia's. The next time we meet, we can get to know each other. Right now, I have to get back downstairs,"
Mike said.

"No problem, take care," Reggie responded.

Mike kissed his wife, and said good-bye.

"I need to get going, also," Angie said. "I have to pick the twins up from soccer. Shay is in good hands." She hugged her sister, then shook Reggie's hand before leaving the room.

Reggie waited with Julia until Shay was settled into a room. As he prepared to leave, he asked Julia what time he should return to pick them up in the morning.

"Thanks, but you don't have to come all the way back here." Thinking she'd misread disappointment in his facial expression, she continued, "I'll arrange for the limo service to drive us home. But it would help if you could have Nikki drive my car home." She handed him the keys.

"I'll see to it," he answered dryly.

Julia walked over and stood in front of him. She reached for his hands and held them as she looked directly into his eyes. "Thank you for being here with me today. I needed someone and you were everything I needed you to be. When I didn't have any strength of my own, you gave me some of yours, and I'll always remember that. Thank you for being a part of my life." She then stretched on her tiptoes and softly kissed his cheek.

Reggie's jaw flexed and his nostrils flared, as if he was struggling with his emotions. "I was just trying to be a good friend."

"Reggie, you are a good friend. Good-bye, Reggie," she said with finality.

"Keep your cell phone on. I'll call you later," he ordered, then abruptly left.

Reggie walked out of the hospital as fast as he could without running. He didn't understand what had just happened to him. Despite his best efforts to prevent it, Julia had managed to touch him in a way no woman ever had. She'd managed to penetrate the wall he'd built around his heart and had captured him. He wanted to give himself to her. Not just his body, but his heart and soul. He wanted to belong only to her. He wanted to hold and protect her. He wanted to love her. The way she looked into his eyes, the sweet words she spoke and the soft touch of her lips against his cheek, made him want to forget he was a Man of God. Julia had reminded him what it felt like to be a man.

"God, you've got to help me understand what's going on. I can't allow anything or anyone to distract me from the job you've given me. Show me how to push past my emotions and concentrate on only you," he prayed, as he headed toward the interstate.

Chapter 15

J ulia busied herself packing for her trip to her parents' home. The family was celebrating Christmas on the San Fernando Valley estate. Originally, she planned to leave on Wednesday, but after the recent turn of events, decided to leave a few days early. She needed to get away from the Bay Area and away from Reginald Pennington. She couldn't get him out of her mind, because he was deep inside her heart. She missed the roar of his laughter and the touch of his fingertips against her skin. He was so good to her that night at the hospital, but he wasn't good for her. Daydreaming and wishful thinking didn't change the fact that Reggie's caring for her didn't extend beyond the "road dog" level. How do you remain just friends with the one you love, she wondered while packing her toiletries.

"Mom, telephone. It's Reggie," Shay said, with a hint of mischievousness. Since meeting him at the hospital, Shay had been singing Reggie's praises.

"He called on the house phone?" Julia knew she hadn't given him her home number.

"No." Shay hunched her shoulders. "I answered your cell phone."

"If I wanted my cell phone answered, I would have answered it myself," Julia snapped and took the phone from her daughter. "Hello, Reggie."

"Is everything all right, sweetheart?"

"I'm in the middle of packing for my parents' house." She paused. "We're leaving today."

"I thought you weren't leaving until Wednesday." He sounded disappointed. "I was hoping we could have dinner at Skates tonight. I have something I want to give you."

"Sorry, but my flight leaves at six o'clock. Maybe we can get together when I get back," she suggested, proud for not yielding to his request.

"When will that be?" he asked, his voice subdued.

Julia fought to keep her voice from breaking. To her, he sounded lonely. She thought for a moment, she couldn't recall him ever mentioning his plans for Christmas. She hoped he wasn't spending it alone.

"Reggie, do you have plans for Christmas? If you don't, you're more than welcome to join us."

"After a short Christmas service, I'll probably visit my aunt and uncle in Stockton."

"You don't sound too excited. Why don't you think about it? Give me a call on Thursday and let me know."

Julia couldn't believe what she was doing. Just five minutes earlier she was trying to get away from him. Now she was inviting him home to meet the family.

"I'll think about it. What airport and airlines are you flying?"

"We're leaving out of Oakland on American."

"Good, I'll meet you there," he said with a burst of excitement.

"You don't have to do that," she protested, even though she really wanted to see him.

"I know I don't. See you soon." He hung up before she could say anything.

* * *

By Julia's estimation, the limo ride to the airport was taking too long. She tried not to be, but she was excited about seeing Reggie. They hadn't seen each other since Shay's accident, eight days ago. She had heard his voice daily, but now as the limo neared the airport, she was anxious for more. He was like a drug to her; one minute she didn't want anymore, the next minute she was having withdrawal symptoms. Her palms were sweaty and her right leg shook. As soon as the limo pulled up to the curb at Terminal 1, she spotted him.

"Give the driver a chance to stop the car. Your man's not going anywhere," Shay teased, when Julia's hand clutched the door latch.

"He's not my man," Julia defended.

"For real? Look at the grin on his face. You've got that man wrapped around your fingers and your toes."

"Shay, stop it. He considers me to be a good friend, that's all."

"That's what his mouth says, but that look in his eyes, says he would love to give you some 'praise and worship' service."

"I can't believe you said that," Julia said just as the driver opened her door. Deep down she hoped her daughter was right.

Julia noticed Reggie smiling as he watched her step from the limo.

"Hello, beautiful," he said, when he met her. "Maybe I should go with you."

"Hello," Shay and Julia said in unison. Reggie chuckled when Julia informed her daughter he wasn't talking to her.

"Mom, I was just having fun." Julia didn't respond.

"Uh huh," Julia grumbled, then directed her attention back to Reggie.

"Merry Christmas, Reggie. I'll leave you two alone to discuss praise and worship service." Shay laughed out loud, then went to check her luggage.

"What did she mean by that?" he asked.

"Nothing at all," Julia answered, while Reggie relieved her of the wheeled suitcase the driver placed beside her.

Reggie stood in line with her while she checked her bags and as she waited at the security checkpoint. As the long line progressed near the front, he gestured for Shay and Julia to grab hands, and he said a quick word of prayer for their safety and quick return.

"I thought you had something for me," Julia said when he finished.

"I do, but don't open it until you get on the plane." He pulled a small gift box from the inside of his jacket.

Julia took the box and placed it in her carry-on bag. "Thank you." She was nearing the ID checkpoint. Shay moved forward to give them a little privacy.

Reggie released her hand and moved so close to her that she smelled the residue of mint on his breath. He cupped her face with his hands at the perfect angle.

Heat began in her chest and rapidly swept through her body in anticipation of what she assumed would happen next. The expectation was too great; she'd fantasized about this moment more times than she cared to admit. She closed her eyes and parted her lips and waited. Then it happened. His lips finally rested against her forehead. Her heart sank at the disappointment.

"Merry Christmas, sweetheart," he whispered and walked away.

When Julia opened her eyes Reggie was near the exit.

Once settled on the plane, she opened his box. Inside was a beautiful crystal angel. The inside of the card read:

Thank you for making my life complete.

Your friend,

Reggie

"I may have made your life complete, but you've made mine incomplete," she moaned as the plane taxied down the runway. "Oh boy, I'm in trouble."

Chapter 16

"Mommy! Papa!" Julia called from the foyer of her parents' home.

After a few moments, Carey Simone Sr. appeared at the top of the stairwell.

"Hey, ma cherie," he exclaimed. "I didn't know you were coming down this early." He opened his arms as he galloped to greet his daughter. "I would have met you at the airport."

Carey Simone Sr. looked good for his sixty-eight years. He carried his two-hundred- pound weight well on his six-foot frame. His firm olive skin was nearly wrinkle-free, framed by a neat beard. His long wavy hair, pulled back in a ponytail, was scarcely sprinkled with salt. Jogging every morning kept him in shape, full of energy and gorgeous. As a child, Julia fabricated a story to her friends that Sean Connery and her father were twin brothers. Connery was just a stage name. One visit to the school by her father on career day, was enough to validate her claim.

"Hello, Papa." Julia rushed to her father and wrapped her arms around his neck. She loved to hug her father; his strong arms always made her feel protected.

Carey Sr. released her and took a step back. "How's ma cherie feeling today?" "Ma cherie" was what Carey Simone called all his daughters and granddaughters. "Each one of you is my little darling," was what the French native explained. Except for a few French words, Carey Simone Sr. spoke very little French. His parents migrated to the United States when he was three years old.

"I'm wonderful, now that I'm here with you."

Carey Sr. studied his daughter's face. "After you get settled, why don't you come downstairs to my office? Then you can tell me the real reason you showed up two days early."

Julia didn't deny he'd read her actions correctly. "Sure, Papa, but first I want to find Mommy."

"Hey, Papa," Shay cried when she entered the foyer. She raced to hug her grandfather while Julia went to find her mother.

"Mommy," she called as she tapped on her parents' bedroom door. Before her mother had a chance to respond, Julia was already inside.

Ana placed the magazine she was reading on the sofa table, then stood and embraced her daughter. "Hey, baby. I didn't expect to see you for a couple of days."

"I decided to come down and spend some time with you and Papa."

Ana's eyes narrowed. "Humph, that's your story and you're sticking to it."

Julia laughed.

"At any rate, you can help me with the last-minute shopping. And you can help me cook the sweet potato pies."

Glad her mother didn't probe further, Julia submitted, "Whatever you say, Mommy, you're the boss."

* * *

Carey and Ana Simone were millionaires and employed a staff of six to maintain the grounds of their property and to keep their home immaculate, but Ana preferred to do most of the cooking herself. The staff had every December off with pay while Ana and her daughters prepared the holiday meals for the family.

Ana, a Houston native, made sure all five of her daughters knew how to cook balanced meals, keep their bodies clean, and keep a clean house, by the time they were teenagers. One of the most important things she taught her daughters was how to respect a man as being the head of the home. She did this by precept and example. In almost fifty years of marriage, Ana had never openly disrespected her husband. What she did behind her bedroom door was another story. Whatever decision Carey Simone made was the law; whether she agreed or not, she followed his wishes, but voiced her opinion.

Because they had so many children so close together, Ana was unable to work outside of the home until the youngest child, Andre, was in school. By that time, she didn't have the need or desire to work.

Money was real low in the beginning, but she didn't complain, she worked with how much or how little her husband brought home. When Carey shared his dream of starting The Simone Company, she didn't see how it was going to happen, but she never voiced it to him. When he would return home from work at night, she would encourage him, but during the day, she would pray constantly for him to succeed. Now, every time she opened her eyes she reaped the benefits of her answered prayers. There's nothing Carey wouldn't do for her and she likewise for him.

After Julia got settled in one of the six upstairs bedrooms, she went to look for her father. She found him sitting at his desk, looking over some drawings.

"Am I interrupting?" she asked with a smile, knowing what the answer would be.

"Not at all, ma cherie. You are just the person I want to see. Come over here and sit down." He patted his leg. Ever since she was a child, she always sat on her father's lap when she went to his office.

"Those chairs are for people who want to do business with me. I'm not doing business with you, I'm being your father," was what he told his children. His sons still preferred to stand beside him.

Julia happily sat on her father's lap. "So, Papa, are you really going to retire in a year?" she began.

"No, I'm going to retire at the end of the month."

Julia's eyes bulged. "But that's just a few days away. Does Mommy know?"

"No. I'm going to tell her on New Year's Eve, at the stroke of midnight." He smiled. "All of the necessary documents are signed and recorded. Chantel and Stephan will officially have control of the company on January first. I'm very proud of them; I know they have what it takes to carry the company to the next level," he said proudly.

"Are you sure about this? I mean you've worked so hard for so long, are you ready to just give it all up?"

"Ma cherie, with the help of God, I have done everything I've set out to do. I've provided a good life for my family by making The Simone Company a highly respected name in the industry. I have everything I want. My children are independent, functioning adults, with a little bit of sense, and are taking good care of their families. But do you want to know the main reason I'm ready to stop?"

"What's that?" she asked.

"I've got a beautiful woman upstairs who deserves my time and full attention, while I'm in good health and of sound mind. I gave her my heart years ago, now it's time to give her *me*. After all of the beautiful years she's given me, I owe your mother that."

"That's very sweet, Papa," she whispered.

Carey remained quiet. Julia had something on her mind. Like Ana, he knew when his children needed to talk.

"Papa," she finally spoke, "how long did it take you to realize you were in love with Mommy?"

"I loved your mother the first time I saw her in my eleventh grade math class. Of course, it was just physical—your mother was a Nubian queen brick house. Still is. After we spent a year getting to know one another, I fell in love with who she was."

"But how did you know she was your soul mate?" Julia asked.

"Ma cherie, it's hard to explain. I just knew in my heart we were made for each other. She made me feel like I could take on the world. She laughed at my jokes and took my dreams seriously. She made me feel like a man."

♪Ain't no woman, like the one I got♪. His face lit up as he sang the words to the classic Four Tops tune.

"So that's the reason behind those sad eyes, you're in love," he surmised.

Julia lowered her head. "Yes, Papa. I am forty years old with a grown daughter and in love for the first time."

Carey lifted her chin. "Ma cherie, that's nothing to be ashamed of. People live their whole lives searching for that very thing and never find it. Thank God you've found it at forty."

"But that's just it, Papa," she whined. "I've found love, but love hasn't found me."

"What do you mean?"

"I've been dating, spending time with the most loving man I've known outside of you, but he doesn't feel the same. He says he just wants to be friends, but in my heart, I know he's the one." She lay against his neck.

"Ma cherie, if that's how you feel, then give him some time. Take your time and discover who he really is. Let him take the lead and pursue you. If he's the one for you, God will bring him around in due time. Trust God, and remember: God moves in His own time. When that man surrenders to God's will, he'll chase you."

Carey kissed his daughter's forehead, then maneuvered and set her on her feet. "I gotta go."

"Where are you going?" Julia asked.

"All this talk about love has gotten me excited. I'm going to go chase your mama around."

Laughter poured from Julia, as her father trotted off, singing in his baritone voice, Barry White's "I Can't Get Enough of Your Love." The only thing white about Carey Simone was his skin color.

Julia spent the next two days helping her mother get ready for Christmas dinner. She enjoyed every moment spent with her mother, even when Ana complained she wasn't doing something right. She'd just smile, and say, "Whatever you say, Mommy, you're the boss."

On Christmas Eve night they prepared the sweet potato pies, 7-Up Cakes, and peach cobblers. It was during family gatherings like this that Ana really appreciated the two-story Mediterranean home Carey had custom built for her. The twenty-thousand-square-foot home contained ten bedrooms—four on the bottom and six upstairs—eight full bathrooms and two half-baths, four fireplaces, a formal dining room that could seat fifty people easily, a library, two fully equipped kitchens, one on each floor, and probably the most important amenity, an elevator. Out back was a pool house with an indoor heated pool. In the backyard, there was an Olympic-size pool and a custom-built barbeque grill.

Julia stood at the center island, kneading dough. Ana was at the counter, mixing cake batter.

"I've waited long enough. What's his name?" Ana asked without warning.

"Who?"

"The man that's got you all messed up, that's who," Ana said. "I've seen you leave the room to talk on your cell phone more than a few times."

"His name is Reginald, but I call him Reggie. He's a pastor of a church in Oakland. As a matter of fact, he's Nikki's pastor."

"He must be a powerful man, if he's Nikki's pastor." Ana laughed as she poured the batter into the pans. "And to have you all messed up, too," she added.

"He is powerful," Julia said with a hint of sadness.

"So what's the problem?"

Julia stopped rolling dough and faced her mother. She didn't feel like beating around the bush anymore.

"Mommy, when I was twenty-two, I married a man that I thought I loved until he gave more time and energy to his work than he gave to me. That's when I realized I didn't love him enough to have married him. Then he died and left me with a daughter to raise. Then I married a man I didn't love because he gave me a little attention and I allowed him to abuse me, in order to keep that attention."

"Now, Mama, at forty, I'm finally in love for real. I love everything about Reggie, from the way he eats his food to the way he laughs when he's happy or frowns when he doesn't like something. But he doesn't feel the same, at least that's what he says. He told me he only wants me as a friend, but I want him as my friend and my lover. The way he kissed me at the airport the other day and the way he strokes my hand, tells me he wants the same." She sighed. "Mommy, I honestly don't know what to think. I don't know if I should continue to see him or just walk away." Julia threw her hands down in resignation.

Ana dried her hands and looked into her daughter's eyes. "Baby, when you don't know which way to go, the best thing to do is simply stand still."

Chapter 17

J ulia stared out of her office window at the vast Pacific Ocean. Her thoughts traveled back over the holidays. She'd had a wonderful time with her family at her parents' home. All of her siblings had made it home, except her older brother, Jonathan. His wife, Theresa, had suffered a miscarriage the week of Christmas.

Then there was Reggie. When she returned home, he called to tell her how much he missed her, as if he hadn't called her every day that she was away. It was hard, but she declined his dinner and movie invitations. She needed some space from him, so she decided it was a good time to perform an in-house company audit. There wasn't much going on at the construction site, especially with the winter weather, so now was as good of a time as any.

"I'll be working a lot, so I won't be able to hang out for a while, but you can reach me by phone," she told him.

He said he understood and that's the way she left it. However, the audit did little to rid her mind and heart of him.

Her cell phone interrupted her thoughts. "Hey, Nikki, what's going on?"

"Nothing much, girl. Just wanted to know if I could count on you to attend True Worship's Annual Scholarship Banquet the fourth Friday of this month. The tickets are a hundred-fifty dollars."

"Sure, you can put me down for a ticket," Julia said.

"Actually, I was hoping to put Pinnacle down as a corporate sponsor and a table of ten." Nikki laughed.

"Why not? But you'll have to sit with me, so I'll have someone to talk to."

"I know someone who would *love* to talk to you," Nikki teased. "You can sit on his lap. He won't mind."

"Girl, you better let that go," Julia warned.

"Whatever."

"What's the attire for the evening?" Julia asked, trying to take her thoughts away from Reggie.

"Formal. I know you have a huge selection in your closet to choose from, but I'm going to Union Square on Saturday to see what I can find."

"That sounds like a good idea. I'll join you." The San Francisco premier shopping galleria was one of Julia's favorite places to shop. "Where's the banquet being held?"

"The Scottish Rite Ballroom, across from the lake," Nikki answered.

"Sounds like fun. Why don't we get dressed at my condo? I'll have the limo service pick us up. That way, we won't have to worry about parking. You know how bad the parking is over there."

"I'll gladly take a free limo ride any day. We'll talk about it on Saturday," Nikki said.

"Talk to you later."

Two weeks later, Julia sat at her desk, reviewing the expense report from the Point Richmond project. So far, things were looking pretty good, as far as the budget was concerned. Interest was growing fast for the waterfront property. Two-thirds of the luxury condos had been reserved for purchase. If all went well, they would be complete by the June deadline. Her ringing cell phone distracted her again. She checked the caller ID and was happy it wasn't Reggie. She'd been dodging his calls.

"Hey, big brother!" It was her brother, Jonathan. He was only fourteen months older than she was, and the two of them had always been close. Even after he moved and started his law practice in Arizona, they still kept in touch on a regular basis.

"How's my favorite sister named Julia doing?"

"Blessed and highly favored." They shared a laugh.

"How are things going with you and Theresa?"

"We're taking it one day at a time. Some days are better than others, but we're hanging in there."

"Trust me, Jon, it does get easier over time," she tried to reassure her brother. Losing a baby at six months wasn't easy.

"I know, sis." He paused. "I was calling to let you know I'll be in town next week for a conference at the Convention Center. It runs from Wednesday to Friday. Mind if I stay at the condo? I don't want to deal with the drama of downtown Oakland."

"Only if you bring your black tux and escort Nikki and myself to a banquet on Friday night."

"You don't have to bribe me to get me to spend the night with two beautiful women."

"Once a hound, always a hound," Julia teased. "I'll tell the doorman to expect you Wednesday morning."

"See you later, sis. I love you."

"I love you, too, and tell Theresa I'm praying for her."

* * *

Reggie looked forward to seeing Julia at the scholarship banquet that night. He hadn't seen much of her lately. He had only seen her a handful of times, and that was with Nikki and Tyrone. She seemed purposefully distant since the holidays. He still talked to her daily, but their conversations were short and impersonal, not like the long engaging chats he'd grown accustomed to. A few weeks ago, he thought he wanted to put some space between them, but she'd beat him to it and he didn't like it. He missed his friend. He hoped to spend some time with her tonight at the banquet, but knew public interaction with her would make the headlines of the church's gossip column—a chance he was now willing to take.

As he straightened his desk, he remembered Julia commenting on how much she liked his goatee and decided to stop by the barber-shop on the way home.

Chapter 18

J ulia and Nikki were dressed—almost. They were running behind schedule, because Nikki decided to have her nails done on Friday at five o'clock.

"That's the only time I could squeeze it in," she said when Julia complained. They were just about done applying the finishing touches on their makeup when the telephone rang. A moment later, Jonathan knocked on the bedroom door.

"The limo's here," he called out.

"We'll be right out," Nikki answered, before Julia scolded her, yet again for being late.

Julia and Nikki took one final look in the full-length door mirror, grabbed their evening bags and headed for the door.

The January weather was perfect for the evening—clear with a slight breeze. Julia was glad she had chosen the royal blue satin, off-the-shoulder, formal V-neck with matching wrap. The dress flattered her shape nicely, like it was made just for her. She wore her hair pinned up to show the matching sapphire and diamond earrings and necklace ensemble. The four-inch matching blue heels completed the look.

Nikki looked equally elegant in her black and gold ensemble and Jonathan complemented them both in his black Armani tuxedo.

Jonathan intended to escort both Julia and Nikki, but when they approached the entrance, Tyrone appeared and extended his arm to

Nikki. Without uttering one word, she gladly accepted Tyrone's hand and left Jonathan and Julia standing outside.

Reggie was seated at the head table with the guest speakers and special guest. From time to time he watched the door in expectation of her arrival. He looked at his watch; she was thirty minutes late. "I hope she's not stuck in traffic," he whispered to no one in particular.

A smile creased his face, but quickly disappeared when he saw Nikki enter with Tyrone. Julia had told him that she and Nikki were riding together. He stood and was about to walk over and ask Nikki where she was, when Julia appeared in the doorway. His eyes zeroed in on her like she was the only person in the spacious ballroom. To him, she was simply beautiful. She was gorgeous in that fitted blue dress. And her hair, her hair was beautiful pinned up like that, revealing the prettiest neck he had ever seen. When she smiled he felt a tug in his heart. He missed her so much and wanted to be close to her. To touch her. Without evaluating his actions, he started walking in her direction. He had to be close to her. He took four steps, then stopped. His smile disappeared and his heart sank when *he* appeared. A man Reggie didn't know placed his arm around Julia's waist and escorted her in the opposite direction.

Reggie's body froze on the vintage carpet. So many questions ran through his mind. Who was that man? Where did he come from? Was he what had been keeping her so busy? Why was he touching her? Why was she smiling like she was happy with him. The voice of the MC finally caught his attention and he held his head down and slowly walked back to his seat.

Julia greeted the guests at Pinnacle's round table of ten. Joining her were Pastor and First Lady Leonard, Michelle and her fiancée, a couple of her employees, and of course Nikki and Tyrone. Julia made herself comfortable and surveyed the room. She spotted Reggie at the head table, looking fine as ever. For a brief moment, they made eye contact. She smiled, but he just gave her a cold stare. Jonathan tapped her shoulder and asked her a question and she joined the conversation going on at her table. Forcing thoughts of Reggie to the back burner.

The evening passed quickly. The food, speakers, and entertainment were enjoyable, but Julia had a hard time focusing on anything or anyone but Reggie and his cold demeanor toward her. Twice she'd caught him glaring at her from the head table. She couldn't stand being this close to him and not being able to hear his assuasive voice explain the reason behind his sour attitude.

"Excuse me," she said to her table guests, when she decided to go out onto the balcony for some fresh air.

When she stepped into the cool night air, she was happy she had the balcony to herself. She had been out there under the dark starstudded sky for only a moment when she smelled his cologne. Her heartbeat accelerated, it had been a long time since she was this close to him. *Too long,* she thought.

She turned to face him. "You look handsome tonight." She expected him to flash that sexy smile of his, but he didn't give her the pleasure.

"Who is that man you brought here?" he asked without preliminary.

"Excuse me?"

"You heard me, Julia. Who is he and why was he touching you?" He raised his voice.

"You're joking, right?" She was teasing, but he was dead serious. "You really can't tell who he is?"

"I don't have time for your silly schoolgirl games, Julia!" She flinched and he lowered his voice. "Is he the reason you haven't had time for me lately?"

"What are you talking about, Reginald?" She metered the words.

"I'm a grown man, Julia. Don't play childish games with me. I don't have time for the kind of games women like you play. If you want to see someone else, then be woman enough to tell me, but don't parade your men in front of my face!"

Now Julia was angry. "Reginald Pennington, you are the biggest hypocrite I've ever seen!" Her fist pressed into her hips and her neck rolled.

Reggie was taken back.

"First of all," she held up a forefinger, "I don't belong to you. I can see whomever, whenever I please and I don't need your approval to do it." She added a finger. "Secondly, I'm a grown woman and I don't play childish games. You've cornered the market on that!"

"What do you mean?" he interjected. "I have never played any games with you."

"What I mean, Mr. I Don't Date, is you have been playing the worst type of game with me for the past three months."

Reggie looked as if he was genuinely confused.

"You have spent the past three months constantly telling me you are not interested in me outside of friendship, yet you call me every day and you send me flowers and tell me how beautiful I am. Every time we are together you hold my hand like it belongs to you and you call me 'sweetheart' more than you call me by my name. One minute you tell me you're thankful I'm in your life, and then the very next minute you tell me I'm not your type. Mr. I Don't Date, I got a newsflash for you: You've been dating me for three months. You're just too stupid and blind to see it!"

Reggie took a step back.

Julia stepped forward and pointed at his chest.

"Do you know why you can't see it? Because you're hiding behind being the pastor of True Worship. You're so caught up in being a pastor, that you've forgotten that you are a man first. You used me to satisfy your need for a woman, but you gave me nothing in return." Julia's voice broke. She felt the tears coming, but she continued anyway. "And finally, Reggie, let me enlighten you on a few things about 'women like me.' We get tired of being alone. We get tired of being penalized for being successful. We deserve to have someone commit to us and love us unconditionally." Her tears flowed freely now, but pride prevented her from totally breaking down. "We get tired of holding our love inside, because there's no one we can trust with our heart. And we are *way* past sick and tired of men like you who don't know what they want!" She closed her eyes and sighed heavily. "I wish I wasn't in love with you. There's nothing worse than being in love with someone who won't love you back."

Reggie had an expression of both shock and horror on his face when she opened her eyes.

"Don't worry, Reggie, I'm going to make it easy for you. I don't want to see or talk to you again. Do me a favor and stay out of my life; I don't need a friend like you!" She walked past him, stopped at the doorway, turned and spoke evenly. "About the man who escorted me tonight. You know, the man you saw with his arm around me. If you weren't so blind and self-centered, you would have seen the resemblance. He's my brother!"

Chapter 19

Reggie sat at his desk, staring at the dark-blue carpet on the floor. He couldn't focus on any one thing in particular, because there were a million thoughts running through his mind and every one of them centered on Julia Simone. Friday night, she knocked his world off its axis.

After she left him, he stayed out on the balcony in the cool air for the rest of the evening. Even when he heard his name called over the microphone, he still didn't move. He wanted to run after her and explain his actions. He wanted to make her understand how he felt. How he had been feeling since the night of Shay's accident, but he couldn't. That would force him to acknowledge the truth.

He warred with his emotions all night Friday and all day Saturday. He couldn't, or didn't want to understand why he reacted the way he did when he saw Julia with her brother. He hadn't really looked at the man's face. The only thing he saw was another man touching her, and he didn't like it. He didn't like the way she gave her smile—his smile—to another man. He knew that he had not committed himself to her, at least that's what he told himself, but it didn't matter. Julia was his special friend and he didn't want to share her with anyone.

His heart constricted every time he envisioned her tear-stained face. He hated himself for being the cause of her pain. In the past, it didn't bother him to see a woman cry over him, and plenty had, but now things were different. Julia loved him, but he had hurt her, and she had walked out of his life, leaving a massive void.

He tried to reach her all day Saturday, but she didn't answer the phone. He drove out to her home in Blackhawk, but got turned away at the security gate. He didn't know what he would have said to her, if she had agreed to see him. All he knew was he had to find a way to keep her in his life.

"I hope you feel better, Pastor," Minister Debra Watson said, as she stuck her head inside to say good-bye.

Reggie had asked her to preach the morning service. After only four hours of sleep in forty-eight hours, he had nothing to give his congregation. He was certain Minister Watson had delivered a powerful message, but he hadn't heard any of it. As he sat in his pulpit, the only words he heard were the ones Julia had yelled at him on Friday night. As much as he desired to rebuke Julia for lying, he couldn't. Her true words pierced his conscience.

"Thank you, Minister Watson," he said and sat back in his chair. He closed his eyes and tried to figure out how to fix his situation.

"The church is empty and locked. Can I talk to you for a few minutes?" The deacon entered unannounced.

"I don't feel like talking."

"Good," Tyrone sat in a chair, "because I don't want you to talk. I want you to listen," Tyrone said.

"Go ahead." Reggie gave Tyrone his attention.

"I'm not speaking to my pastor," Tyrone began, "I'm speaking to my friend, Reggie. From Nikki, I heard about the argument you had the other night with Julia." Tyrone paused before continuing. "I have watched you, for the past five years, give yourself completely to this ministry and you have asked for nothing in return. For three years, you refused to take a salary, because you said the ministry could use the money on better things. The only reason you receive a salary now is because the administrative staff out-voted you."

"For five years, I watched you drive around in an old Honda while you helped people in your congregation buy new cars. If the church hadn't purchased that Mercedes as an anniversary gift, you would still be driving that old Honda. Despite the fact that True Worship has experienced phenomenal growth and is financially stable, you still refuse to do anything for yourself.

"In the beginning, I thought you were just a humble person, but that's not it. Don't get me wrong, Reggie, you are one of the most humble people I know and you really do love God's people. I know from personal experience, how you are willing to, and have given the shirt off your back to help someone else. But it's deeper than that. Reggie, most of your self-denial deeds have been done out of guilt."

Reggie shifted in his seat.

"You preach to us constantly about forgiveness. You teach us the importance of forgiving our brothers and sisters for the harm they have caused us in the past. But you leave out what's probably the most important part: We have to learn how to forgive ourselves for the harm we have caused ourselves in the past."

Reggie's right palm massaged his bald left fist. His temporal vein flared, but he didn't debate with Tyrone.

"Reggie, after all these years, you haven't done that yet. What you did happened almost eighteen years ago. God forgave you eight years ago when you got saved. Don't you think it's time that you forgive yourself? The guilt that you're carrying is controlling your life and you don't even know it."

Reggie's jaws flexed and his eyes watered, but Tyrone continued.

"I've watched you these past three months. I've heard you laugh more in that short period of time, than I have in the last five years. I have seen you relax and have fun like a normal person. I have seen how your face brightens when you are with Julia. You are in love with her, but this guilt you're carrying is preventing you from loving her. Because of what happened in your past, you don't think you deserve a good woman now. You don't think you deserve to have another woman love you, because of what you did. You have tried to convince yourself that True Worship is all you need, but it's not. You need Julia. She can help you in ways this church never will, and I don't mean physically." Tyrone stood. "Reggie, I hate to see you like this. Please let it go. Just forgive yourself and let it go. If you don't, your life will never be complete. Think about it. Don't let your past dictate your future. I love you, man." Tyrone turned and left out the side door.

As Reggie sat there, the weight of the last seventeen years hit him like a ton of bricks and constricted his breathing. Everything Tyrone said was true. He'd been trying to make retribution for his mistakes, when Jesus had already paid the debt over two thousand years ago. His refusal to deal with his true feelings had cost him the only woman he ever loved. Reggie couldn't contain himself any longer. He fell on his knees and wept uncontrollably. He wept for the people he hurt, but he wept hardest for himself. "God, please help me," he cried out.

Chapter 20

"Good morning, Michelle," Julia said when she entered the office suite on Monday morning.

"Good morning to you," Michelle replied, with what Julia considered to be an extra serving of perkiness. She dismissed her assistant's excitement and continued the trek to her office suite. After the fight with Reggie she had little to be excited about. He was out of her life.

"I hate him," was what she had told Nikki on Friday night when Nikki followed her into the ladies' room after her argument with Reggie.

"You don't mean that, you are just hurt right now." Nikki's attempt to comfort her was only half-effective.

"Maybe I don't hate him, but I hate what's he's done to me. How could he play with my emotions like that?"

"I don't know," Nikki answered. "But I know he really cares about you. Why else would he have acted so jealous?"

"Because he's an egotistical, self-centered jerk, that's why," Julia shot back.

"I know you're angry with him right now, and you have every right to be. Just don't make any hasty decisions. Take some time and think about it, maybe you two can still work things out," Nikki said hopefully.

For Julia, time had run out for Reginald Pennington. She had turned her cell phone off over the weekend, so he couldn't reach her. She even instructed the security office to deny him access. She wanted nothing more to do with him. Three months was long enough to waste on him. "I'm a big girl. I know how to nurse my wounds and move on." She'd been repeating the declaration all weekend, but had yet to convince herself. Her heart revealed her life would never be the same without their one-sided relationship.

"Michelle, could you please hold my calls this morning?" Julia called over her shoulder.

"Sure thing, Ms. Simone."

Julia decided to just keep walking at that moment. She really didn't care why Michelle was so happy. She unlocked her office door, turned on the lights and stepped into her office. She gasped and dropped her briefcase as she surveyed her private space. Inside her office were at least two hundred carnations of various colors spread throughout.

"Michelle, what's—" her words evaporated when she turned around and stood face to face with Reginald Pennington. He was wearing the black tuxedo with a white shirt and red cummerbund he wore on Friday. In his hand was a single red carnation.

She swallowed hard and pretended his unexpected presence meant nothing. "What do you want?" she asked flatly, then turned to walk away from him.

He gently grabbed her elbow in an effort to stop her. "I want to go back to Friday night and continue our conversation. I want to tell you, now, what I should have told you then."

She turned to face him. "I think you've said enough, Reverend. I don't have time for this, I have work to do," she said impatiently. "Besides, my office isn't big enough for your ego."

"Please, just give me a few minutes."

Julia wanted him to leave, but the look in his eyes tugged at her heart. They displayed a pleading she hadn't seen before. "All right, Mr. Pennington, you've got two minutes," she said and sat in one of the chairs usually reserved for guests. Reggie had sat in that same chair the first day he walked into her office. She leaned back with her arms folded.

Reggie seemed to have plenty of time on his hands. With slow metered steps, he closed the door and placed the carnation on her desk. He looked down at her and opened his mouth to speak, but didn't. Instead he knelt down on his knees in front of her.

"Reggie, what are you doing?" she asked, as she unfolded her arms and leaned forward.

He covered her hands with his. "I don't want to talk down at you, I want to talk to you."

Uh-oh, she thought.

"Sweetheart, I heard everything you said. And you are absolutely correct. I have been a hypocrite. Not only toward you, but to my congregation as well. To both of you I have preached one thing and lived another. I have used my job as a pastor to hide my inner struggles. You were correct; I have been playing a game with you. I've told you one thing and done another, because I was afraid to be honest with myself. I demanded all of you, but I wasn't willing to give you me in return."

Julia blinked her eyes rapidly, trying to push back the flood of tears she felt coming. She hadn't expected to hear those words coming from him. In her dreams maybe, but not live in the flesh.

With a shaky voice, Reggie continued, "For using you and taking advantage of you, I am sorry. For expecting more from you than I was willing to give, I am sorry. For not being honest with you about my feelings for you, I am very sorry." Reggie paused and closed his eyes. When they reopened, two tears trailed down his cheeks.

Julia's breathing accelerated. This was more than she'd expected. A sincere apology and tears? She needed to escape before all of her defenses wilted.

Reggie brought her hands to his mouth and kissed them. He looked into her eyes and continued, "Julia, I have loved you since the first day I saw you dancing at my church. I have been in love with you since the night of Shay's accident."

Julia gasped.

"There's not a day that goes by that I don't wake up with you on my mind. There's not an hour that passes that I don't wonder what you're doing and if you're all right. You are so beautiful to me. When I'm not with you, I feel empty and incomplete. I *need* you in my life. Sweetheart, please, can we start over? Give me the chance to redeem myself. I promise, you won't regret it."

Julia couldn't stand it anymore; she had to get away from him while she still had control over her emotions. She snatched her hands from him and stood in an effort to escape. But he wrapped his arms around her waist and she couldn't move. He looked up at her with eyes full of desperation.

"Baby, please don't walk away from me. You're the first woman I've ever loved. I need you. I don't want to go back to the way my life was before you. I'm sorry. I need you. I love you."

The dam broke along with her heart and Julia fell back down into the chair. When Reggie reached for her this time, she accepted and returned his embrace. When she felt his tears fall onto her shoulder, she squeezed him tighter. He held onto her as if his life depended on it. They remained that way until Julia reluctantly, but gently pulled away.

"I need to get some tissue," she said, as she sniffled and attempted to clean her face with the back of her hand.

Reggie reached inside his tuxedo jacket, pulled out a handkerchief and handed it to her. She dried her face and then proceeded to wipe his.

"Thank you, sweetheart." The grin resting on his face was one of serenity. Like it didn't matter to him that he'd just finished crying like a baby. He was in love, and the woman he loved had just agreed to give him another chance.

"Sweetheart, I want to be completely honest with you regarding my intentions. My rules on dating have not changed. I'm only willing to date someone if I believe it's going to lead to marriage."

"What are you trying to tell me?"

"I know that I love you, and I know that I don't want to be without you. But first I have to find out if what I want is what God has planned for me. I want us to take our relationship slow and really get to know one another. When I do get married, it will be for the rest of my life. I don't want to rush. I want to move in God's time. I promise you that I'm totally committed to making this relationship work on a permanent basis."

"I understand and I accept that. I don't want you to do anything you're not ready to do. Besides, the next time I get married, it will be my last."

"I hope you've saved the best for last," he asked, openly flirting with her for the first time.

"I most certainly have," she replied.

Chapter 21

"I knew it, I knew it," Nikki screamed into the phone when Julia told her the latest developments between her and Reggie. "I knew he was going to make a move soon. I could tell by the way he sat in the pulpit looking depressed yesterday. Girl, he looked like Jesus had called the roll in heaven, and his name wasn't on it!" Nikki hollered.

"Well, he just left here with a big smile on his face."

"He's got himself a woman now. He's going to smile so much now, his cheeks are going to beg him for a break." The two friends laughed and shared a few more wisecracks. Then Nikki's tone turned serious. "Now, how do you *really* feel now that things are serious with you two? I mean, how do you feel about marrying a powerful preacher and being a pastor's wife?"

"Don't you think you're moving a little too fast? He hasn't proposed, we've just agreed to stop lying about not being in a relationship. We are going to take things slow and see what happens."

"Girl, have you forgotten who you're talking to? You know good and well y'all are in love. If that man asked you to, you'd meet him at the courthouse by five o'clock today."

"Girl, you know I would." Julia laughed. "But seriously, I want this to be right, so I'm willing to wait until we're both ready. Remember, I've been down this road before."

"But not with anyone you've loved," Nikki interjected.

"I know, Nikki," Julia's tone turned serious, "and, girl, that's what scares me. I'm scared that this is not real. Like I'm going to wake up and find out this morning was just a dream. It happened so fast."

"Trust me, it's real. That man loves you. When the two of you get married—and you will—you're going to be so happy that you're going to forget about the rough beginning. The two of you really want and need the same thing."

"What's that?" Julia asked.

"Someone for you to give your love to," Nikki answered, plainly. "It's that simple."

"That's why you're my best friend; you always know what to say."

* * *

Reggie sat at his desk admiring the blueprints for the new building. Construction was set to begin in early summer, thanks to Julia's charitable contribution. Reggie thought back to one of their earlier conversations. "I believe in your vision," was what she had said. "Thank you for believing in me," he voiced and made a mental note to tell her so.

Earlier in the day, he joined in the Noonday Prayer session with Mother Elsie. He couldn't remember the last time he felt such peace and freedom. He was now ready to accept his life the way it was, free from guilt and shame. And he was in love with a wonderful woman.

"Pastor, I'm so glad you finally got yourself together," Mother Elsie told him after prayer. "I don't think I could stand to see you looking as pitiful as you did last Sunday. I went home and worked overtime in prayer for you."

"Thank you, Mother. I love you for the way you look out for me."

"I know you love me, but you need to tell Sister Julia from House of Prayer, that you love her." Mother Elsie's reprimand was sweet, but firm.

For a quick second Reggie was shocked that she knew about his love for Julia, but then again, Mother always said that God talked to her.

"You are right, Mother, I do love her and she knows it."

Mother Elsie started speaking in tongues and did a holy dance without the music as he laughed and walked back to his office.

Reggie was still laughing about Mother Elsie when Tyrone knocked on his door.

"Can I come in?" Tyrone asked.

Reggie waved him in. "You're just the person I want to see," Reggie said as he stood and walked around his desk. For the next few minutes neither man said a word. They just stood there embracing one another.

"Thank you for being a real friend to me and telling me the truth. Thank you for not sitting back and watching me make one of the biggest mistakes of my life," Reggie said when he finally let go.

"I'm just glad you acted on what I said."

Reggie looked puzzled. "How did you know?"

"Come on, man, you know Nikki and Julia are best friends. I bet before you got to the elevator, Julia was on the phone, running down the details."

"Oh really?" Reggie smiled. "Speaking of Nikki, how are things going with you and Sister Thompson?"

"She doesn't know it yet, but Sister Thompson is going to be Sister Davis as soon as I finish with my degree," Tyrone said with a big smile.

"What do you mean, she doesn't know?"

"I haven't told her my full intentions, but she knows that she's very special to me."

"Well, looks like God is about to turn both our lives upside down," Reggie concluded.

"Yeah, and I can hardly wait."

Chapter 22

"Good morning, beautiful," Reggie's suave voice sounded in her ear. He had made it his job to be her alarm clock every morning since they officially started dating, two weeks prior.

"Is it morning already?" Julia moaned. She stretched and turned over to read the bright red numbers on her alarm clock.

"Did you sleep well? You had sweet dreams, I hope."

She imagined a confident grin on his face. "No, every time I closed my eyes I saw images of you. It was horrible," she teased.

"Well, I had wonderful dreams of you, but I won't tell you about them, because it's your meditation time and you need to be able to concentrate."

"I see you can give as good as you get."

"I don't want to keep you. I just wanted to know if you'll have dinner with me on my birthday."

Julia cleared her throat. "When is your birthday?" She was glad he had changed the conversation, her mind was starting to wander to places it shouldn't. Like how much warmer her bed would be with him lying beside her.

"Today."

"Today? I didn't know today was also your birthday. Why didn't you tell me?"

"When you get to be my age it's no big deal, but I would like to spend the evening with you." He paused. "There's something I want to share with you."

"Where did you have in mind?" she asked flirtatiously.

"My house. I'm going to cook you dinner."

Julia snickered. "You're going to cook me dinner? Do you really know how to cook?"

"Why don't you come see for yourself? Dinner will be served at six o'clock sharp," he said with confidence.

"I'll be there, just don't forget to throw out the take-out cartons." She laughed.

"Funny. Until later, sweetheart."

"Reggie," she called, before he hung up.

"Yes, love."

"Happy Valentine's Day," she said, with more giddiness than she'd ever felt.

"Happy Valentine's Day," he said in kind, then added, "I don't recall a woman ever telling me that, at least not one I cared about."

* * *

Reggie wanted the evening to be perfect. The maid service had stopped by earlier that morning, so the house was spotless. He spent the afternoon shopping and preparing the night's meal. He was on a mission to prove Julia wrong. His mother had taught him how to cook, and in his opinion, she had done a great job.

He set the table with his mother's fine china, just like she taught him. For a centerpiece, he used a crystal vase filled with fresh-cut red carnations. He lit red tapered candles and dimmed the lights. Sounds of Kirk Whalum's saxophone permeated the atmosphere.

He prepared a feast of Caesar salad with homemade croutons, broiled lobster tails and shrimp scampi. As complements, he chose asparagus with cream sauce and wild rice. For dessert, there was red velvet cake, which he purchased from his favorite bakery. He had just finished chilling the nonalcoholic champagne, when the doorbell sounded.

"Happy Birthday," Julia said when she stepped inside.

"Happy Valentine's Day," he said as he helped her out of her coat.

"This is for you," she said when he returned from the coat closet. In her hand was a small black velvet box. "It's your Valentine's Day gift."

"You didn't have to get me anything," he said as he took the package from her.

"I know I didn't, but I wanted to."

She watched him open the box and was satisfied when a smile spread across his face.

"Do you like it?" she asked.

"Do I like it? I love it!" he exclaimed.

"I had it custom-made for you. Your initials are engraved on the back."

Reggie turned the gold cross over and rubbed his finger across *RLP* in script letters.

"Do you think the chain is the right length?" Julia asked.

"It's perfect, thank you," he whispered, then hugged her. "I hope you're hungry," he said as he led her into the dining room, hoping she hadn't noticed the water in his eyes.

"Wow," Julia said when she entered the dining room. "This is beautiful. Did you do all this yourself?"

"I sure did," he said proudly and pulled out her chair.

"Thank you." She paused. "What's this?" she asked, pointing to the red velvet box on the table in front of her.

"That's your Valentine's Day gift."

He watched her excitedly open the little box. She stared down at the gold heart outlined in diamonds for a long moment, before she finally whispered, "Thank you."

Reggie assumed the delayed response was due to the simplicity of the gift. "I know you probably have a lot of jewelry already that's worth way more than this, but it's just a little gift, from my heart to yours." When she remained silent, he continued, "If you don't like it, I'll take it back and you—"

"No," she said, shaking her head. Unlike him, she wasn't embarrassed by her outpouring of emotions. She looked up at him with tears trailing down both cheeks. In her eyes he saw her sincerity.

"Reggie," she began softly. "This is the first time that a man I truly love has given me something, and it's perfect."

The announcement confused Reggie. Julia had been married twice. Surely she loved one of the men she'd pledged her devotion to.

She continued, "I've never been in love before. Reggie, you're my first and only love." She stood and placed her arms around his neck. She looked deep into his eyes, and said, "Baby, the things I have acquired before now and how much they cost, don't matter to me. You do. Every gift you give me takes precedent over what I've accumulated in the past, because I know it's from your heart. And because I love you." Julia's fingertips caressed his cheeks.

This time he didn't try to hide his emotions. "I love you, too, sweetheart." His voice cracked as he held her.

An hour later, Julia helped Reggie clear the table. She tried to help with the dishes, but he wouldn't allow her to, so she went into the living room and enjoyed the view from his bay window. From where she stood she could see the illuminated outline of three bridges. As she stared out at the city, she rubbed the gift around her neck. "We both selected the same type of jewelry for each other," she said.

She walked over to the fireplace and picked up Reggie's baby picture. She smiled and outlined his baby face with her fingertips.

"You really like that picture, don't you?" She didn't hear him come into the room.

She turned to face him. "Yes, I do. You were such a handsome baby."

Reggie watched her for a moment. He'd rehearsed this conversation all week in his head, but now he was nervous. He walked over, stood beside her and rested his arm around her shoulders.

"That's what I want to share with you." He took a breath. "This is not a picture of me."

"Reggie, anybody can see that this is a younger version of you. That cute dimple of yours is a definite giveaway."

"I know this looks like me, but it's not me. The baby in this picture is my son."

Julia's mouth gaped as she looked at Reggie and then back at the picture. "What? You have a son? Why haven't you mentioned him before?"

"Yes, I have a son. The reason I haven't mentioned him is because I don't know where he is." Reggie hung his head. "I haven't seen him since shortly after this picture was taken. At the time of this picture, he was six months old."

His answer unleashed more questions. "How old is your son? What's his name? And why is it that you don't know where he is?"

Reggie walked across the room and sat on the couch. He leaned forward and rested his elbows on his thighs. Julia stood in front of him with a puzzled expression, waiting for answers.

"My son's name is Brian Deshawn Pennington. He'll be eighteen in June. I don't know where he is, because his mother ran off with him when he was eight months old."

"Are you saying you haven't seen your son in seventeen years?" She nearly yelled the question.

"I haven't seen him or talked to his mother in seventeen years," he said flatly.

"Oh, my God," she said, and sat next to him on the couch, looking straight ahead.

Reggie didn't comment, deciding to let the new information sink in.

Leaning against him, she broke the silence. "The Reggie I know is not the deadbeat-dad type. You are soft, loving and sometimes selfish, but I believe you would've made a great father. You told me you were once engaged. Is his mother the woman you were engaged to?"

"Yes. Her name is Patricia Robinson."

"I'm not sure I really want to know the answer to my next question, but I need to ask."

"Go ahead. You can ask me anything," he assured her.

"What did you do to make her run away with your son?"

For the first time in years, Reggie didn't feel shame about sharing his past. He still regretted his actions, but he wasn't ashamed of himself anymore. Maybe he just felt comfortable with her or maybe it was because he had finally forgiven himself. He turned his body, so he could face her.

"The man I am today is not the person I was back then. When I was in college, I was a horrible person. I was selfish, demanding and callous. Apart from my mother, I didn't respect or value women. I played with them like they were toys and used them to satisfy my physical needs. I saw women as a means to get what I wanted. And I wanted everything—their time, their attention and their bodies. I wasn't willing and didn't give anything in return."

"Wow," Julia said and looked down at the picture in her hand.

He continued, "I met Patricia at the start of my junior year. I thought she was attractive, so I decided to have some 'fun' with her for a while. When she shared her history with me, I should have left her alone, but I didn't. Patricia grew up in the foster care system. She went from one foster home to another from the time she was a baby until she was of legal age. She never knew her real parents and didn't have any known relatives. She saw our relationship as a way to bring stability into her life. She trusted me and said she was in love with me. I, on the other hand, just used her for sex. I was seeing other women the whole time I was with her."

"When she became pregnant, I tried to change and commit to her, but that didn't last long. The day my son was born was the happiest day of my life. I watched him enter this world. I cut his umbilical cord and I even held him before his mother did." He cleared his throat in an effort to gain control of his voice.

"While holding him in that hospital room, I decided it was time for me to stop my foolishness and settle down. I knew that I didn't love Patricia, but I loved my son and I wanted to be a part of his life. So, I proposed to Patricia. She gladly accepted, because all she ever wanted was a family of her own and because she loved me. My parents tried to talk me out of it. They knew I wasn't ready to be committed and they knew I didn't love her. But I refused to listen." He stood, walked back to the fireplace and stared at the portrait of his parents.

"Turns out my parents were right. By the time Brian was three months old, I was at it again. It all came to a head when Brian was eight months old." He turned to face Julia who was still seated on the couch. "It was two weeks before our wedding and I was at her apartment, watching Brian while she was at work. She returned early and found me on the couch having sex with her roommate, while Brian lay in his playpen a few feet away. Three days later, she left me a note telling me she hated me and never wanted to see me again. She said that I didn't love anyone but myself, and she didn't want someone as coldhearted as me in her son's life. I haven't seen or heard from her since."

Julia remained silent, processing what he had just told her. The person in his story didn't match the person standing in the room with her. She didn't judge him. She felt sorry for him, but she also felt sorry for Patricia. She had been betrayed in the worst way.

"Have you tried to find her?" she finally asked.

"I've tried on numerous occasions, but have always come up short. It's hard to find a person with no real family roots. As far as I knew, she didn't have any friends outside of her roommate. I stayed in the Bay Area because I hoped one day she would change her mind and contact my parents or me, but she never did." He rubbed his freshly cut hair. "I've paid a high price for my actions and will continue to pay every day that I'm away from my son. I not only cheated myself, but I cheated my parents as well. My parents weren't able to have children after me, so they cherished Brian. And I cheated them out of their only grandchild. The first year, my mother cried every day. After that, she lit a candle for him on his birthday and every holiday. She even bought him birthday gifts. There are boxes in the garage filled with old birthday gifts. My mother refused to throw them away; she believed he would return one day."

"How did you deal with it all?"

"I didn't. At first I was angry with Patricia. I knew what I had done was wrong, but I felt I didn't deserve the punishment she handed down. I still don't. Then I was angry with God for allowing her to take my son from me. It wasn't until ten years ago when I joined church, that I started to soften. Even after that it took me two more years before I took responsibility for my actions," he paused, "and just a couple of weeks ago, I was finally able to forgive myself and let go of the shame and guilt I had been carrying."

Julia stood and walked over to the fireplace and placed the picture back on the mantle, then faced him.

"Do you think you'll see him again?" she asked as she took his hands in hers.

"That's up to God and Patricia. I don't know what, or if, she's told him about me. I'm hoping when he turns eighteen, he'll try to find me."

"Is this why you had a hard time committing to me?"

Reggie's chest pounded, but if he and Julia were to have a solid relationship, he had to be open and honest.

"Making a commitment would have forced me to admit my physical attraction to you. I couldn't be honest about my feelings for you, because doing so would make me vulnerable to the very thing that controlled me so long ago and cost me my son."

"And what might that be?"

Her voice was so soft, he wasn't sure she'd asked the question or if he'd imagined it. The gentle squeeze on his hands confirmed her genuine desire to get to know all of him.

"Sex," he plainly stated.

Her eyebrows narrowed.

"To put it plain, I enjoyed having sex to the point I allowed my flesh to control not only my body, but my ability to think rationally. I wouldn't go as far as to say I was a sex addict, but I can't count, nor remember how many women I've been with. And what's more pathetic is I didn't love none of them. After I got what I wanted, I usually lost interest. For me, it was all about conquering the prey."

Julia flinched.

"Once I saw how easy it was to manipulate women into submission, I had no boundaries. Depending on my mood, I'd change partners often. I just couldn't get enough. I loved having sex."

"What about now?" Julia bit her lower lip. "You seem to have it all under control. If it weren't for you calling me beautiful and holding my hand, I wouldn't think you were attracted to me."

Nervous laughter escaped from his lips. "Trust me, I noticed your physical attributes the first day I saw you in church. And I more than liked what I saw. And yes, I've fantasized on more than one occasion about all the naughty things I'd like to do to your body." His eyes swept her body.

Julia blushed.

"When I surrendered my life to Christ eight years ago, I also vowed not to engage my body in any activity that doesn't glorify Him. That's why I won't kiss your lips or touch you in certain places. I know once I taste your lips, chances are I won't stop until I have all of you."

Julia studied the face of the man she loved. "If it's possible, I love you more at this moment than I did when I entered the house. I love you for being transparent with me and for trusting me with your intimate feelings. You're right, the man you are today is not the person you were back then. You are an anointed and powerful man of God. I believe the God you—we—serve can fix what you've messed up. I believe He will restore your son back to you." Julia then closed her eyes and squeezed his hands and prayed fervently. She prayed until he felt the peace only God could give.

Chapter 23

He may not have voiced the reasons behind the changes in his behavior, but Reggie's congregation sure noticed the difference. Reggie smiled and laughed much more now than he ever had. He seemed more relaxed and at peace. On Sunday mornings, he danced more and praised God more vigorously. His preaching was more powerful than ever. Not a Sunday went by that people didn't come to the altar and commit their life to Christ after hearing him preach. Last Sunday, True Worship's membership exceeded eight hundred.

Julia had the chance to see the new-and-improved pastor, as Nikki called him, in action at the Fifth Sunday Fellowship service at True Worship the previous Sunday. Julia was standing in True Worship's dining hall, waiting for Nikki, again. This time she wasn't late, she was helping set the tables for the after-service fellowship meal. Julia set her purse down and gave her a hand.

Just as she spread a tablecloth, she felt the vibration from her cell phone on her waist. The text message read: *U look beautiful*. Julia looked around the room and blushed when she spotted Reggie standing on the opposite end, smiling at her.

Moments later Reggie walked over with Minister Johnson and greeted her and Nikki. Trying not to be obvious, Reggie gave Nikki a light hug and then did the same to Julia.

"You look mighty fine yourself," Julia quickly whispered in his ear when he hugged her.

"I hope you enjoy the service this afternoon, swe-Sister Julia. I'm sure Pastor Leonard is going to preach a wonderful sermon," he said, trying to make small talk.

"Did you almost call her sweetheart in public?"

Reggie waved off Nikki's question and subsequent laughter at the slip.

Julia ignored her, too. "I'm sure he will," Julia answered with a smile.

Noticing that more people had entered the hall, Reggie said, "I'll see the two of you later."

"I hope you don't think I fell for that little exchange," Minister Johnson said to Reggie as they left the hall. "You're forgetting that I'm the one who introduced you to Ms. Simone."

Once inside his office, Reggie greeted Pastor Leonard, "God bless you, sir."

"God bless you! You're doing a great work over here." Pastor Leonard pointed to the model of the new building on Reggie's desk.

"Thank you, sir." As Reggie hugged him, he felt a need to express himself. "Reverend Leonard, I know I've never told you this, but I really appreciate you for all of the help and encouragement you have given me over the years. There were many occasions when I wanted to give up and you called and spoke life into me when I needed it the most. I'm pleased to tell you that I have finally been set free of my past."

Reverend Leonard's eyes glossed over. "I'm proud of you, son. I never doubted God would work things out for you. Have you contacted your son yet?"

"No, but I believe God is going to work that out, too."

Reverend Leonard patted his shoulder. "I know He will." He took note of Reggie's neck. "Son, that's a nice cross around your neck. I can't recall seeing one like that before."

"This," Reggie said, looking down, "this was given to me by a very special person. She had it custom designed for me," he said proudly.

Reverend Leonard's eyes lit up. "Would this *special person* happen to be Sister Julia?"

"Yes, sir. She is my special person." Reggie didn't try to hide how much that pleased him.

Reverend Leonard was so excited, he let his thought slip out, "Boy, you finally went and bought you some sense!"

Reggie laughed along with him. "I guess I did."

"How special is she?" Reverend Leonard asked expectantly.

"Well, right now we're getting to know each other and I believe she's the one for me, but I'm seeking God for direction and the proper timing."

"You are aware that she's accepted her call into the ministry and will be ordained soon?"

"Yes, I am, and I think it's wonderful."

"Praise God. God is good," was all Reverend Leonard could say.

"I guess that's my cue," Reggie said, when chords from the organ penetrated the thin walls of the office. "I'll see you in service."

After the opening prayer and scripture reading, the Praise and Worship Ministry took the platform. Reggie was pleasantly surprised to see Julia leading the group, along with Brother Moore, the leader of True Worship's team. Reggie and Reverend Leonard thought it was a good idea to combine the music ministries for the fellowship services, but Julia never told him that she was going to lead Praise and Worship.

Standing on stage, Julia looked like a true minister. Like she belonged there. She had changed from the fancy black-beaded suit, into a simple black cassock. She and Brother Moore took turns leading the twelve-member group through a medley of worship songs. Between selections, she exhorted the congregation to praise God.

Reggie surveyed the sanctuary and took note of the audience. Everywhere he looked, people were praising God for real. He noticed some of his members, who never participated during Praise and Worship, were now on their feet. Maybe it was the energy she exhibited. Maybe it was her sincerity. Or maybe she was just doing what she'd been born to do. Whatever it was, Reggie enjoyed watching Julia praise God.

To conclude Praise and Worship, the combined choir joined them on stage, and Julia led them in a foot-stomping, version of "Thank You, Lord." She sang with so much energy and conviction that the whole congregation was on its feet clapping and singing along with her. She got so excited that she started dancing and couldn't finish the song. Brother Moore took the microphone and carried on like that switch was part of the original plan. Reggie enjoyed watching her dance. How she could move that fast in high heels was inconceivable to him.

Julia's dancing in the spirit was the calm before the storm. In no time, half of the congregation, including Reggie and Reverend Leonard, joined in. The praise marathon was off and running. For the next thirty minutes, the musicians put in a good workout, dripping with sweat trying to keep up with the praisers. As soon as one side would calm down a little, the other side would start up. Even the balcony was jumping. A few ladies broke their heels trying to dance. Others simply took their shoes off. Even Mother Elsie did her two-step across the front. By this time, Julia was tired. She sat down and watched everyone else.

Reggie finally stopped dancing long enough to walk to the podium. He figured this was the perfect time for Reverend Leonard to preach. Between shouts of "Glory," "Hallelujah," and "Thank You," he attempted to introduce Reverend Leonard. He was only able to get one sentence out.

"The Bible says, 'Let everything that hath breath praise the Lord'." That was it. The congregations of True Worship and House of Prayer decided that at this Fifth Sunday Fellowship service they would obey the Word. The praise party shifted into overdrive.

* * *

Julia sang along with the CD as she drove her Jaguar down Interstate 80. She had just finished a tour of the Point Richmond project and was pleased with the progress. The project was now ninety percent complete and she had reservation of purchases for all of the luxury condos. She made up her mind to take some time off from developing once the project was completed. She wasn't quite sure what she would do, but whatever she decided, it would include Reggie.

"Maybe she'd help Reggie with the new building," she said, and contemplated her options. After helping True Worship acquire the building, she doubted Reggie would ever ask her for anything else. He was too much of a man for that, and he was her man.

They'd been dating for eight weeks now and in her opinion things were going very well. They talked on the phone at least once a day, even when one of them was out of town. They ate dinner together at least twice a week and enjoyed countless lunch dates together. She even had the garage reserve a parking spot for him, so he wouldn't have to waste time looking for one. "You can spend the time you save with me," is what she told him when at first he objected.

The closer they grew, the harder it became to conceal their relationship. Reggie didn't want to publicize the relationship until they were absolutely sure they were headed down the aisle. She agreed; in fact, she respected him for it.

The ringing of Julia's cell phone interrupted her thoughts. "Hey, you."

"Hello, love," Reggie said.

"Are you packed yet?" Julia had convinced him to accompany her to her parents' home for their fiftieth wedding anniversary party on Saturday. To persuade him, she had to promise to have him back in time for Sunday morning service.

"That's what I'm calling about. What's the attire for this party?"

"It's not really a party. Think of it as a family barbeque."

"A barbeque?" he questioned.

"Yes. My parents didn't want to do anything fancy. They just wanted the family to get together. Oh, don't forget to bring your trunks, just in case you decide to swim. And don't forget your tennis shoes, my family loves shooting hoops. Do you like horseback riding? If you do, we can do that, too." She took a breath and slowed down. "I know I'm rambling, but I'm excited about you meeting my family."

"I can tell you're excited, but do you think we'll have enough time to do all of those activities and still make it to your parents' home?"

It took a moment for Julia to understand his question. "I'm sorry, honey. I guess I didn't make myself clear. All of these activities are on my parents' estate."

"Oh, I see." He was quiet for a moment. "What time does our flight leave?"

"CJ and Angie will meet us at the Oakland Airport at seven-thirty a.m. We're scheduled to take off at eight."

"You never did tell me how much I owe you for my ticket," he stated.

"Didn't I tell you, we're flying in The Simone Company private plane?"

After a long moment he said, "I see."

"Are you okay with this?" she asked nervously. "I hope so, because this really means a lot to me. I love you and just know my family will."

"If I'm going to be in your life, there are some things I'll just have to get used to," he said in resignation. "I'll meet you at your condo in the morning. I'm sure you've already arranged for the limo service to take us to the airport." His response was peppered with a hint of sarcasm.

"You're getting to know me already." She tried to lighten his mood, but failed.

"Bye."

As she exited the freeway, Julia prayed Reggie wouldn't cancel.

Chapter 24

During the entire drive to Julia's condo, Reggie tried to talk himself out of going to southern California with her. He would have to meet her family, eventually, but wasn't sure if he was prepared for them. He really didn't know what to expect. Julia constantly told him how fun and easygoing the Simone family was, but he considered her observation biased, because she was one of them. It wasn't that people with money intimidated him, because he was content with who he was. He just didn't care much for snobbish people who looked down on those who had less than they had. Although Julia had never given him any indication that, that was the case with her family, he was still cautious. He also wondered if Julia's loving behavior would change once they entered her family's presence.

On the elevator ride up to her condo, he decided he wasn't ready to meet the Simone family. Julia wouldn't be happy about it, but he hoped she would understand his reasons. He was just about to press the bell when she opened the door.

"Hey, you." She was bubbling with excitement. She already had her purse on her shoulder and her travel bag in hand. "I hope you're ready to have a good time. I just know you're going to love my family. This means so much to me. Thank you for agreeing to join me."

Reggie stood stuck in place, as he studied her. She was simply gorgeous in her black jean outfit. The underlying V-neck top brought attention to the heart pendent he'd given her for Valentine's Day. On her face was the smile he loved. Suddenly, all of the doubts he had moments earlier were now insignificant. The only thing he wanted to do was make her happy, and if that meant getting on a plane and spending the day with her family, then that was exactly what he was going to do.

"Lead the way," he said after kissing her forehead and taking the travel bag.

Within minutes of Julia's limo arriving at the airport, the two limos transporting CJ and Angie arrived. Shay rode with Mike, Angie and their three children. Angie's sisters used to tease her because she was the oldest sister, but she was the last one to have children. Ryan was twelve and twins Trevor and Tre'ana were ten.

As each limo emptied its passengers, the siblings greeted each other and their spouses with hugs and kisses. Reggie stood in the background, watching Julia interact with her family. The affection exchanged appeared genuine.

Julia was so excited; she nearly skipped over to Reggie and grabbed him by the arm. "Come on. I want to introduce you to everyone." She was walking so fast, he had to quicken his pace to keep up with her. Reggie surveyed the group and took notice they all bore expressions of shock.

"Everybody, this is Reggie, I mean Reverend Reginald Pennington. He's the pastor of a very progressive church here in Oakland. As a matter of fact, he's Nikki's pastor." Julia took a breath in an effort to calm herself.

"Hi," the four said in unison.

Shay leaned against the limo, laughing at her mother's behavior. "Mama, I can't remember the last time I saw you this excited about anything."

Julia continued with introductions. "You probably remember their faces from the picture in my office, but I'll introduce you. This is my oldest brother, Carey Jr.," she pointed him out, "but you can call him CJ, like everyone else does. He's the oldest child in the family. That's his wife, Alaina. She's my sister-in-law, but we're more like sisters. It's like that with all of my in-laws, but you will see that later. Anyway, this is their youngest. They have two more, but they're not here now. You'll meet them when we get to the San Fernando Valley." She pointed to Angie. "You remember Mike and Angie from the hospital, don't you? Angie's the second born. These are her three children." She pointed in their direction. "The younger two are twins, but I'm sure you've noticed that." She finally took a breath.

Reggie's face now bore the same shocked expression as her family did. The whole time he had known Julia, he had never seen her so giddy or heard her talk so fast. The five adults stood there staring at Julia, like she'd just stepped out of the twilight zone.

"It's good to see you again, Reggie," Angie finally said. That seemed to have brought everyone back to earth and they exchanged greetings with him. Reggie was not prepared for their type of exchange. He extended his hand, but instead of accepting it, everyone hugged him and said, "Welcome to the family."

Reggie wasn't sure how to respond, outside of a polite, "Thank you."

"Mr. Simone, we'll be ready for departure in fifteen minutes," the pilot called down.

"Thanks, Sam. Let's board," CJ said to the group, then headed up the stairs.

Angie and Alaina pulled out their cell phones, leaving Julia little doubt they were calling other family members to tell them about Reggie.

Once everyone boarded, the family joined hands for a quick prayer. During CJ's prayer Angie squeezed Julia's hand, indicating a discussion would take place in the very near future.

To his surprise, the hour-long plane ride was enjoyable. Reggie was sure he would be bombarded with questions about his economic status. But not once did his stock portfolio or what type of car he drove come up. What did come up was his church. He felt at ease, as he shared his expansion plans over a game of chess with CJ. Mike and CJ seemed genuinely interested. Mike even promised to visit one Sunday.

Julia, on the other hand, didn't enjoy herself as much. For the entire ride Shay, Alaina and Angie teased her.

"Girl, are you sure you didn't pee on yourself?" Alaina started. "Stand up and let me check, because you are just too excited."

"You forgot you were at the airport, out there skipping around like you were in the forest or something," Angie added. "My twins can't jump as high you did over that man."

"Mama, your smile is so wide, you need to grow some more teeth to fill in the space."

"Forget y'all," Julia said, laughing at their assessment.

The laughter caught Reggie's attention and he turned toward the back. "I wonder what they're laughing at back there," he said to CJ and Mike.

"Reggie, I wouldn't worry about that if I were you. You will hear that laughter all day," CJ answered.

* * *

The limos pulled onto the Simone family estate shortly before 10:00 a.m. The half-mile drive from the security gate to the house was taking too long for Julia. She fidgeted and her left leg shook.

Reggie squeezed her shoulder. "Calm down, sweetheart. By the way you're acting, one would think this was *your* first time here."

"I just want you to have a good time, that's all," Julia answered.

"As long as I'm with you, I will," he said and kissed her forehead.

Julia rolled her eyes when she saw Alaina and Angie texting at rapid speed.

"Reggie, my man, I hope you're wearing the whole armor, because in the next five minutes you're going to need it," Mike teased.

"Leave him alone, Mike," Julia scolded.

Reggie didn't have a clue as to what Mike was talking about. When Reggie stepped out of the limo, he surveyed his surroundings. Luxury vehicles and SUVs lined the horseshoe-shaped driveway. In the center of the green, manicured lawn was a gigantic fountain with two cherubs. As the limo driver unloaded the luggage, the walkway leading to the arched entrance caught his attention. The walkway contained multicolored marble squares with some of his favorite scriptures engraved on them.

"Do you like that?" Julia asked.

"Yes, that adds a nice touch."

"Come on inside." Julia grabbed his arm and he willingly followed. Angie and Alaina trailed close behind.

CJ shook his head as he said, "Sheep going to the slaughter."

If Reggie knew what was on the other side of the door, he probably would have run back to Oakland. He never saw it coming. As soon as Julia led him through the foyer, into the oversized living room, Reggie got ambushed. Instantly, the introductions, which felt more like an interrogation, began.

"Hi, Reggie, I'm Chantel, third born, it's so wonderful to meet you."

"Welcome, man. Stephan, number six."

"How's it going? I'm Greg, Chantel's husband."

"Hello, Reggie. Raquel, number seven. I am so happy to meet you."

"Number four, Jonathan. Hey, didn't I see you at that banquet a while back? Welcome to our family."

"Hi, I'm Janice and I'm married to Stephan."

"How are you? Theresa, Jonathan's wife"

"What's up, Reggie? I'm Antonio and I belong to Raquel."

"Hey, man, I'm Andre, the baby of the family and the only woman I belong to is my mama."

Reggie got a hug and a bright smile with each introduction. He was speechless. When the siblings finished introducing themselves, they then introduced their children—all twenty-two of them.

Julia was bursting with joy as he made his way around the room. She searched for her parents and spotted them standing in front of the fireplace. "Come," she said, and steered him in their direction. As she neared her parents, the crowded room seemed to quiet down.

Julia was so excited she could barely contain herself; she leapt in the air. She faced her parents and took a breath before she began.

"Papa, Mama, this is Reverend Reginald Pennington. Reggie, these are my parents, Carey and Ana Simone."

Reggie was impressed with how young they looked. He assumed the picture in Julia's office had been taken years earlier. Ana Simone was surprisingly petite, considering she had birthed eight children. Besides a few gray strands, Carey Simone didn't look a day over fifty-five. *This is where she gets her youthfulness from.*

"It's an honor to meet you both." Reggie's light bulb still wasn't working, for the umpteenth time that day he extended his hand. He became uncomfortable when neither of her parents said a word, or acknowledged his hand.

Carey and Ana looked at their daughter, who was literally glowing, and then at each other. For what seemed like hours to Reggie was actually thirty seconds. They took turns studying Reggie and Julia's faces. Reggie was about to withdraw his hand, when Carey Sr. yelled, "Welcome to our family, son!" He then pushed Reggie's hand away and gave him a big bear hug. Ana followed suit with a lighter, but just as affectionate, hug. The noise level in the room suddenly increased.

"Thank you, Mr. and Mrs. Simone," a winded Reggie said.

Carey Sr. dismissed his formalities. "Call me 'Papa.' When I'm conducting business, that's when I'm Mr. Simone. Here with my family and friends, I'm simply Papa. And stop offering your hand. That's what you do when you close a business deal. There's no business deal here, it's just family. So you can save that for your church members. Around here we show our affection. Do you think you can handle that?"

Reggie was humbled by the reprimand. "Yes, Papa, I can," he answered.

"And I'm Mom, Mother, Mama or Mommy; whichever one you feel comfortable with," Ana added.

"Hey, Reggie, you look like you can shoot hoops. We're going to get a game started in about twenty minutes," Stephan called out.

Julia was about to respond, but her mother beat her to it.

"Stephan, he'll be out in thirty minutes. He needs to get settled into his room and eat something before he plays. Julia, go into the kitchen and fix him something to eat," Ana ordered, then turned to Reggie. "Follow me, son, I'll show you to your room."

"Whatever you say, Mother, you're the boss," he said and followed Ana down the hall.

"Oh, he's going to fit in *real* good," Chantel remarked.

"He sure is," Ana's remaining three daughters agreed.

Julia was about to leave the room when Raquel's sassy tone stopped her. "And as for you, young lady, we'll meet you in the downstairs kitchen in thirty-five minutes."

* * *

Reggie remained quiet as he rode the elevator with Ana. It fascinated him to see an elevator inside of a residence. He was truly overwhelmed by the Simone family. They were nothing like he imagined. They weren't stuck up and snobbish, but friendly and sincere. In a few short minutes, Carey Simone had earned his utmost respect.

Ana's voice interrupted his thoughts. "Son, I know I just met you, but I want to thank you," she said as she stepped off the elevator.

"For what, Mother?" he asked as he followed her around a corner. She stopped in front of the bedroom door and faced him.

"For loving my daughter." Reggie was stunned by her directness. "I haven't seen my baby smile like that in years. To be honest, she hadn't been happy in years. You're the first person she's brought here, since that sorry ex-husband of hers, and that was only once. After the objections she received from her father, brothers and me, she distanced herself from us. When she did return, she wasn't the same. For a long time she was hurt and angry. Even after she worked through her pain, I could still see the sadness in her eyes. But, son, I didn't see that today. What I saw, was a woman in love with a man that loves her. Son, I don't know anything about you, but I can tell you need her just as much as she needs you."

"I do, Mother, I do," Reggie managed to say after swallowing the lump in his throat.

Ana raised her eyebrow. "I know you do. I'm just waiting for you to say, 'I do'."

"All things in time, Mother."

Once inside the room, Reggie walked over to the window and scanned the grounds. The second floor bedroom offered an extended view of what was supposed to be the backyard. To Reggie, it looked more like a resort.

Closest to the house was the biggest grill he'd ever seen. The brick-encased surface was at least ten-feet long. Mounted on the lawn were two regular-sized grills. All three were loaded with various kinds of meat. The lawn was covered with picnic tables and lawn chairs. Off to the right, family members enjoyed the Olympic-sized pool. In the far left corner of the grounds, he could see the horse stables. On the other side of the fence were the tennis and full basketball courts. Julia's brothers were out there warming up. Reggie quickly changed into his shorts and court shoes and walked out the door.

Once in the hallway, he was confused as to which way to go.

"Need some help?" Julia asked. He hadn't seen her standing at the other end of the hall.

He smiled. "Not anymore."

She returned his smile and guided him to the stairs.

"Is your room up here?"

"No. Shay and I are sharing a room downstairs."

"How many rooms are there in this house?"

"Ten, plus the three-bedroom guest house out back. That's where the older grandchildren hang out."

"There are nearly fifty people here, are they all going to stay here tonight?"

"There's more than that, if you include my aunts, uncles and cousins." Reggie's eyes widened. "Don't worry, only my siblings and their families are staying."

"Where will everyone sleep?" he asked.

"That's the easy part. Each sibling shares a room with their spouse. Since I'm single, I usually share with Shay, and the spoiled brat, Andre, gets a room all to himself. Like I said before, the adult grandchildren like to stay in the guesthouse and the younger ones usually camp out in the den or wherever there's space."

"Wow, you guys are very organized," he remarked.

"With a family this size, you have to be."

"Where are we going?" he asked as he started down the stairs.

"To the downstairs' kitchen," she answered.

"How many kitchens are in this house?"

"Two. One on each floor."

"I see."

Inside the kitchen Reggie sat at the counter and enjoyed a light meal of yogurt, fresh fruit and freshly squeezed orange juice. Julia stood across from him, silently admiring the way his tank top accented his muscles. This was the first time she'd seen him without a shirt. When he caught her staring, she quickly looked away.

Knowing the answer, he asked, "Do you like what you see?"

Deciding to play with his ego, she rolled her eyes and answered, "It's aw-right."

He opened his mouth to respond, but stopped when her young niece entered the kitchen. When he finished eating, she walked him to the basketball court. When Julia returned to the kitchen, the Simone women were waiting.

The Simone women busied themselves making collard greens, macaroni and cheese, candied yams, potato salad and baked beans, as they began Julia's interrogation.

"Girl, what's this I hear about you skipping down the runway?" Theresa started in.

"And cheesin' like you just won Super Lotto," Chantel added.

Raquel jumped in. "Honey, she did, that man is *fine!*" She and Chantel gave each other high-fives.

"Girl, I ain't mad at you. If he was my man, I'd skip and do back flips," Janice added.

"Girl, shut up. Stephan has made you turn so many cartwheels that you've forgotten how to stand up straight," Angie hollered.

When the laughter subsided, Raquel started in again. "So, big sister, what kind of circus tricks has Reggie taught you?"

Julia gasped at her question.

Alaina jumped in. "Raquel, for someone with your education, you sure do say some stupid things. You know Reggie's a pastor and Julia's getting ordained soon."

"That doesn't mean they are not human."

Ana responded for her daughter. "No, it doesn't, but not everyone wears an *Always Open for Business* sign between their legs like you do."

"Ooh!" echoed throughout the kitchen.

"Antonio's not complaining," Raquel shot back.

"That's because you've whipped him like he stole something," Julia threw out.

"And you know this. A girl's got to do, what a girl's got to do!" Raquel showed no shame whatsoever, taking a moment to "drop it like it's hot."

"When did you two become serious?" Angie asked. "I knew there was something brewing between you at the hospital."

"And why didn't you tell us you were bringing him?" Ana asked.

"I wanted to be sure he could make the trip before I told everyone. We started our relationship at the end of January," Julia said, answering Angie's question.

"We don't have to ask how you feel about him. Stevie Wonder can see that you're in love," Chantel said.

Julia blushed and pressed her hand to her chest. She looked around at the women she loved. Her eyes watered. "Yes, I am. I am in love for the first time."

Sounds of "oh" and sniffles were heard through the kitchen.

"How long do the two of you plan on dating?" Alaina asked as she dabbed her eyes.

"I don't know, but I hope it's not too long. I don't know how much longer I can keep myself from kissing those luscious lips," Julia hollered.

"You mean you haven't kissed him yet?" Janice asked. "We heard about him kissing a dent in your forehead."

"No, we've agreed not to kiss on the lips until we are married. We also agreed not to touch each other."

"Are you tempted?" Theresa asked.

"Girl, yes! But I know if I buy *that* horse, I'll *have* to ride it."

"That's my girl," Raquel said and gave Julia a high-five.

"You're doing right, baby," Ana said. "What's the Simone women motto?"

"Say 'I do,' then do the do," the women said in unison, although not all of them followed that rule.

By early afternoon, the Simone estate was overflowing with relatives and friends, there to congratulate Carey and Ana on their fiftieth wedding anniversary. The sunny spring weather was perfect for the occasion. At least two hundred people were scattered around, enjoying everything from swimming to barbeque ribs and good music through mounted speakers.

After a friendly, but competitive game of basketball with the Simone men, Reggie showered and changed into a tan, casual two-piece outfit. The above-the-elbow cut sleeves revealed his strong muscular arms. Julia, now wearing a floral print wrap dress, smiled proudly as she strolled around on his arm, introducing him to her relatives.

"How was your game?" she asked him.

"It was great. Your brothers and nephews can really play ball. It's a good thing I work out four days a week. Otherwise, I wouldn't be able to keep up."

Without thinking about it, Julia rubbed his arm and said in a sultry voice, "It is a good thing."

Reggie stopped and faced her. He was about to respond when someone announced in the microphone that it was time for the Simone family dance.

"Come on, let's dance." She grabbed his hand and took off before he could protest.

In no time, every Simone, and most of their guests, were up and doing the Simone family dance, to a Kirk Franklin tune, with Carey and Ana leading the pack. The dance steps were similar to the Electric Slide. It took Julia a minute to teach the steps to Reggie, but once he caught on, he added a few moves of his own. Julia was surprised when he continued dancing for two more songs.

Reggie's happiness poured from him as they walked back across the lawn. He picked Julia up and spun her around. "I don't know the last time I had this much fun. Thank you for inviting me."

She wrapped her arms around his neck. "I'm glad you're enjoying yourself. You had me worried for a minute. I thought you were going to cancel at the last minute."

"I was, but I'm glad I didn't. Your family consists of wonderful people. Your brothers are hilarious. We're meeting in the game room later on to play pool." Reggie stopped walking. "Hey, I didn't know Andre was a cop. You should have seen the look on my face, when he pulled out his gun and told me to give him my wallet, so he could check my ID."

Julia laughed. "That's Andre, the prankster. How he's taken seriously as a lieutenant, I'll never know."

"And you know what else? I could kick myself for not realizing Jonathan was your brother. The two of you look so much alike."

"I told you, you're blind," she reminded him.

His expression turned serious and set her on her feet. "Not anymore."

"Do you think my family is something you could um, be a part of?"

Reggie slid his arm around her waist and squeezed her to him. "Without a doubt," he said and kissed her forehead.

* * *

"That's what you get for playing your little joke on Reggie," Julia said after she hit Andre on the back of the head. She had caught up with him on his way to the game room.

He rubbed the spot. "You know I had to welcome him into the family."

"But did you have to use your gun?"

"You should have seen his face." Andre laughed. "That dark brother turned red. I'm on my way to play pool with the guys now. Maybe this time I'll pull out my hand grenade?"

"You are sick, you know that, right?" Julia said. "Hey, before you go to the game room, I want to run something by you."

Andre leaned against the wall with his arms folded. "What's up?"

* * *

Just before midnight, Reggie walked Julia to her room.

"Don't forget, family prayer is at eight a.m. sharp," she reminded him.

"Shall I pick you up?"

"Sure. I'll be waiting."

"Sweet dreams, beautiful," he said and turned to leave.

"Reggie," she called to him. "I love you."

"I love you, too, sweetheart."

By 8:00 a.m., the Simone family had eaten breakfast and assembled for family prayer. Everyone joined hands as a symbol of their never-ending bond. Carey and Ana opened the prayer with thanksgiving for their family. Then each sibling, from the oldest to the youngest, took turns praying for everything from the health of their marriages to the healing of the sick. Normally, Carey and Ana would close the prayer by pronouncing blessings over their children and grandchildren, but today they decided to do something different.

"This morning we are going to have the newest addition to our family pronounce the blessings over our lives and also traveling mercy," Carey said.

The room remained silent as everyone waited for the conclusion of the prayer. It remained that way until Julia finally whispered into Reggie's ear, "Honey, he's talking about you."

Reggie's knees nearly buckled at the gesture. The Simones knew little about him, yet they accepted him into their family without reservation. He hadn't experienced that kind of love since the death of his parents. Reggie swallowed the lump in his throat and summoned the right words for the task at hand.

On the plane ride home, Reggie tried to review the notes for his sermon, but he had a hard time concentrating, so he put them away. He couldn't believe how wrong he had been about the Simones. They were nothing like he prejudged them to be. Silently, he asked God for forgiveness.

The Simone men were real and genuine. They treated him like an old friend. They even exchanged numbers with him. And what could he say about Julia's parents? They treated him as if he was their son. It had been a long time since he'd been part of a family, and then it was a small family. It would take some time to get used to the camaraderie, but he looked forward to it.

Watching Julia sleep across from him, the words Ana spoke to him came to mind. "You need her just as much as she needs you."

"What can a woman who has so much, need?" he questioned himself.

Love, he heard a small still voice answer.

Chapter 25

J ulia tried to calm her nerves by looking out the window as Reggie drove through the Altamont Pass. After having such a wonderful time last weekend with the Simones, Reggie thought it was time for Julia to meet his family. It wasn't a big family like hers, just his aunt, uncle and his two cousins, but he was excited nonetheless. He looked over at her watching the cows grazing in the sunburnt hills along Highway 205. As if reading her thoughts, he lifted her hand to his lips and said, "My family's going to love you, just like I do." After he kissed the back of her hand she placed his hand in her lap.

"How did you know what I was thinking?" she asked.

"I could tell by the way you were staring at those cows back there."

Her brow furrowed. "What do you mean?"

"The last time you paid a cow that much attention, it was dripping with A1, and sautéed mushrooms on the side." They both laughed and she relaxed a little.

When Reggie took the March Lane Road exit, Julia pulled out her compact and checked her makeup one final time. She normally didn't wear much makeup, but today was special. She put on a full face, including foundation.

After making a couple of turns, Reggie parked his Mercedes in front of a two-story white house with yellow trim, then walked around and opened the passenger door.

"Do you think this dress is appropriate?" she said in reference to the light-blue scoop- neck, short-sleeved linen dress she was wearing with the four-inch ankle-wrap sandals. After she was out of the car, she turned in a circle, so he could view the dress from all angles.

"You look *very good* in that dress," he said in a voice that she didn't recognize.

She snapped her head up to find his eyes focused on her hips. She blushed, but couldn't resist flirting back. "Gives you something to look forward to, doesn't it?"

Just then his cousin, Edward, pulled up. After he got out of his SUV, the six-foot, dark- brown, medium-build brother greeted Reggie with a playful hug. He then turned his attention to Julia.

"So, you're the person my cousin can't stop talking about and I see why. You are a beautiful woman. My name is Edward, if you ever get bored with him, give me a call."

Julia knew Edward was only joking, because Reggie told her both of his cousins were happily married with more children than they could handle. She looked up at Reggie who now stood with his arm around her shoulder. She instantly knew what he was doing. Edward being his cousin didn't stop him from marking his territory.

Julia shook his hand. "It's nice to meet you, Edward. I have heard a lot about you. I'm sure I won't get bored because this fine man standing next to me is more than I can handle."

Pleased with her response, Reggie kissed her on the forehead.

Edward pretended to be wounded. "I guess I'll have to settle for my wife and five kids."

The three shared a laugh and followed Edward up the red brick walkway and into the house.

The moment she stepped into the bungalow-style house, she was instantly welcomed by the smell of fresh collard greens and fried chicken. Before she got a chance to complete a visual survey of the living room, Reggie's aunt and uncle came bustling in from the kitchen.

"Reggie, she's beautiful!" his aunt exclaimed. The elderly, robust, medium-brown skinned woman held her arms out and headed straight for Julia. The hug she gave Julia was so strong, Julia nearly lost her balance.

"It's a pleasure to meet you, Mrs. Pennington," Julia said, returning her hug. "Reggie talks about you all the time."

"Welcome to our home, baby. I wish my brother was alive to see this, he would definitely be pleased," Reggie's uncle said, after he hugged her.

"Thank you, sir."

Reggie's aunt, still smiling, looked down at Julia's hands. "Where's your ring?"

Julia and Reggie looked at each other before Julia answered, "I'm not sure I understand your question."

"Your engagement ring. Where's your engagement ring?" his aunt clarified.

"Auntie, we're not engaged yet?" Reggie answered for Julia.

Reggie's aunt threw her hands down. "You're not? I assumed since she's the first woman you've brought to meet the family, and by the way your face lights up every time you mention her name, that you two are headed down the aisle. Shoots, I don' went and bought me a new dress to wear to the wedding."

Julia laughed, but Reggie looked embarrassed.

Reggie's aunt took Julia by the hand. "Come on in the kitchen with me. Reggie tells me you can cook; you can help me finish up dinner. Maybe by that time Reggie will be don' made up his mind."

Julia obediently followed the sweet elderly woman into the country-sized kitchen. The two women talked and laughed and talked some more, while Julia made homemade cornbread and Aunt Mae added the frosting to a homemade German chocolate cake. Julia was surprised to learn that Reggie had told his family everything there was to know about her. Aunt Mae asked about Shay and the rest of the Simone family. Julia was blown away when Reggie's aunt asked how her company was doing. Julia had no idea that Reggie was now comfortable enough about her business to tell others about it.

"Reggie told us how you're redesigning Emery Bay and Point Richmond," Aunt Mae said. "He said you're doing a wonderful job."

"Really?"

"Brags about you all the time. He's amazed at how you were able to turn an idea into a multimillion dollar company, while being a single parent."

Julia placed her left hand over her heart and listened as Aunt Mae went on and on about how much Reggie talks about her and how proud he is of her.

When Reggie brought his cousin James into the kitchen to meet Julia, she kissed Reggie on the cheek.

"What's that for?" he asked.

She offered him a smile. "Just for being you," she answered and then greeted James.

During dinner Julia laughed at stories about Reggie's childhood and his Jheri curl-wearing days.

"You should have seen that boy, just slinging juice every where," Reggie's uncle said.

"I hated to see him coming, because I would have to wash my couch covers as soon as he left," Aunt Mae added.

"Let's not forget the time Mr. Big City kid came out here to the country and thought he would show us how to kill a chicken," James added. "That chicken got so tired of Reggie flinging it around, it popped its own neck."

"You should have seen Reggie running and screaming around the yard from the headless chicken." Edward laughed.

"Whatever, man." Reggie took it all in stride.

After dinner, Julia helped Aunt Mae with the dishes and then joined Reggie in the living room on the floral-print couch. Reggie put his arm around her shoulder. "I hope you're having a good time."

She leaned into him. "I'm having a wonderful time. I love your family."

"Do you think my family is something you could be a part of?"

Julia looked directly into his eyes. "Yes, just as long as you don't revert back to wearing a Jheri curl."

Aunt Mae watched as Reggie laughed out loud and then kissed Julia on the cheek. "I'll get to wear my new dress after all," she said and bustled back into the kitchen.

Chapter 26

J ulia sat on her bed, sorting through mail. After tossing out the junk mail and reviewing her personal bank statements, she decided she was ready to open the package from her brother, Andre.

For weeks, she warred with herself. Maybe it was best if she didn't get involved, but she was curious and she loved him. If there was any way she could help Reggie, she would. The pain she saw in his eyes on Valentine's Day was still etched in her memory.

Reggie smiled and laughed a lot more now, but she could still see his pain, especially when Shay was around. There were times when his eyes glossed over while watching their interaction. She saw it two weeks ago at her parents' home when he interacted with her brothers and nephews. That's why she'd asked Andre to use his law enforcement resources to help find Patricia Robinson.

"Thanks, Lieutenant, you're crazy, but you always come through," she told him two days ago when she phoned after the package arrived.

"Anything to keep you skipping down runways," he teased.

"When are you going to find someone to make you skip?"

"I've been thinking about it." He grew quiet. "Hey, sis, how did you know you were ready to start a relationship with Reggie?"

"I didn't. I just thought he was attractive, but the more time I spent with him, the more I wanted to be with him."

"I can relate to that."

"What's her name?" Julia asked knowingly.

"Candace."

"Is it serious?"

"Hey, I got to run, but I hope things work out for Reggie."

Julia didn't press him. If this Candace was special, they'd meet in the near future. "And I hope things work out with Candace," she said then hung up.

Now that she had all the information she needed to find Reggie's son, she was having second thoughts. If things didn't work out, would he blame her? She held the Federal Express envelope for a long moment, then after taking a deep breath, opened it.

The next morning, she confirmed her itinerary with Sam, the family's pilot, then called Michelle and cleared her schedule for the next two days. Including the weekend, that would give her four days to talk with Patricia Robinson and hopefully get her to agree to a meeting with Reggie.

Well aware of the Arizona heat, she packed appropriately and headed out the door. On her way to the airport, she phoned Reggie.

"Hey, sweetheart, I was just thinking about you. How does PF Chang's sound for dinner?" he asked.

"It sounds wonderful, but I'm going to have to take a rain check." She paused. "I was calling to tell you that I'm leaving town for a few days."

"Oh really, you didn't mentioned that before."

"I know." She stalled. "Something's come up. I'm on my way to the airport now."

"Where are you going?"

"Arizona," she said quickly and changed the subject. "How's your aunt?"

"She's fine," he answered, but his concern was for her family. "Is everything all right with Jonathan?"

"He's fine, but I'm not going to see him. I have some business to take care of." She stammered, "I-I have to run. I'll call you later on tonight."

"Sure, have a safe trip." He hung up without saying good-bye.

She looked down at the phone in her hand and blew a sigh of relief. She hated not being able to tell Reggie what she was doing, but it had to be this way until she had more information. She heard the disappointment in his voice, but couldn't risk giving him false hope. She started to call him back, but changed her mind after she punched in the last number. "You've waited seventeen years; just a little while longer," she mumbled.

During the two-hour flight to Phoenix, Julia read through the information she had on Patricia Robinson once again. According to Andre's sources, she no longer used the name Patricia. Instead she went by her middle name, Alysse. And for the last three years, she'd been married to a man ten years her senior, named Mark Green. They lived just minutes outside of Phoenix. Mark Green was the owner of a local travel agency in Goodyear, Arizona. Julia would start her search for Alysse Green at the Desert Travel Agency.

The fourteen years prior to marrying Mark, she'd lived like a vagabond, moving through eight states in fourteen years. She'd held various job titles from waitress to secretary. Outside of Brian, Patricia had no other children.

In an effort to cool off, Julia stopped at Starbucks for a caramel Frappuccino, after she picked up her rental car. "Thank you, Jesus, for air conditioning," she said out loud, driving down Interstate 10.

Ninety minutes after she arrived in Phoenix, Julia was parked at the strip mall that was home to the Desert Travel Agency. Julia sat in the car and said a quick prayer, not knowing what to expect.

Trying to avoid the Arizona sun, she quickly walked inside the small business. A woman who appeared to be in her early sixties greeted her.

"May I help you?" the woman, whose voice was as dry as the desert, asked.

Julia fidgeted and scanned her surroundings. "I hope so. I'm looking for Alysse Green."

"Is she expecting you?"

"No, but I was directed to her by a good friend," Julia answered honestly.

"Hold on a minute," the woman said, and disappeared around a corner.

Julia tried to calm her nerves by looking at the pictures on the walls of popular tourist spots. She had firsthand knowledge of most of the destinations.

"Hello, can I help you?" a dark-complexioned woman, wearing a blue denim skirt, white tank top and sandals, appeared from around the corner. She wore a bob hairstyle and silver hoop earrings. Her face was attractive, but there was evidence of a rough life in her dark-brown eyes.

Julia swallowed hard. "I'm looking for Alysse Green."

"That's me. What can I do for you?" she asked cheerfully.

Julia looked over her shoulder, then behind her. She didn't want to have this conversation out in the open. "Is there someplace private we can talk?"

"Ms....I'm sorry I didn't get your name."

"Julia. You can call me 'Julia'."

"All right, Julia, have a seat at my workstation. Betty just left for the day, so we're all alone," Alysse stated. She led her to the desk and gestured for Julia to sit down. After Alysse took her seat, she cheerfully asked, "So Julia, what fabulous vacation can I plan for you?"

Julia didn't respond right away. Two pictures on Alysse's desk held her attention. One was a photo of Alysse with Mark on their wedding day. In the other wooden frame was a dark- chocolate teenage boy, with a dimpled left cheek. He was wearing a baseball uniform and the same smile that Julia had come to love.

"Is that your son?" Julia asked.

"Yes, that's my Brian," Alysse answered with a proud smile.

Relieved that she had found the right person, Julia exhaled. She didn't know how to begin, so she did what her mother had always done. She went straight to the point.

"Alysse, I'm not here to plan a vacation. I'm here to talk to you about your son's father, Reginald Pennington."

Alysse looked as if she'd seen a ghost. "What…what are you talking about? What…what do you know? Who are you?"

Julia continued, "My name is Julia Simone, and I know your name was Patricia Robinson, and almost eighteen years ago you gave birth to a son named, Brian Deshawn Pennington. I know you were engaged to Reggie and I also know the reason you ended the engagement and left with Brian."

Alysse's mouth hung open.

"Reggie," Julia continued, "is a special friend of mine and he's been trying to find you and his son ever since you left."

"So, Reggie told you all those things about me?"

"Yes. Well, most of it anyway."

"Well, did he also happen to tell you he's a bonafide dog who can't be trusted?"

"Not exactly." Julia swallowed hard. "Let me be perfectly clear. I think how Reggie treated you was deplorable and there's no excuse for him. He was wrong. I understand completely why you ran off with Brian, but I don't agree with it. If your goal was to pay Reggie back for how he treated you, then you've accomplished that and some."

Alysse leaned back and folded her arms. "So why did he send you here? Why now?"

"Reggie, didn't send me here. He doesn't even know I'm here. He has no idea that I've found you. Why now? Because the person who hurt you back then is not the man I love today."

Alysse raised an eyebrow.

Julia didn't mean to disclose their relationship, but it was too late now, so she continued,

"Reggie is a changed man and he's sorry for his past behavior. He doesn't do the things he did back then. He's the pastor of a very productive church in Oakland."

"Reggie's a pastor?" Alysse interjected. "I can't believe that."

"Yes, and more than anything else in the world, he would love to have a chance for a relationship with his son."

"Doesn't he have more children by now?" Alysse asked.

"No, he doesn't. And his parents died seven years ago." Julia paused. "Brian is all he has left."

Alysse appeared genuinely saddened. "Sorry to hear about his parents. They were wonderful to me and Brian."

"You know, he still has Brian's baby picture on his mantle. He's never forgotten his son or what he did to you. Please consider allowing him to see Brian," Julia pleaded.

Alysse remained silent.

Julia continued, "Alysse, in a couple of months Brian will be eighteen and Reggie won't need your permission. In fact, Brian might try to find his father on his own."

Alysse's tone sharpened. "I can guarantee you my son will never look for Reginald Pennington."

"How can you be so sure?"

"Because he thinks his father is dead," Alysse said flatly.

Julia gasped in disbelief. "Why...why does he believe that?"

"That's what I told him the first time he asked me at age three." Alysse threw her arms up. "He thinks his father was killed in a car accident."

Julia was stunned. "Why would you tell your child a blatant lie like that? What if something had happened to you? Brian would have thought he was alone. What if Brian had medical problems and needed Reggie's help?"

"Look," Alysse snapped, "at the time Reggie was dead to me. I hated him and I didn't want to have anything to do with him. The lie was enough to stop Brian from asking questions about his father's absence. So I never told him anything different."

"What about now, do you still hate him?" Julia asked softly.

Alysse sighed deeply and massaged her forehead. "No, I don't hate him anymore, and no, I don't want to punish him anymore. I've moved on and I'm happy with my life now. But I'm not willing to disrupt my son's life."

"I think you did that a long time ago," Julia snapped before she could stop herself.

Alysse stood and raised her voice. "Look, Julia, I don't have to explain myself to you."

"No, you don't, but when Reggie knocks on your door, you'll have to explain to Brian why he looks just like him," Julia snapped back.

"That'll never happen!"

"Yes, it will," Julia said and stood to meet Alysse's gaze. "Because if you don't contact Reggie soon, I will tell him how to find you. In fact, I'll bring him here myself."

"I can take *my* son and leave," Alysse said vengefully.

"Go right ahead, but I guarantee you I'll find you, just like I found you today." Julia felt like she was negotiating a real estate transaction as she stared at her, unflinching.

When Alysse realized that Julia wasn't going to back down, she slowly sat back down and focused on her wedding picture.

Julia interrupted her thoughts. "Your husband doesn't know the truth either, does he?"

Alysse's voice was shaky and her eyes watered. "No, he doesn't and I don't know how he's going to react when he finds out that I lied to him when I didn't need to. He trusts me and I don't want to hurt him. I love him." Her tears now flowed. "After all of my years of searching, I finally have a family of my own and place to call my own. I can't take a chance on losing that."

Julia handed Alysse a tissue from her purse and gave her time to regroup.

"Alysse," she began softly, "I know firsthand what it's like to search and want something so much, that it scares you to death when you finally get it. I know what it's like to think you've found it, only to have someone take it away from you. And I know what it's like to love someone so much that it hurts. If Mark loves you, and I believe he does by that smile on his face, he'll understand and he'll appreciate you for trusting him with your frailties."

She pressed harder. "Think about all the years Brian has lost with his father. Moments he can never get back. You know firsthand how painful it is to grow up without a father figure. You know what it's like not to have your father read you a story or tuck you in at night. You know what it's like not to have your father's smile of approval when you perform in a school play. You know what it's like not to have your father teach you how to ride a bike. You know what it's like not to have a father's love. You have succeeded in hurting Reggie, but you also hurt Brian. I'm sure Mark is a good father figure, but you can't substitute him for Reggie. Brian needs his father. He can learn things from Reggie that he'll never learn from you."

Alysse stared down at her desk.

"Alysse, do you believe in God?"

She sniffled. "Mark and I started attending church about six months ago."

"That's good, but do you believe in God?"

"Yes, I do, but I'm working on learning to trust Him."

"Well, trust this, God has not given us the spirit of fear; he has given us power and love. Alysse, you have the power in you to overcome your fear of losing your husband and son and you have enough love in your heart to give Reggie and Brian a chance for a relationship."

Alysse put her head in her hands and cried. Julia walked around and consoled her. When she finished crying Julia prayed with her.

Alysse gave her the picture of Brian from her desk to take to Reggie. Julia pulled up True Worship's website for Alysse. She was impressed with the church. Alysse did a double take when the picture of Reggie opened. She hadn't seen him in seventeen years.

"Wow, he's still fine!"

"Yes, he is," Julia answered.

"Earlier, you said you're in love with him."

"Yes, I am," Julia said with pride.

"I hope things work out for you," Alysse said after a prolonged silence.

They talked a while longer.

"I can't believe that no one has interrupted us," Alysse said, as she walked Julia to the door. "We've been in here going on two hours."

"God knows what he's doing," Julia said.

Alysse promised she would get in touch with her in a few days. She needed time to talk to Mark and Brian. Julia said she understood and hugged Alysse good-bye.

Julia drove down Interstate 10, heading for the hotel, elated that she found Alysse so easily. "Thank you, baby brother," she said out loud. She knew in her heart, Alysse would be in touch soon.

She looked down at the clock; it was quarter to six. With her mission accomplished, she didn't feel like sleeping in a strange bed. She grabbed her cell phone and called Sam, then exited the interstate and headed toward the airport.

Chapter 27

Reggie spent Friday morning working at the church. Earlier, he'd met with the project manager for the new building project. He was satisfied with the progress so far. The church was about the only thing he was happy about.

He was concerned about his relationship with Julia. For reasons he couldn't explain, she'd changed in the last week. The shift started when she suddenly flew to Arizona. She said she would be gone for a few days, but came back late that same evening. If he hadn't called her, he wouldn't have known she was back in town. And since then she had been avoiding him. Whenever he called, she only talked for a few minutes and she always made an excuse about why she couldn't see him. He loved her, but he wanted to know what was going on with her. He had been completely honest with her, now he wanted the same from her. He made up his mind; after he made a few phone calls he was going over to her office to find out what, or who, was going on.

Julia's nerves raced violently as she walked toward Reggie's side office door. Tyrone told her Reggie would be down at the church until the afternoon. She felt guilty that she'd kept him in the dark, but she didn't have a choice. She had to make sure everything was in place before she said anything. She couldn't stand to see Reggie disappointed. Alysse had called her two days prior with the final arrangements, but Julia wanted to wait until the plane landed, just to be sure. She pressed the brown envelope to her chest, took a deep breath and knocked on Reggie's door.

Reggie was about to grab his jacket when he heard the knock. He quickly walked over and opened the door.

He stared at her for a long moment without saying anything. He hadn't seen her in eight days and he missed her terribly, but he didn't let it show. He couldn't until he heard the reason for her distance and evasiveness.

"Hello, Julia," he said plainly.

"What? I'm not your sweetheart anymore?" she said nervously.

"Not until you tell me why you have been avoiding me for the last eight days."

She turned serious. "That's why I'm here."

"I'm listening," he said and sat down on the couch.

Julia sat on the couch next to him. She took deep breaths before she continued, "Reggie, I don't know how to tell you this. I mean I don't know where to start."

He didn't like the sound of that or the fact that Julia's left leg was shaking. "Why don't you start from the beginning?"

"All right." She took another deep breath and looked him in the eyes. "Do you remember last Thursday, when I suddenly flew to Arizona for the day?"

"Yes, I do." He nodded for her to continue.

"I told you that I had some business to take care of, but then came back without telling you."

"Yes, and I want to know why." He really didn't like the tone of the conversation. "That's the same day you started pushing me away."

"Well, honey," she said with a smile, "with Andre's help, I found them."

Her response confused him. He thought she was about to say she'd met someone else. "You found who?"

She took his hands. "I found Patricia Robinson and Brian."

Reggie went into shock. He couldn't speak; he just stared at her with his mouth open.

She explained further. "I had Andre search, and he located her. She lives just outside of Phoenix. She doesn't use the name Patricia anymore; she uses her middle name, Alysse. She's known as Alysse Green."

Reggie slumped back against the couch, staring at the ceiling. "Oh, my God. I can't believe it," he said repeatedly.

Julia removed the brown envelope from her jacket pocket and handed the picture to him. "Honey, she gave me this, for you."

Reggie's hand shook uncontrollably as he took the picture and slowly brought it to his face. The ache started in his chest and dropped to his stomach. Unable to contain himself he pressed the photo to his chest and cried out, "Oh, God. My son, my son!" His entire body shook and Julia put her arms around him, holding him tightly. He moaned deeply while she rocked him.

When he calmed down, she whispered in his ear, "Honey, they're here. Tyrone is on his way from the airport with Patricia, her husband, Mark and Brian. You're going to see your son in a few minutes."

Reggie felt like he was going to pass out. His breaths came in short rapid pants. He fell back on the couch and tried to calm himself.

Julia opened the window next to the couch.

"Are you sure you're going to be able to handle this? Let me get you some water," she said when he didn't respond, but he grabbed her and pulled her back down next to him. She put her arms around him and he laid his head on her shoulder.

"Honey, there's something else you need to know," she said as she stroked his head. "Brian didn't know you existed until recently. Patricia...Alysse told him you were killed in a car accident when he was a baby. Up until five days ago, Brian didn't know he had a father."

He moaned and she felt his body constrict. She told him more about Alysse and her husband. She told him how she had moved around, but now was settled in Goodyear. He sat there quietly resting in her arms, except for an occasional moan.

Tyrone quietly entered the office.

When Reggie saw him, he started shaking again.

Tears outlined Julia's cheeks when Tyrone walked over to the couch, and said, "Come on, friend, it's time to meet your son."

Tyrone helped him stand on his feet and supported his weight. Reggie reached back for Julia and she grabbed his hand.

With the help of his best friend and the woman he loved, Reggie walked into the sanctuary to meet his son for the first time in seventeen years. He didn't say a word, but breathed heavily with each step.

Inside the sanctuary, Reggie was greeted first by Patricia. She said hello and introduced her husband to him.

Reggie was too afraid to speak. He'd dreamed about this moment for seventeen years and didn't want to ruin it before holding his baby boy. He nodded his head. The water cascading down Patricia's eyes told him that she understood his emotions were unstable.

Reggie looked to the left of Mark and gasped. Standing there, just an inch shorter than him, was Brian. Logically, Reggie understood seventeen years had passed and Brian was no longer the baby in the sailor suit, but he was not prepared for the young man standing before him. Looking at Brian was like looking at a reflection of himself.

Suddenly, Reggie regained his strength. He stood straight up and walked toward Brian, who was already crying, with his arms opened wide. As Reggie embraced his son, he lost all control. He sobbed uncontrollably. "My son, my son," he cried out repeatedly, as he felt Brian's tears against his neck. Reggie squeezed him tighter. "I've missed you so much."

Father and son remained that way. Even after the sobs ended, they stood there holding each other.

Between her silent tears, Julia said, "Thank you, God." She then hugged and thanked Mark and Alysse for allowing Reggie and Brian to reunite.

Tyrone thanked them, too, and then took the liberty of handing everyone fresh tissues.

Emotionally drained, Reggie finally sat down on the platform stairs. Brian sat down beside him and his father put his arm around him. Everyone else sat in the front row, facing them.

"Wow," was the only word in Reggie's vocabulary as he took in his flesh and blood. He studied him from head to toe. They shared the same complexion, the same left dimple, the same full lips, and the same nose, and the same dark eyes. Even their heads were shaped alike. He had Patricia's ears though.

It amazed Reggie that his son was as big as him. In less than two months, Brian would be eighteen, but he had the build of a grown man. He guessed they even wore the same size clothing. Brian's arms were as big as Reggie's. He figured it was from playing baseball.

"I saw your picture. You play baseball; what position?" Reggie asked his son.

"Left field," Brian answered shyly.

"You must have some powerful arms to throw from way out there."

"They're all right," Brian responded, but still held his head down.

"I'll have to come and see you play before the season is over."

Brian didn't say anything, but when he lifted his head, the big grin highlighted his dimple.

They spent the next half-hour getting acquainted with one another, while the others sat and watched.

"Wow," Reggie said again, as he squeezed his son. "I wish my parents were here." He looked at his son's mother and stepfather. "Patricia, I mean Alysse, Mark, how long are you going to be in town?"

"Our flight leaves Monday morning," Mark answered.

"What are your plans? Where are you staying?"

"We really don't have any plans. Our sole purpose for being here is so Brian could meet you. We're staying at the Marriott near the airport," Mark answered again.

"So you don't have any plans for tonight or this weekend?" Reggie asked, wanting to be sure. The thought of spending three solid days with his son excited him.

"No, we thought we'd leave that up to you and Brian," Alysse clarified.

Reggie turned to his son. "Well, son, what would you like to do? After you get settled into the hotel, I can pick you up and we can do whatever you like. Hey, the A's are in town tonight. We can catch a baseball game, if you want," Reggie offered.

Brian lowered his head and hesitated before he spoke. "A baseball game sounds great, but I really don't want to stay in a hotel," he paused, "I would like to see where you live."

Trying to contain his enthusiasm, Reggie asked, "Are you saying that you would like to stay at my house with me?"

"Yes," Brian answered shyly. "If you don't mind."

Reggie made eye contact with Alysse. She glanced at Mark and then nodded her head in approval.

Reggie's grin nearly showed all thirty-two of his teeth. "Son, you can come to my house anytime you want."

"Can we get something to eat first? I'm hungry."

"Of course, we can. Why don't we all go have a late lunch?" Reggie suggested.

"That sounds like a good idea," Mark confirmed. "We can get to know each better."

Reggie directed his question to his son. "What do you like to eat?"

"Everything," Alysse and Mark said in unison.

"Why don't I take them to pick up a rental car, then they can meet you at the buffet on Washington?" Tyrone suggested.

"That's fine," Alysse said.

Reggie gave Brian his car keys and Brian followed his mother and stepfather out to Tyrone's car, removed his bag and placed it in Reggie's trunk.

Back inside his office, Reggie grabbed Julia and squeezed her so tightly every muscle in his arms flexed. When he released her he cupped her face.

"Woman, I love you, forever," he said, then kissed her forehead.

"Does this mean I'm your sweetheart again?" she asked playfully.

"Always, until the day I die." His tone purposefully conveyed the sentiments of his heart.

They walked outside hand-in-hand, to find Brian sitting in the front seat of Reggie's Benz, adjusting the satellite radio.

Julia laughed. "Welcome to parenthood."

Chapter 28

Reggie watched with disbelief, as his son consumed more food than he thought humanly possible in one sitting. At least he doesn't have any food allergies, Reggie thought. Brian was an equal opportunist when it came to food. Reggie's stomach was still doing flip-flops, so he couldn't eat anything. In an effort to calm his nerves, Julia made him drink some hot tea.

Sitting directly in front of her, Reggie studied Alysse's face. She was still an attractive woman. For the most part, she'd kept herself up well. As he studied the interaction between her and her husband, he wondered if the older gentleman viewed him as a threat. Mark made sure he had one arm around her at all times, which men regard as a show of possession. If he had asked, Reggie would've gladly told him he was completely satisfied with the woman sitting next to him.

He wondered what was going through Alysse's mind, seeing him after all these years. Did she still hate him? On the outside she seemed happy, like she was okay with him seeing Brian, but her eyes revealed signs of worry.

While Brian piled his third plate, Reggie decided it was a good time to do what he should have done a long time ago.

"Alysse," he began, "there's something I'd like to say to you." Julia held his hand while he talked.

"Go ahead," Alysse said, as Mark stroked her arm.

"When I knew you before, I was not a good person. You were right; I didn't love anyone, including myself. I took advantage of everyone I met, especially you. I used your vulnerability to satisfy my selfish desires, and I was wrong. Alysse you were—are—a good woman and you deserved better. I don't blame you for what you did. After the way I treated you, you had more than enough justification to do what you did." Reggie looked at her steadily. "For all the pain I caused you, I'm sorry. I pray you can find room in your heart to forgive me and allow me the chance to build a relationship with our son."

Alysse dabbed her eyes. "Thank you for saying that. I don't hate you anymore, but I can't honestly say I've forgiven you. I won't stand in the way of you and Brian. But if you hurt him…" She let the statement hang.

"Fair enough." He then turned his attention to Mark. "Mr. Green, I understand you have taken care of my son for the past three years. I thank you for that. I hope that you and I can maintain a cordial relationship, because from here on out, I'm going to be a visible part of my son's life, physically as well as financially."

"You can call me 'Mark'," he answered. "I have no problem with you being in Brian's life; every boy needs his father. Brian is a respectable young man. Alysse has done a good job with him," Mark answered.

"Alysse, you have done a great job," Reggie seconded.

"Thank you, but, Reggie, I need your help."

He noticed she appeared nervous. "What's wrong?" he asked.

Alysse took a deep breath. "My son—our son—hasn't spoken two words to me in five days, since I told him about you. He hates me." Her voice broke. "He blames me for his growing up without a father and for the hard times we had. He feels—and he is right—that if he'd known you and your parents, he would have had a stable environment and would not have had to move around so much."

Reggie agreed with his son. It hurt him to know Alysse chose to drag Brian around the country and barely survived, when all she had to do was make a simple phone call. He would have sent her money, even if he didn't get to see Brian. He would have gladly paid her rent or she could have stayed in his parents' house for as long as she needed. He would have done anything to make sure his son was provided for. *That's in the past,* he reminded himself. He had his son now, and that's all that mattered to him.

"He doesn't hate you, he's just upset. I'll talk to him sometime this weekend and explain what happened," Reggie offered.

"Not even twenty-four hours and you have your first parental assignment," Julia teased.

"Feels good," he said just as Brian returned with his plate piled high.

"Where do you put it all?" Reggie asked.

"Into those size-twelve feet," Alysse answered.

Just as Reggie thought, he shared the same shoe size with his son. Reggie smiled proudly.

"I'm eating light. I have to save room for the baseball game," Brian announced, causing the four adults to burst into laughter.

"Reggie, I'm glad you're here," Mark said. "Now he can eat you out of house and home."

"I look forward to it."

Outside in the parking lot, Reggie said good-bye to Julia. "Are you sure you don't want to join us?"

"No, you need some one-on-one time with your son. But if you want, I can have Michelle leave you two tickets at Will Call for Pinnacle's luxury box," she offered.

"Thank you, sweetheart, but you have done enough already." He wanted to hug her, but they were in public, so he mouthed, "I love you," then said good-bye.

* * *

Reggie went home, so he and Brian could change clothes for the baseball game. Brian gave Reggie his approval when he realized his dad lived on a hill overlooking the entire city.

"This is tight," he said, looking out the bay window.

Reggie gave him a tour of the three-bedroom, two-bathroom house. He showed Brian the portrait of his parents. Brian's eyes looked sad when he saw himself as a baby.

"This picture has been here all this time?" he asked.

"It sure has," Reggie answered. "We never forgot about you."

"What were my grandparents like?" Brian wanted to know.

Reggie told him all about his parents and how much they loved him. "From the day you were born, you were spoiled. My parents bought you everything they thought you would want. They would be so proud to see what a respectable young man you are." Reggie had an idea. "Follow me to the garage. I have something to show you."

Reggie turned on the garage light. "These are unopened Christmas and birthday presents my mother bought for you up until seven years ago, when she passed away."

Brian scanned the walls. "For real?"

"Yes. Son, we always loved you."

Brian carefully opened some boxes and emptied their contents. Then his shoulders heaved; he was crying quietly.

Reggie put his arm around his son. "What's wrong, son?"

Brian sniffled and wiped his cheeks with the back of his hand. "I knew it. I knew we didn't have to struggle like we did. I knew we had a family somewhere. I knew we weren't all alone, like Mama said." He looked at Reggie, and asked, "Why did my mother lie to me? I know she was mad at you, but why didn't she care enough about *me* to tell me the truth?"

"We went from apartments to shelters and sometimes we didn't eat. A lot of times, there wasn't money for clothes and I wore shoes that were too small. I had to put up with her no-good boyfriends beating me when she wasn't around and I really didn't have to. I had a family. I know she hated you, but why did she make me suffer?"

Reggie cried for his son and with his son.

"Your mother didn't mean to make you pay for my mistakes. In her mind, she was getting back at me. She never intended to hurt you in the process. She loves you more than anything in the world. You are the only person that she can really call hers. Don't blame her without blaming me. I'm just as much at fault as she is."

"But she's the one who left."

Reggie stared at him, wondering at what age did the bass overtake his baby's vocal cords. "True, but she was only reacting to my actions."

"I know she wanted you to suffer, but why did I have to?" Brian asked, pleadingly.

"Son, I can't answer that," Reggie responded honestly. "I know that God orders our steps before we're born. It's in those hard steps that we learn who we are and who God is. It's in those difficult times that our character is built."

"Are you saying God wanted me to suffer?" Brian questioned.

"I'm saying that before your mother and I conceived you, God knew what you would deal with and He knew you would make it through. He knew it would not consume you."

Brian was quiet for a while. "I need to think about that one."

"Take all the time you need. In the meantime, try to see things from your mother's point of view. Remember, you weren't suffering alone, she suffered, too."

Brian wiped his face and sat down on one of the boxes. "Do you mind if I stay down here for a while?"

Reggie understood he wanted to be alone. "No problem. I'll go get cleaned up and changed."

As Reggie walked to his room, his heart was heavy for all his son had endured. He prayed Brian would be able to forgive Alysse soon.

Chapter 29

Father and son were inseparable all weekend. At the ball game Friday night, Reggie and Brian carried on like old school-mates. Reggie was sure the concession stand would have to put an *Out of Business* sign up, after Brian went back for the third time. Reggie had to buy a team gym bag to carry all of the team paraphernalia he purchased for his son.

Back at home, they were too wired to sleep, so they popped in a DVD, microwaved popcorn and hung out, talking about everything and nothing, into the wee hours of the morning. They fell asleep on the floor with Reggie's arm securely holding Brian.

Saturday morning, Reggie awoke to the smell of bacon. He rubbed his eyes and looked around the den. Brian had cleaned up the evidence of the previous evening. Reggie stretched and made his way to the kitchen, where he found Brian wearing a black Reebok sweat suit, cooking breakfast.

"Hey, Dad, how do you like your eggs?" Brian asked when he saw his father.

Reggie wrapped his arms around himself to make sure he wasn't dreaming. This was the first time his son called him "Dad." He stared in amazement. After seventeen years his son was standing in his home, cooking breakfast.

"Hello, Earth to Dad. This is an egg," Brian said, waving the egg. "How would you like to eat it?"

Reggie laughed at his son. "Scrambled is fine."

"That's how I eat mine, too."

Reggie sat at the table. "I see your mother has taught you how to cook."

"Mama said I eat too much not to know how to cook," Brian answered.

"And she's absolutely right," Reggie agreed. "I like that sweat suit you're wearing. I have one just like it and the shoes to match."

Brian lifted his left foot and smiled. "You mean these shoes?"

Reggie chuckled. "Well, I see you've found my closet."

"I was just looking around. You know, trying to see if you have good taste," Brian answered.

"Well, how did I score?"

"You're all right. I saw a *few* things that I could work with."

"I'm lucky it was just a *few* things." Reggie thought back to when he was his son's age. He was always into his father's things, especially his cologne.

"Do you know you're running low on Tommy Hilfiger? I had to use Calvin Klein instead," Brian said, placing two plates on the table.

"Sorry for the inconvenience."

During breakfast, Brian talked about his plans to become a lawyer. He'd already applied to Berkeley, but he hadn't heard anything.

"Mom wants me to attend Arizona State, because it's cheaper and closer to home. But Berkeley has one of the top law schools in the country and I figure I'd have a better chance of getting in if I went there as an undergrad."

"It's a possibility, but no guarantee."

Brian continued, "Mama said we can't afford Berkeley, but I can apply for scholarships or grants, and if all else fails, I can get student loans like most college students. So I was thinking, maybe you could talk to her for me. Since you're here I won't be by myself and she might be willing to let me go."

Reggie wanted nothing more than to be able to see his son on a regular basis, but decided to take things slow.

"Let's get that acceptance letter first, and then we'll tackle your mother."

Father and son finished breakfast, discussing Brian's baseball season. Then spent the day sightseeing at San Francisco's Pier 39. They took a ferry ride underneath the Golden Gate Bridge and toured Alcatraz Island. Then they went to the Waxx Museum and Ripley's Believe It or Not!

Reggie felt like he was taking his son on all the field trips he'd missed.

For a snack, Brian wanted to try some clam chowder, inside of a famous San Francisco sourdough bread bowl. While Brian stood in line, Reggie phoned Julia.

* * *

"Girl, I can't believe this! I didn't know Pastor had a son," Nikki said as she walked down the grocery aisles with Julia.

Reggie wanted to have a family dinner in honor of Brian at his house after church the following day, so he asked Julia to help him arrange it.

"What's his mother like? Do you feel threatened by her?"

"Girl, not at all, she's happily married," Julia answered.

"Yeah, but she was once intimate with him."

"I know, but he didn't love her like he loves me."

"Now I know why he always tells us not to judge anyone's past, because we all have one. Including him. So when do we get to meet Brian?" Nikki asked.

"Tomorrow. The three of them will be at True Worship and afterward we're having dinner at Reggie's house."

"Aren't you coming?" Nikki questioned.

"No. Reggie hasn't asked me to come."

"Girl, do I need to buy you a new light bulb while we're here? You know he wants the woman in his life there when he introduces his son to the congregation. Especially since you're the reason he's here," Nikki scolded.

"You forgot, our relationship is still private," Julia reminded her.

"And? He still would love to see your face there for support. Besides, your relationship won't remain a secret much longer."

"And why is that?" Julia asked.

Nikki pulled a nail file from her purse. "Girl, let me tighten your screws. You and Reggie will be married before the year is over."

"Whatever you say, girlfriend," Julia said and continued shopping.

Chapter 30

Reggie grinned through most of Sunday's worship service. Before he preached a heartfelt sermon, he proudly introduced Brian to the congregation. The news came as a shock to everyone except Tyrone and Mother Elsie. He tensed, but only for a moment, when he heard gasps and murmurs from the audience. All anxiety left once he looked over at Julia sitting between Nikki and Shay.

"Finally," he concluded, "like the Apostle Paul wrote, I count not myself to have apprehended. I don't understand why God decided to take me through the fire. But this one thing, I do. I am forgetting those things that are behind me, because even when I was in the fire, God was there. God was there for every disappointment and for every tear. When I felt like giving up, God was right there and He carried me. It was God who took me through the fire, and then through the water, and now He's brought me into my wealthy place.

"And God has a wealthy place for each one of us. A place where there's peace, nothing lacking and nothing broken. A place where God restores everything that we've lost and even some things we gave away. A place where there's joy unspeakable. A place where the joy of the Lord is our strength.

"If you want to get to that place, stand to your feet, raise your hands and talk to God. Tell Him all about it. Let Him fill you with His love. Let His presence soothe your pain."

People stood all over the sanctuary and cried out to God as Praise and Worship ministered in song. Many came down to the front for prayer. Reggie looked up to heaven and mouthed words of thanks, when he saw Alysse and Brian standing together.

Julia cried when Alysse, Reggie and Brian shared a hug at the altar.

Nikki leaned in her ear, and whispered, "All he needs now is his wife."

After service, Reggie's family from Stockton joined Reverend Leonard and First Lady Leonard, Mother Elsie, Tyrone, Nikki, Alysse, Mark, Shay and Julia for dinner at Reggie's house. Before everyone dove into the meal Julia had prepared, Reggie asked Brian to say grace.

The room erupted in laughter when Brian said, "Jesus wept," then reached for a plate.

Chapter 31

Reggie sang along with the CD as he drove down Mandela Parkway. He'd just left his realtor's office and was on his way to Emery Bay. Three days had passed since Brian went back to Arizona, and although he'd talked to him every day, he still missed him.

It still amazed him how alike they were. He guessed Brian agreed with his taste in clothing, because he went on a shopping spree in Reggie's closet. He even "borrowed" Reggie's leather jacket. Reggie couldn't fathom why anyone would wear a leather jacket in Arizona. He made a mental note to retrieve it when he went down for Brian's high school graduation.

And then there was his sweetheart, his love, Julia. He thought he loved her before, but after the recent turn of events, his love for her had deepened. She'd shown him that she was committed to him and would be there for him, no matter what. She'd shown her love for him and he felt it in the core of his being.

He talked to her every day, but hadn't seen her since Sunday night. That was three days ago. He avoided seeing her on purpose. If it weren't for Brian and Shay's constant bickering interrupting them, he would have lost the battle with his flesh.

They'd just finished cleaning up the kitchen, when he embraced and thanked her for preparing dinner. He was about to kiss her on the forehead, like he'd done many times before, but when he looked down at her beautiful face, his emotions overwhelmed him and he wanted to kiss her lips and taste the inside of her mouth. He lifted her chin and lowered his head as his will and emotions warred with each other.

Her lips parted and she brushed them with her tongue, but she didn't turn away. He softly stroked her chin and parted his lips.

"Reggie, would you tell your know-it-all son, that Iverson is a better basketball player than Kobe!" Shay yelled as she stormed into the kitchen.

Feeling like busted teenagers, Reggie and Julia instantly separated. Julia turned on the faucet and splashed her face with water. Reggie was too embarrassed to face Shay, so he turned his back to her.

"Excuse me," Shay said mischievously.

Julia swallowed hard. "Actually, it's perfect timing. Let's go."

Julia said good night to Brian, grabbed her purse and ran out the door without looking back at Reggie.

"I'm sorry," he said when he called to say good night.

"Don't be. Now I know you want me just as much as I want you. But I'm willing to wait until the time is right," she responded.

"Soon, sweetheart, soon," he said before ending the call.

As he crossed Hollis Street, he acknowledged the time would come sooner than he anticipated.

He pulled into his reserved parking stall at Emery Bay. Just as he was about to open the door, his cell phone rang.

"Guess what, Dad? I got in, I got accepted into Berkeley," Brian said excitedly.

"Congratulations, son."

"I can't believe it, I'm going to Cali. That is, if you can get Mom to agree."

"We'll talk to her after the graduation, all right?"

"All right," Brian said.

They talked for a few more minutes, before Reggie took the elevator to Julia's office.

"Things are going to work out just fine," Reggie said as he exited the elevator.

"Hey, you," Julia said, as she stood to greet him.

"Hey, beautiful. I have some free time before Bible Study, do you want to grab a bite."

She winked. "As long as you're buying."

Julia and Reggie ate lunch at PF Chang's and he told her the good news about Brian.

"Are you prepared for a college student?" she asked.

"Mentally, no. I would love it if he could remain a kid for a while, so we could do some of the father-son things we've missed. Financially, yes. I have some money my parents left for him and my stock portfolio. I'm also selling one of my properties."

"You're not selling your parents' home, are you?" she asked.

"Of course not. I'm going to give that to Brian some day. The sale of one duplex will be more than enough to pay for undergrad and law school. Also, I'll need to buy him a car. The rest I'll invest, so he'll have something to start with when he finishes school."

"You're a good father."

"Thank you. I hope he thinks so," Reggie said.

"He does," she assured him.

Back inside her office building, they stepped off the elevator arm-in-arm. Rounding the corner, they collided with a man of medium build and a light-brown complexion. Both the man's clothing and breath reeked of cigarette smoke. The collision nearly knocked the man to his knees.

"Excuse us," they said and tried to help steady the man.

The five-foot, ten-inch man looked familiar to Julia, but she couldn't place him. "Are you all right, sir?" she asked.

"I'm fine, Julia," the man said as he straightened his clothes.

"I'm sorry, sir, do I know you?" she asked.

The man looked at Julia strangely, like he was insulted. "Of course you know me, Nay Nay."

Julia strained her eyes in disbelief. There was only one person who called her by that ghettofied version of her middle name. "David?"

"Hello, Julia. You're a hard person to catch up with."

Still in shock, Julia asked, "David, what are you doing here?"

"I've been trying to meet with you for two weeks, but you've cancelled both of my appointments. So I decided to just show up today," he answered.

"I didn't notice your name on my schedule."

"The appointment was for DW and Associates," he explained.

"I see," Julia said and tried to visualize her schedule, but couldn't. She continued to stare at David in disbelief. Reggie's stroke on her arm caught her attention.

"David this is Reginald Pennington. Reggie this is my ex-husband, David White."

Instead of extending his hand, Reggie put his arm around Julia's waist, and said, "Hello."

Instead of responding to Reggie, David focused on Julia. "So, Nay Nay, do you think you can see me today? It'll only take a few minutes for me to show you a good time, I mean, a good investment." He smiled and looked at Reggie.

Julia felt Reggie's arm tense around her and answered before Reggie could speak.

"My name is Julia and if you plan to discuss business with me, that is what you'll refer to me as. I don't need you to show me a good time. I have all the good time I need next to me."

David raised his hands. "Hey, I don't want to cause any problems. I just want to discuss a business idea with you, Julia, nothing more."

Julia took a hard look at the man in front of her. David looked at least ten years older than his age. Instead of the usual tailored suit, he wore casual slacks and a sports coat. It was clear to her that David had fallen on hard times, especially since he was coming to her for help after all these years.

"Michelle, show Mr. White to my office, please," she called over her shoulder. As soon as those words left her mouth, Reggie stepped away from her.

"Thank you. I guarantee you, you won't regret it," David said with a wink and followed Michelle.

Reggie didn't waste time voicing his disapproval. "Why did you agree to see him?"

"I'm not *seeing* him Reggie, this is business."

"What possible business can you have with him after all this time?" His voice escalated.

"I don't know, but at least I can hear what he has to say." Julia matched his voice. "That's what I do, Reggie. People present ideas to me and I listen, just like I listened to you when you first came here."

"This is not the same thing, Julia, and you know it. I came here with pure motives. There is nothing pure about that man. That man doesn't mean you any good, he's only here to see if there's more of you left to use." He looked at her with contempt. "Maybe that's what you want."

"What is that supposed to mean, Reginald?" she snarled.

"Maybe you like being used, or maybe he didn't hurt you bad enough the last time."

His words hurt her deeply and she fought the urge to cry. "Why would you say something like that?" Her voice quivered.

He lowered his voice. "Julia, you're not blind. You saw how he looked at you, practically undressing you with his eyes. He may start with discussing business, but he has other things on his mind. I don't feel good about this, and I'm asking you not to do this."

Julia bit her lip and lowered her head. The only reason she'd agreed to meet with David was because she felt sorry for him, strange as that sounded. She wanted to tell Reggie that, but she knew at that moment he wouldn't understand. "Reggie, let me handle this, okay. I know what I'm doing."

"Fine!" he yelled. "You can do whatever you want. But don't you *ever* compare me with David White again." He turned and stormed toward the stairwell.

Julia stood there wondering what had happened. It didn't make sense to her for Reggie to have gotten so angry over David. She wanted to go after him, but didn't want to prolong David's visit. She needed him to leave as soon as possible.

"Some things never change," she mumbled. David hadn't been back in her life five minutes, and had already managed to wreak havoc. Inside her office, she found David sitting in her chair. "What do you think you're doing?"

"Waiting for you to get rid of your boyfriend." He smirked.

What she ever found attractive in that lopsided grin of his, she didn't know. "David, get out of my chair. You are a guest here and if you can't act like one, leave." She was beginning to agree with Reggie's assessment.

"Whatever you say, boss." David relinquished her chair. As he settled in a chair he licked his lips and studied her body. "Nay Nay, excuse me, Julia, you've kept yourself up well. I like the way that skirt hangs off those luscious hips and that tight behind—"

She cut him off. "Look, David, I don't have time for this. What did you want to discuss with me? You've got five minutes."

"All right. I have a business proposition for you."

"I'm listening and the clock is ticking," she said, looking at her watch.

"I want to develop Point Molate. I want to do there what you have done here in Emery Bay. Since you have been so successful here, I would like to take you on as a partner."

"You want to partner with me?" she asked incredulously.

"Yes, I think we would make a great team. How can we go wrong with my designs and Pinnacle's reputation?"

Julia restrained herself from laughing. She couldn't believe David had the audacity to sit in her face and try to play her for a fool. "David, have you seen the environmental report on Point Molate?"

David shifted in his seat. "Yes, I have. I know we'll have to do some clean-up, but it's nothing we can't handle."

Julia wanted to slap herself for not listening to Reggie. David hadn't changed one bit; he was just as conniving and manipulative as he'd always been.

"David, let's save us both some time. Point Molate is practically a toxic waste dump. That's why I turned it down two years ago."

"But I...we can still develop it after proper cleanup," he insisted.

"David, stop playing with words. You're here because you don't have the money for the cleanup and you want me to finance it. That's not going to happen," she said flatly.

"Why not?" he yelled.

"Because it doesn't make good business sense. With the cost of cleanup and development, it's nearly impossible to break even. Besides, David, there's no way I'll ever do a joint venture with you."

"What? Why is that?" He seemed surprised. "Don't tell me you're still tripping over the past? You need to let that go. Doesn't that Bible you read say it's not healthy to hold grudges?"

"Please, you're not worth that much energy," Julia stated. "Frankly, David, I don't like your business ethic. I've worked very hard to maintain an impeccable reputation and I won't see it dissipate because of your shady practices."

"So now you think you're better than me?" He banged his fist on her desk.

"No, I don't, but I've outgrown you," she answered plainly.

David sat down and rubbed his forehead. "Julia, I really need this project. I need financial backing to stay afloat."

"I'm sorry, David, but I can't do it."

"Can't or won't, Julia? The way I see it, you owe me," David countered.

"I don't owe you anything. Nothing I have came from you. I've built my business with my sweat and tears, not yours."

"You could have spent some of your time helping me build my business, but you were too selfish for that. You don't care about anyone but yourself. That's why I left you."

"David, that's in the past. Leaving me was the best thing you ever did for me. If you weren't so mean and evil, you would have been successful. Don't blame me for your lack of morals."

"You didn't question my morals when I was banging you every night," he said nastily.

"No, but I did question them when you banged me upside my head the next morning," she shot back.

David started toward her. "How would you like it if I banged you around now, you know, for old time's sake?"

Julia remained seated as she stared at David towering over her. She was afraid, but she wasn't going to let him know it. "David, leave my office and my building. Don't ever bother coming back."

He stood over her, huffing, but she turned her back to him and turned on her computer. Finally, she heard him walk away.

"One day, you're going to pay up, Julia," he said, before he slammed the door.

She exhaled and laid her head on the desk. "You were so right," she said as she stroked the heart around her neck and thought of Reggie.

An hour later, Julia locked her office and said good night to Michelle. She was mentally drained and wanted to disappear in a hot bubble bath. She had attempted to phone Reggie at least three times in the last hour, but got his voice mail. Except for the time when he thought Jonathan was her date, he'd never been angry with her. This time, he had every right to be angry. She decided to try him again later after his Bible Study.

Just as she was about to insert the key into her Jaguar, he came from behind her and snatched her arm from behind her back, causing her keys and briefcase to fall to the ground. With his other hand, he covered her mouth. Over muffled screams, she inhaled his scent. His hot fresh cigarette breath was nauseating. He released her arm and groped her breasts with his free hand. Horror rippled through her when he licked the side of her face, and said, "It's payday, Nay Nay."

In desperation, her eyes scanned the parking garage. He'd just jammed his hand underneath her skirt waistband when she elbowed him in the groin. He cried out and bent over. That was enough for Julia to make a break for the emergency alarm switch in the garage. Just as she grabbed it, he spun her around and slapped her so hard she fell to the pavement. She lay there, dazed.

Just as he was about to undo his belt buckle, Reggie hit David so hard he landed on the hood of a parked car and slid off the opposite side. David never saw it coming. Reggie ran and stood over him until security came seconds later.

"Ms. Simone, are you all right? Do you need an ambulance?" the head of security asked when he saw Julia on the pavement.

"No, I don't need an ambulance. I'm fine, I think," she answered, trying to get her bearings.

Her voice caught Reggie's attention and he went to her. As the security officer helped her to her feet, Reggie fixed her clothes.

She noticed him rubbing his hand. "I didn't know you were still here." She lowered her head. "You were mad, I thought you left."

Reggie shook his head. "Woman, after all the things this man has done to you, do you honestly think I would leave you alone with him?"

The security officer left, just as David was carried away in handcuffs.

Julia didn't respond to Reggie; she kept her head down and cried softly.

"Come here." He held her and she cried harder. His words were so soft. "Sweetheart, I love you. I would never leave you unprotected. Even when you do something I don't like, I'll always be here for you." He stepped back and lifted her head. "Do you understand?"

"Yes."

He lifted her and carried her to his car. On his way to her condo, he phoned and asked Minister Watson to teach Bible Study.

Julia took a long shower and threw out the clothing she had worn that day in an effort to rid herself of David. Her arm ached and her face was discolored, but she was grateful because it could have been a lot worse. Memories of David's viscous attacks were still fresh.

She opened the door for Reggie. He had walked back to the garage and drove her car back to the condo. He went straight to the freezer and got some ice.

"Put this on your face," he said and sat down at the kitchen table. She obeyed and sat down opposite him. They sat there quietly until he finally spoke.

"Julia, we need to talk."

She sensed the seriousness in his voice. "If this is about David, you were right about him."

"This is not about him. This is about us," he answered.

"What about us?"

"Do you know what upset me the most today? It wasn't the fact that David showed up out of nowhere; it was because you didn't trust my judgment nor respect my wishes?"

"What are you talking about?" she asked.

"Julia, I specifically asked you not to see him. I clearly told you he was bad news. But because you didn't agree, or maybe because you didn't see it, you totally disregarded what I said. You're only conceding now, because you have proof."

"That's not true," she protested. "I've always valued what you said."

"That's because, up until now, you've always agreed with me." He sighed deeply. "Look, Julia, you are a bright and intelligent woman. I've watched you work for the past six months and you are a master at leading Pinnacle. You're a great single parent. You're used to giving the final word on everything. But if we are going to have a permanent relationship, you can't be the leader and you can't have the final word."

Julia opened her mouth to object, but didn't.

"You have to be willing to trust me and allow me to lead, even if you disagree with me. Even if I do things differently from you, or out of the ordinary. You have to be willing to follow me and respect me as the man in your life and eventually the head of our home." He paused and allowed the words to penetrate. "Sweetheart, I know you love me, but you need to ask yourself if you love me enough to submit to me. Do you love me enough to allow me to be the head of our home? Do you trust me enough to know that I would never take advantage of you?"

"I do trust you and I know you wouldn't take advantage of me."

"Then why was it so easy for you to compare me with someone like David White?"

She thought hard. "I don't know, maybe it's because sometimes you don't seem real to me."

"What do you mean?"

"Sometimes I think our relationship is too good to be true. I have never been this emotionally attached to anyone. Sometimes I'm scared that I'm going to wake up and find out that this was all a dream." Her voice was just above a whisper.

He wanted to take her into his arms and reassure her, but used his words instead. "Julia, you have to stop exhausting your energy on making everyone else happy, and realize that you deserve to be happy and not just from a distance. What we have is not a dream or an illusion. It is very real and designed by God. It's time for you to start thinking about how good our future together is going to be."

"I know. I'm working on it."

"Do I make you happy?" he asked.

She smiled. "Of course you do."

"So why don't you think you deserve me?"

"I don't know." She fidgeted. "It's just that I have waited a long time for someone like you, I'm scared that you're going to walk away," she finally admitted, turning her head away from him.

"Julia, look at me," he said and turned her chin to face him when she didn't comply. "I love you, and I am not going anywhere. If you don't know that after today, you'll never know it." He massaged her cheek with his thumb.

As he prepared to leave, she asked, "Don't you want to know what David wanted?"

"I already know. He wanted what I already have. He wanted you," he answered and left.

Chapter 32

The Arizona sun didn't have any mercy on Reggie. He'd heard stories about the Arizona heat. Unfortunately, for him they all proved to be true. Reggie wiped his head and stepped toward the front; he wanted to make sure he got a good picture. His eyes misted as he took in the scenery. There wasn't a clear spot anywhere as hundreds of excited parents like him flooded the high school football field in hopes of catching the momentous occasion on film.

Reggie felt a tug of jealousy as he thought about the parents around him. For sure this day would be the climax to the many celebrations they had shared with their children over the years. But for him, today was all he had outside of Brian's birth. Just a few short weeks ago he didn't think he would see this day, but God had performed a miracle for him. After adjusting his digital camera he looked through the lens and listened for the announcer.

"Brian Deshawn Pennington."

Reggie snapped the picture just as Brian received his high school diploma with honors.

"Did you get it?" Alysse asked anxiously when he returned to his seat.

"I sure did," he answered with a smile and showed Mark and Alysse the images in his camera.

"Look at my baby," Alysse said as she put her hand over her heart.

"He's not a baby, he just received his high school diploma and will turn eighteen in a few days," Reggie reminded her.

"He'll always be my baby," she pointed out.

"Are you planning on following him off to college?" Reggie teased.

"I don't have to. He's going to school right here in Phoenix."

Reggie didn't feel this was a good time to upset Alysse, so he remained quiet. There would be plenty of time later on to ruffle her feathers.

After the ceremony, Brian took turns taking pictures with his parents.

"Nice tie, I have one just like it," Reggie said as they posed.

"Not anymore." Brian grinned just as the flash blinded Reggie.

Mark took a picture of the three of them. Reggie didn't want Mark to feel left out, so he asked the gentleman behind him to get a picture of the four of them. Mark seemed pleased by the gesture and even told Reggie so."

"We'd better get going if we're going to beat the crowd at Chevy's," Alysse suggested.

The four of them made their way through the crowded football field to the parking lot. Alysse wasn't the least bit surprised when Brian opted to ride in the rental car with Reggie.

Father and son sat opposite Mark and Alysse in the crowded restaurant. After the waitress took their orders, Reggie stopped putting off the unavoidable. He just prayed Alysse wouldn't cause a scene.

"Alysse, have you and Brian decided on a school yet?" he began.

"Yes."

"No," Mother and son answered simultaneously.

"I told you earlier, Brian is going to Arizona State," she answered firmly.

"But I don't want to attend Arizona State, I want to attend Berkeley," Brian protested.

"Look, Brian, I've told you already, Berkeley is too far. And you're too young to live on your own."

"Mom, I just graduated high school and I'll be eighteen in a few days. Legally, that makes me an adult." Brian pouted.

"I don't care what the law says." Alysse elevated her voice and rolled her neck. "You are my baby and Berkeley is too far and too loose for you without supervision!"

"He won't be alone, Alysse. I'll be around," Reggie interjected.

She snapped her head in Reggie's direction. "You'll be where, Reggie? You already have your hands full with your church and your girlfriend. How are you going to find the time to look after him?"

"He's not a little kid, Alysse. He doesn't need a babysitter." Mark's voice of reasoning interrupted the argument. "Honey, you can't hold on to him like he's a baby forever."

Alysse frowned at her husband. "Mark, you don't understand, Brian is all I have. And I am not going to allow him to run off to a strange city with strange people. I remember the Bay Area quite well, and Berkeley is a strange place for a young child."

"Reggie's not a stranger; he's his father," Mark countered. "If he's a stranger to Brian it's because of the decision you made to keep them apart."

Alysse glared at Brian. "That's what this is all about? You want to be with your father? After all I've done for you?"

"Mom, you know I've been talking about Berkeley for over a year now, long before you told me about Dad," Brian answered. "You know I plan to attend Boalt School of Law at Berkeley when I'm done with undergrad."

"I think he should attend the school of his choice. He'll be motivated to do well if he's happy," Reggie offered.

Alysse rolled her eyes at Reggie as if she really didn't care what he thought. "Look, Reggie, that sounds good, but I can't afford Berkeley. I can barely handle Arizona State."

Brian started to speak. "Mom, I told you —"

Reggie interrupted his son. "Alysse, I'll take care of the tuition."

Brian and Alysse looked at Reggie with stunned faces.

Reggie's last statement didn't surprise Mark at all. "That's great."

Alysse searched for another objection. "What about housing? The cost of living is astronomical in Berkeley, especially near campus."

Reggie had an answer. "Brian can live in my house. Since I'll be moving soon, having him there will save me the hassle of renting it out."

Alysse was desperate. "How is he going to get to class from your house in Oakland?"

"Alysse, you know it's only a ten-minute drive."

"Reggie, I don't know if you've noticed, but Brian doesn't have a car!"

"I'll take care of that, too," Reggie responded plainly.

Alysse was out of objections and Brian couldn't have been happier. Looking defeated, she folded her arms and scowled.

"Let me get this straight, Reginald Pennington. Are you telling me that you are going to pay for his college education, allow him to live in your home and buy him a car?"

"That's exactly what I'm saying. After lost time, it's the least I can do for my only offspring. I owe him at least that much."

"Thanks, Dad," Brian said and gave his father an appreciative hug, but Alysse was fuming.

"Well, Mom, what do you say?" Brian knew his grin always had a weakening effect on her.

"I guess so." She smiled at her son, but gave Reggie the death stare. "I'm happy I don't have to worry about Brian's education, but I'm not happy about my son leaving me."

"That settles it for me," Mark said, just as their food arrived.

"Hey, Dad, are you going to buy me a Benz like yours?" Brian asked expectantly.

"Absolutely not, but I will get something reliable and appropriate for an eighteen-year-old college student," Reggie answered.

"How about a RAV4? Shay says they're reliable and good on gas," Brian said, after he took a bite of his burrito. "I asked her how she knew, since she drives a PT Cruiser. You know she thinks she knows everything."

"She used to drive a RAV4 before her accident," Reggie clarified.

"That's what she told me last night."

Reggie set his fork down. "You talked to Shay last night?"

"She called to congratulate me on my graduation. Actually, she said, 'The diploma's not edible, so don't try to eat it'." Everyone at the table shared a laugh.

"I didn't know the two of you exchanged numbers," Reggie said. "The way you guys argue, I thought you disliked each other."

"Oh, no," Brian defended. "Shay's all right; that's my buddy. We have a lot in common, that's probably why we argue so much. She's only eleven months older than me, but she acts like it's eleven years."

"Sounds like the two of you are good friends," Alysse interjected.

"We're very good friends," Brian said and took another bite of his burrito.

Chapter 33

"Lil sis, you looked so good in your clergy attire," Angie said, looking at pictures from Julia's ordination service. "It was such a nice service, sacred, like God had planned it," she continued.

"I believe it was planned by God," Nikki commented.

"Look at my fine daddy and mama beaming with pride," Angie said of the photo with Julia and their parents. She placed the photo book on the counter. "Why didn't you tell us Reggie was participating in your ordination?"

"Girl, she didn't know," Nikki answered for Julia.

"You didn't?"

"No. Both Reggie and Reverend Leonard withheld that information from me," Julia said over her shoulder, as she peeled potatoes at the kitchen sink. "Can you imagine how surprised I was when he walked up and anointed my head?"

"You almost came out of the Spirit, didn't you, girl?" Nikki teased.

Angie's family, along with Tyrone and Nikki, had driven out to Blackhawk for a mini family barbeque. The men were in the den, watching baseball. Shay and Brian were out on the patio debating, among other things, which had the best football team, Stanford or Cal Berkeley. The debate wouldn't be settled until the annual Big Game between the two schools.

Angie searched for a tray and a knife to cut the watermelon. Nikki worked at the center island, preparing a green salad.

Reggie quietly entered the kitchen and leaned against the wall. He grinned as he watched Julia work over the sink. Even while peeling potatoes, she was beautiful. As he stood and watched her, he couldn't think of a time when she wasn't beautiful to him. He honestly loved this woman with his soul.

For him, the time had come. He was ready to make their relationship permanent. He was ready for the world to know how he felt about her. He was ready to love, protect and cherish her. He was ready to be her husband.

Brian had settled into his new home and everything was in place for him to start Berkeley the following month. The addition to True Worship was on schedule and membership steadily grew.

For Julia, the Point Richmond project was finished and completely sold out. She now had free time to devote to the ministry, or do whatever she wanted.

After getting Papa and Shay's approval last week, Reggie wanted to plan the perfect moment. He believed Julia knew eventually that he would propose, but when he did, he wanted to catch her off guard. As he watched her work over the sink, he decided this was the perfect time. He had planned a romantic speech, but now the words escaped him. When he opened his mouth, "Marry me, Julia," were the only three words he could remember.

She didn't turn around, just yelled over her shoulder, "Can I finish these potatoes first?" and continued peeling.

"Oh, my God!" Nikki's screams were so loud and intense that Mike and Tyrone came running into the kitchen. Brian and Shay rushed through the patio door and Angie dropped the watermelon on the floor.

Julia dropped the vegetable peeler into the sink and spun around. "Nikki..." she couldn't finish when she looked down at a smiling Reggie, on one knee, holding a ring. She gasped and covered her mouth with her right hand and followed Nikki's lead. "Oh, my God," she whispered.

Reggie took her free left hand. "Well, sweetheart, are you ready to be my wife?"

Julia couldn't find any words, so she just kept blushing and repeating, "Oh, my God."

Angie had enough words for everybody. She pulled out her cell phone and took Mike's from his waist. She worked both phones like an air traffic controller.

Shay and Nikki watched in tears.

Julia still stood with her hand over her mouth, except now she too was crying. "Oh, my God," she still repeated.

Reggie teased her. "You've called on God ten times, but you haven't given me one answer. Will you be my wife, lover and friend for the rest of my life?"

Julia removed her hand and screamed, "Yes!"

Everyone cheered, as Reggie placed the two-carat diamond engagement ring on her finger. He stood and wrapped his arms around her. "Thank you. I promise you won't regret it."

Within minutes the Simone family blew up both Reggie and Julia's cell phones. This time Reggie was prepared when her brothers and sisters congratulated him, and he wasn't surprised when each of them asked to speak to Brian also.

Ana called Julia's house line. Shay answered and filled her grandmother in on the details.

"Grandma and Papa want to know when's the wedding," Shay yelled over the noise.

Julia looked at Reggie and shrugged her shoulders. Reggie thought for a second. "September," he answered. "The third Saturday in September," he said with finality.

Julia's eyes bulged. "But that's only seven weeks away! That's not much time to plan a wedding."

He licked his lips. "As far as I'm concerned, that's seven weeks too long."

"Tell Papa the third Saturday in September," Julia yelled back to Shay.

* * *

Julia tried to calm her nerves by singing a praise song as she pulled into the parking lot at True Worship. Her eyes searched for a parking space when Tyrone waved and caught her attention. She rolled down her window and he leaned in and teased her.

"Yo man asked me to save you a spot."

They shared a smile and he directed her to a space near Reggie's Mercedes. When Julia got out of the car, Nikki ran over to meet her.

"Girl, I can't believe you're on time."

"Honey, I wouldn't miss this for the world." Nikki looked around. "Where's Brian and Shay?"

"They're on the way. Brian wanted to drive his new RAV4, and of course, Shay had to show him how to do it right."

"Those two are a mess." Nikki lowered her voice. "Are you nervous?"

"Girl, yes! What if the church doesn't agree with his decision?" Julia asked.

"You don't have anything to worry about," Nikki answered. "Now, there are a few sisters who will need therapy after today, because they were absolutely positive the Lord told them that Pastor was their husband. Other than that, everything will be fine."

The friends walked into the sanctuary and found seats in the second row. Julia didn't have a chance to sit, before Mother Elsie approached her.

Mother looked down at Julia's left hand. "God sure is good. Congratulations, baby. Pastor has reserved a seat next to me on the front row for you. That's where he wants you to sit from now on."

The huge grin on Nikki's face told Julia that her friend knew about this arrangement.

"Okay," Julia said as Mother Elsie pointed out her seat.

"Where are Brian and your daughter?"

"They're on the way, Mother," Julia answered.

"Good, because the two seats next to you are for them. Do you have any family members coming today? Pastor gave specific instruction; he wants his family up front."

That's so sweet of him, Julia thought. "My sister's family is coming. You might know them, the Sorensons? They've been visiting for the last month."

"Are you talking about the two doctors with the three children?"

"Yes."

"I thought the young lady looked familiar," Mother Elsie said, then gave instructions to an usher. A moment later, Mike and Angie joined her on the front row.

The ministerial staff of True Worship took their places on the dais. Julia wasn't sure, but they appeared to be smiling in her direction. She was relieved when the musicians started playing and the Praise and Worship Ministry took their places for service to begin.

After the scripture reading, Reggie joined the ministers on the platform. To Julia, he looked gorgeous in his black-and-gold cassock. She couldn't wait to explore what lay underneath.

He waved at the rest of his new family, but he gave Julia a knowing smile and she blushed, because she knew he was pleased with her attire. She was wearing his favorite suit. The blue one with the rhinestones and matching shoes. Her hair hung in the long loose curls he liked.

Julia's nerves took a break long enough for her to enjoy the service and Reggie's sermon, but they went into overdrive after the ministers administered prayer and Reggie returned to the podium. Julia breathed deeply and looked straight ahead.

"I have a special announcement to make to the congregation this afternoon," he began. "For the past five years many of you have asked me why I'm not married. I've repeatedly stated that I didn't desire a wife." He paused and grinned at Julia. "But now that's changed."

Reggie continued, despite several sisters jumping up and yelling, "Thank you, Jesus."

"The Bible states, 'He that findeth a wife, findeth a good thing.' I'm pleased to announce that I have found my good thing."

People stood all over the congregation and applauded. Some even shouted, "All right, Pastor."

"I told you," Nikki said, as Julia looked around the sanctuary. She inwardly laughed when she saw a number of hopeful sisters adjusting their clothing and trying to fix their hair.

Shay and Angie shared a look of bewilderment, as several sisters even tried to make their way into the aisles.

Reggie continued after the applause. "Please receive the love of my life, whom I will marry in this church seven weeks from yesterday."

Julia held her breath.

"From the House of Prayer Community Church, please welcome the future First Lady of True Worship, Minister Julia Simone."

The congregation erupted in cheers and applause as Reggie helped her up the stairs and onto the platform. He made her blush when he asked the congregation, "Isn't she beautiful?"

Julia was overwhelmed by the warm reception True Worship had given her. In her mind she thought back to that first Sunday in October, when she first entered True Worship's doors and how she felt like she was at home. Soon she would be.

Chapter 34

Julia's two-bedroom condo looked more like Grand Central Station, as seven women and two girls prepared for the wedding. Julia's nerves were in overdrive as the hair stylist and makeup artist worked on her. Her left leg shook in addition and she had sweaty palms. She tried to calm her nerves by focusing on her wedding party.

She'd chosen her three sisters as bridesmaids. Julia thought they looked simply gorgeous in the emerald dresses she had chosen. Shay and Nikki, who served as her Maids of Honor, looked equally outstanding in the gold version of the dress.

"Ladies, you look beautiful; the matching gold jewelry really tops it off."

"Auntie, how do we look?" her two nieces who served as flower girls asked.

"Beautiful," she said just as Ana shooed them away.

"You two, go and sit down in the living room, so you don't mess up your hair and dresses," Ana instructed. "How are you feeling, baby?" she asked Julia.

"Oh, Mama, I'm so nervous. I can't believe this is finally happening. It seems so unreal."

"Why?"

"Because he's everything I want. I love him so much. Mama, I really love him."

"He loves you, too, baby."

The doorbell sounded in the background.

"I know he does and this time, I know I'm marrying the right person for the right reasons."

"I'm happy for you, baby," Ana said as she placed her strand of pearls around Julia's neck.

"Mama, the courier just dropped this off for you." Shay stepped in the room and handed Julia an envelope. It wasn't addressed, just her name written on the front in gold script letters.

"What is it, girl?" Nikki asked while applying mascara on her eyelashes.

"I don't know," Julia answered nervously. She was afraid to open it, so she turned to her mother. "Mama, can you read this for me?"

Ana removed the contents. She read the first line silently and stopped. "Baby, I think you should read this yourself."

Julia's nerves settled as she read.

Dearest Julia,

Thank you is not enough to express my gratitude for you allowing me to become your husband. If the word perfect could be adequately defined, it would have to include a picture of you. Your love has made my life complete. Before you, I merely existed, but now I'm alive. I look forward to being awakened by the sunshine of your smile for the rest of my days.

My heart warms when I try to envision the portrait of perfect beauty you'll be as you walk down the aisle, or when I think of the sweet symphony we'll create on this night. I anxiously await the moment I can finally kiss your lips and feast on their sweetness. I promise I'll take my time and give you EVERYTHING!

Until Later,

Reggie

"Hurry up, ladies, I have a wedding to get to!" Julia yelled.

* * *

Reggie's cousin, James, tried to calm him down. "Hey, cuz, you're going to sweat out that tux, if you don't stop pacing."

Reggie's office made him claustrophobic. He was too nervous to remain still. His future happiness lay in the balance of one event. "What if she changes her mind?" he asked no one in particular.

"My sister's not going to change her mind, she loves you too much," Andre answered.

Reggie listened to his future brother-in-law's advice and prayed love would conquer all. He looked at his Best Men, Brian and Tyrone. "Did you guys remember the ring?"

Brian patted his jacket. "It's right here, Dad."

"Man, I'm going to throw some water on you, if you don't calm down," his cousin James said.

"Don't make me pull out my gun, again," Andre warned.

Just then, Reverend Leonard entered the office, bubbling with joy. "How are you doing, son?"

"I'll be fine when this is over." Reggie massaged his forehead. "What's taking so long?" he asked impatiently.

Reverend Leonard chuckled. "Son, the wedding's not scheduled to start for another twenty minutes."

Reggie looked at his watch, then resumed pacing.

"Reverend Leonard, now would be a good time to pray," Tyrone suggested.

Ten minutes later, an usher knocked on the door with a delivery for Reggie. "Pastor, the bride has arrived and she asked me to give you this."

Reggie loosened his tie and read the simple, handwritten note.

What instrument will you be playing?

It took a moment for him to catch the reference to the symphony he'd mentioned in his note to her. He let out a huge sigh of relief, smiled and slipped the note into his inside pocket. The rest of the room exhaled.

* * *

While the rest of the bridal party vacated the two limos, Julia waited out front in CJ's Bentley. She surveyed her surroundings. Both the parking lot and street were filled to capacity. She knew it was standing room only inside, because several guests were standing outside. On any other day, the fifteen-hundred-seat sanctuary would have been adequate. But not today. Not with True Worship and House of Prayer, plus family and friends. According to the final guest count, at least two hundred of Julia's family members were in attendance.

Inside, after Ana and Reggie's aunt Mae was escorted to their seat, Reggie and his groomsmen followed Reverend Leonard to their places on the platform.

Outside, an usher rolled out the red carpet and Julia's stomach turned cartwheels as her father and one of the wedding coordinators assisted her out of the Bentley.

"Ma cherie, you look beautiful," her father complimented her.

"Thank you, Papa, for everything." Julia was well capable of paying for her own wedding, but her father insisted he foot the bill. "Daddy, you know you're the finest man here."

"Don't I know it." Her father laughed and struck a pose.

* * *

The church was packed beyond capacity. People lined the sidewalls, some just stood in the back. The self-proclaimed bachelor's wedding announcement shocked the local religious community. Many came to see if Reggie would follow through and some females came to pray he wouldn't.

Reggie was impressed with the decorations. He'd never seen True Worship look so elegant and royal. The emerald green, gold, and ivory color scheme gave the church a regal ambiance. He particularly liked the archway under which he and Julia would stand. It was covered with ivory netting and at least one-thousand green, gold and ivory carnations created specifically for this day. The aisles were lined with gold candelabras with more netting and flowers.

He forced a smile as Julia's sisters, the bridesmaids, made their entrance, then his heart nearly stopped after the flower girls made their way to the stage and the music ended.

Julia's legs wobbled as she walked through the entrance. Her father smiled and kissed her forehead. The sound technician and hair stylist gave her one last check.

Carey Sr. extended his arm. "Ready, ma cherie?"

"Ready," she said and placed her arm in her father's. Just before the ushers opened the double doors, she looked at her father, and said, "Papa, no matter what happens, don't wake me up for at least another hour."

Carey Sr. smiled at his daughter. "Ma cherie, dreams do come true."

Inside, Ana Simone stood and faced the entrance. The rest of the congregation followed suit. The double doors opened and soft notes played. Reggie was confused momentarily, because he thought Julia's nephew and sister-in-law were performing "Endless Love," but they didn't come forward. Reggie turned his attention back to the door, he didn't care who was singing as long as Julia walked down the aisle.

♪*My love, there's only you in my life, the only thing that's right.*♪

Reggie's earlier confusion was erased when he heard the sweet voice of the woman he loved.

The wedding party, as well as the audience, had no idea that Julia was going to sing her way down the aisle. Her father was surprised, too, because even he didn't see the small cordless microphone hidden behind her bouquet.

Reggie's eyes flooded with tears as she slowly, but steadily, walked toward him. She was singing with her nephew, but singing directly to her man. Tears rolled down her face, but she never took her eyes off of Reggie. When she reached the front, the entire bridal party and most of the audience were in tears.

Her father handed her his handkerchief at the same time Brian gave Reggie his. After dabbing her face, Reggie helped her onto the platform, while the audience openly admired the detail of the six-foot beaded train on her ivory dress. When she placed her arm in his, he leaned toward her ear, and whispered, "Portrait of perfect beauty."

Reverend Leonard, who had just dried his face, began, "Dearly beloved, we are gathered together here in the sight of God, and this company, to join together this man and this woman in holy matrimony. Let us invoke God's divine presence upon the union."

After Reverend Leonard prayed and read a scripture, he began with the vows.

"Reginald, do you take this woman to be your wedded wife? Do you earnestly promise, before God and these witnesses, that you will love her, comfort her, honor and keep her in sickness and in health; and forsake all others for her alone, perform unto her all the respect that a husband owes to his wife, until God by death shall separate you?"

Reggie looked deep into her eyes and with a strong voice, said, "I do."

Julia held his gaze as Reverend Leonard repeated the question for her. "I do," she answered as she wiped the lone tear that trailed down Reggie's cheek.

"Who gives this woman to be married?"

"I do, with pleasure," Carey Sr. said and took his place next to Ana.

Julia handed Shay her bouquet and joined hands with Reggie as they took turns reciting the traditional marriage vows.

After Janice sang The Lord's Prayer, Reverend Leonard asked for the rings. Nikki handed Julia the custom-made wedding band.

Reverend Leonard admired Julia's five-carat wedding band. "Daughter, you're going to need shades to handle the glare." He laughed, then held the rings and blessed them. After the ring exchange, they continued holding hands.

"Now the bride has a special song she'd like to sing to the groom."

Reggie didn't know what to expect. Julia looked deep into his eyes and when the music started with all her heart and soul, she sang, "You Bring Me Joy."

Reggie couldn't contain himself as she belted out the words with passion. The tears flowed in a steady stream and gathered in his fresh trimmed goatee.

Julia stroked his cheek as she sang. ♪*I believe this is gonna be what you want it to be.*♪

"Sing, Mama," Shay called out as the audience cheered and rose to its feet.

By the time she finished, both of their faces were soaked. Reggie released her hands and pressed her into him.

"We better hurry and wrap this up. I don't know how much more my son can take," Reverend Leonard said, and the audience agreed.

"For as much as Reginald and Julia have consented together in Holy Wedlock, and have pledged their faith to each other. I pronounce that they are husband and wife in the Name of the Father, and of the Son, and of the Holy Spirit."

Still embracing each other, Reggie and Julia burst into laughter as the audience and wedding party cheered.

"Those whom God has joined together, let no man put asunder. Son, you may now kiss your bride."

Julia threw her head back and laughed as Reggie prepared his lips for their first real kiss. Her laughter subsided, the closer his lips got to hers. As he lowered his head she parted her lips and received all he had to offer.

"Save some for later, cuz."

"Handle your business, man."

"Work it out, Pastor."

The audience heckled as he took a whole minute getting acquainted with his newfound treasure.

His appetite satisfied, he moaned, and whispered, "Mine. All mine."

After an extensive photo session, Julia and the ladies went inside Reggie's office to remove her train.

"Lil sis, that was beautiful," Chantel started.

"I've never heard you sing like that," Nikki added.

"Girl, you broke the brother down!" Raquel joked. "Had the preacher crying like a baby in front of his congregation."

"I wasn't trying to break anyone down, I just wanted him to know how I feel, that's all," Julia answered.

Angie jumped in. "By that kiss, I'd say he broke *you* down. You're going to know how he feels before the night is over."

"Ooh, Mama, you're gonna get it," Shay teased.

"Yeah, girl, I think you're in trouble," Nikki agreed. "I hope you took your vitamins."

Julia rolled her eyes. "I've got three words for y'all."

"What?"

"BRING IT ON!"

Reggie was waiting for her by the Bentley with CJ. "There's my bride." He met her with a kiss. CJ held the door, while they settled into the backseat. "You," Reggie said after CJ closed the door.

"Excuse me?" she asked, turning her head to face him.

"You asked what instrument I'll be playing in our symphony. My answer is, you."

The smile he offered wasn't his normal casual smile; it was laced with desire and endless possibilities. Julia used her hand for a fan and exhaled. "In that case, you'll need to practice 'cause I need some fine-tuning," she flirted back.

Reggie spent most of the ride to the Convention Center practicing.

Chapter 35

"Let me hear you make some noise for the couple of the hour in their first appearance together. Give it up for Reverend and Mrs. Reginald Pennington."

The room, which was filled to its eight-hundred-seat capacity, erupted as Reggie and Julia strolled through the entrance of the reception hall.

Once they were seated at the head table, dinner was served. They feasted on prime rib, roasted chicken and grilled shrimp. The couple wanted Skates to cater the reception, but Henry complained he couldn't do so without closing down the restaurant for the day. Of course, when he realized how much he'd make at fifty dollars a head, he reconsidered and happily closed the doors for the day. In fact, Henry was on hand to personally serve the wedding party.

After the meal, the newlyweds took to the dance floor for the traditional first dance. They'd never slow danced before, but quickly fell in sync. Between the lyrics, Reggie whispered words of adoration and nibbled on her ear.

As soon as the song ended, Carey Sr. and Ana had their turns with the bride and groom. Reggie's aunt and uncle followed suit, then the dance floor flooded with the Simone clan and their guests. Reggie was caught off guard when the Simone women, including Ana, surrounded him on the floor. He took it in stride and did a little two-step move. They were just about to sit down, when the DJ put on an old school Motown tune and announced it was Simone family dance time.

This time Reggie led Julia onto the floor just a step behind her father. "I Got to Give it Up" for the late Marvin Gaye," Carey Sr. said as he passed them.

The Simones taught the simple step to the new family members. Brian caught on quickly, but Nikki had to work with Tyrone a little longer. By the time the second song started, most of the guests from True Worship had joined in. Even Reverend Leonard tried to keep up.

Before the cake cutting, Tyrone and Brian gave the traditional toast.

Tyrone went first. "In life, many people cross our paths, but very few we can truly call friends. When you find a true friend you hold on to them with all of your strength. Reggie and Julia, my prayer for you is that you will hold on to each other, always. On the good days and on the bad days. That you will never forget that before you became lovers, you were friends. God bless you." Tyrone lifted his glass of non-alcoholic champagne to the newlyweds.

Now it was Brian's turn. He cleared his throat first. "I'll start with my Mama J. I call her that because she said she won't treat me like a stepson, so I can't treat her like a stepmother." The Simones echoed her sentiments.

"When she asked me how I felt about her marrying my dad, she explained that he and I are a package deal, just like she and Shay are." He raised his glass. "Mama J, I think you are a wonderful woman and I know you are good for my dad. Thank you for loving my dad enough to change both of our lives."

Brian took a deep breath. "Now, as for my dad. I've only known my dad for four months. In this short period of time, I've learned a lot about him and from him. My dad is a man of great integrity and love. I felt his love the first day I met him and every day since." He took another breath. "This is the first time I've verbalized this to my father." He wiped his eyes. "I love you, Dad, and I pray that someday, I can be half the man you are. Congratulations."

Shay interrupted the embrace Brian shared with his father. "Here, fathead, take this before you start slinging snot everywhere." She handed him a tissue after she wiped her own eyes. Several other family members and friends gave expressions after that.

As soon as Nikki caught the bouquet and Andre snatched the garter, Reggie and Julia were ready to leave. They said their good-byes, changed clothes and dashed out the door while dodging bubbles.

Chapter 36

B y the time they made the ninety-minute drive to the seaside home Reggie rented for the week in Bodega Bay, it was almost midnight. Reggie unloaded the Benz while Julia went inside to look around. She loved the cozy, romantic atmosphere. The two-story beach house had all the amenities of home. Inside the kitchen, the refrigerator was fully stocked with things she liked. She looked around the living room, where carnations were spread throughout and around the fireplace. She climbed the stairs to the second level where the bedrooms were.

Inside the master bedroom were more carnations and her favorite scented candles. *That looks like fun,* she thought, regarding the Jacuzzi tub in the bathroom. She thought the same of the large plush bearskin rug positioned between the fireplace and the king-sized bed. She opened the sliding glass door and stepped out onto the deck. Minutes later she felt his arms wrap around her from behind as she looked up into the clear starry sky and inhaled the fresh ocean scent.

He nibbled on her ear. "Do you like it?"

"I love it." She tilted her head to give him better access to her neck. She moaned and said, "I'll be right back."

That was forty-five minutes ago. She had planned carefully for this night. She had purchased the perfect little blue teddy. She carefully dabbed his favorite fragrance in areas of interest and styled her hair loosely, the way he liked it. But she was afraid to leave the bathroom.

She was a forty-one-year-old woman with a nineteen-year-old daughter, but she felt like this was her first time being intimate with a man. In a way, it was. This would be the first time she shared her body with a man she loved. The thought occurred to her that, in all of her planning and preparation, maybe she never really believed tonight would finally come. It all felt like a dream to her.

Inside the bedroom, Reggie didn't fare any better. The candles were lit and the fireplace glowed. The non-alcoholic champagne was chilling on the nightstand and the CD of love songs he'd had made specifically for tonight was playing, but he was still nervous.

It had been a long time since he had had sex and tonight would be the first time he actually made love with his heart and soul. Tonight would always be special to him, but his number-one priority was pleasing Julia. Unlike any time before, tonight he would take his time and love her. He turned his attention back to the fireplace and squatted in front of it.

"Nice."

He hadn't heard the bathroom door open. Her voice startled him and he quickly stood and faced her. He gasped and slowly forced himself to exhale. He'd imagined what she would look like at this moment, but the reality far exceeded his expectation.

"Very nice," his mouth said as his eyes roamed her body. He swallowed hard, then beckoned her with his arms.

She walked slowly toward him, because she was afraid her legs would give way any second. She gave his full body a visual inspection. He was without a doubt the finest man she'd seen in all of her life.

He pulled her into his arms and kissed her gently, but passionately. When he cupped her face, her cheeks were wet. He stepped back and asked her what was wrong.

She moved her lips to verbally respond, but no words would come. She timidly touched his massive chest as "Tonight I Celebrate My Love For You" played in the background.

He understood completely now. He looked deep into her eyes and reassured her. "You are not dreaming. This is real. I'm real and I'm all yours."

He then lifted her, placed her on the rug and loved her. He loved her slowly and completely, taking his time to acquaint himself with every part of her. He loved her not only with his body, but also with his heart and soul. Between whispering words of love and adoration, he kissed her tears away, which flowed in a steady stream.

Julia accepted everything he offered and freely gave herself to him, holding nothing back. Finally, she had a love of her own. "Mine," she whispered as she lay in his arms later.

If Reggie had any doubts as to whether he satisfied her, they were erased three hours later when they finally made it to the bed, where Julia helped herself to another serving. Exhausted and completely satisfied, she peacefully slept with a smile.

Just before he dozed off, he whispered in her ear, "Good morning, love," as the rays from the sun peeked through the window.

* * *

Eight days later

"Welcome home, Mrs. Pennington," Reggie said, as he carried Julia across the threshold of their Blackhawk estate. He didn't think it was fair to ask her to downsize from her estate and move into his house. They agreed that it would be better for him to move out to Blackhawk, than to buy a new home, because Julia's house was already paid for and had everything they needed. Any doubts he had about Julia allowing him to be the head of the house were alleviated when she added him to the deed. He did likewise with his properties, so everything they owned, they owned together.

He let her down and kissed her, first gently then passionately.

"We could have a welcome home celebration." She licked her lips and started to unfasten his shirt buttons.

He pressed her to him. "Your place or mine?"

"Right here." She kissed him again before leading him into the den.

Julia was just about to sit on his lap when...

"I see you guys have made it back," Shay said, as she walked in from the pool.

Just that quickly they'd forgotten that they'd seen Shay's car in the driveway. Startled, they worked quickly to fix their clothing.

"I forgot you were home," Julia said, embarrassed.

"Brian and I were out in the pool; if you need anything, holler. And, guys, get a room. There's nothing more disgusting than catching your parents making out."

They laughed as Shay headed for the kitchen.

"This is going to take some getting used to," Julia said.

"I think we should take her advice and get a room." Reggie took her hand and led her upstairs to their bedroom.

Chapter 37

First Sunday in October

Julia pulled into the parking lot and smiled when she saw the sign *Reserved for First Lady Pennington*, next to Reggie's Benz. They'd driven separate cars because he wanted to get to the church early. He hadn't been inside the doors of True Worship for two weeks and wanted to meet with his staff before service.

From the time she stepped out of her car, members greeted her.

"Hi, First Lady."

"Welcome First Lady."

"Good Morning, First Lady."

Julia made sure she responded to everyone with a smile.

She spotted Nikki and Tyrone in the vestibule. "Hey, guys."

"My, don't we look all rested and stress-free. Girl, look like you done laid your burdens down!" Nikki teased.

"I'm not going to go there with you today," Julia answered. "I'll just say God is good."

"Yes, He is," Tyrone said and directed her attention to Nikki's left hand.

Now it was Julia's turn to scream, "Oh, my God!" She hugged and congratulated both of them. "Have you set a date yet?"

"We're thinking about early summer," Nikki answered, leaning up against Tyrone.

"Count me in," she said as the music started. "I'd better get inside."

Inside, Julia waved at Mike and Angie as she made her way to the front row. They had decided to join the Sunday before the wedding.

"Good morning, Mother." She gave Mother Elsie a hug and sat down.

"Baby, what are you doing down here? You're the First Lady now. Your seat is up there next to your husband."

"Oh," Julia said as she saw the two new chairs on the dais for her and Reggie.

"Go on and take your place," Mother Elsie encouraged.

Julia stood in front of the new chair and looked out over the congregation as the reality of it all hit her. She was married to a pastor. A gorgeous pastor. A loving man and good friend.

Moments later, service began and her handsome husband, and now pastor, joined her.

"Hello, First Lady," he said when he kissed her cheek. "You're beautiful as always."

"Hello, Pastor," she said, blushing.

As the choir sang, "I've Got a Testimony," Reggie and Julia were consumed with their own thoughts, but yet the same thoughts. It was one year ago today, on the first Sunday in October, when they first laid eyes on each other.

To him, she was the most beautiful woman he'd ever seen.

To her, he was a Black Adonis.

He loved the way she praised the Lord and she loved the way he preached. His life was empty and incomplete, so was hers. He was alone, so was she.

Reggie looked out at the son he thought he would never find and the new daughter God had given him.

Julia thanked God for her new son.

They both were grateful for their family members, who recently joined the church.

Maybe it was because they were now one, or maybe they just felt the Spirit at the same time. Who knows? When the choir finished singing and while the congregation yelled praises to God, Reverend Pennington and First Lady Pennington simultaneously jumped up and started dancing in the Spirit. The members followed the lead of their spiritual parents and joined them.

Chapter 38

J ulia crawled back into bed, thankful she didn't have to go into the office anymore. Having decided to take a break from developing, she turned the day-to-day management operations over to Michelle. Now, she only worked at Emery Bay once a week, usually on Fridays. The rest of the time she spent getting acquainted with her new husband of three months.

This Friday morning she didn't have the energy to go anywhere. She felt tired a lot lately and had cut her morning workout sessions in half because she would tire easily.

Today, she figured she was suffering from a stomach virus, since this morning like the two prior mornings, she woke up feeling nauseated and she couldn't hold any food down during the day.

"You should go to the doctor and get something for that," Reggie said, after her second trip to the bathroom.

"I'll be fine, it should pass by tomorrow," she answered and turned into his embrace. He covered her head with the green-and-gold Down comforter. "If it doesn't, I'll go in on Monday."

On Saturday, she felt a little better, but she still couldn't hold any food down. Shay and Brian stopped by on their way to the Monterey Bay Aquarium. Julia was standing over the sink, running water, when she felt faint. Shay walked in just as she fell to the floor.

"Mama!" Shay cried and ran to her. Brian, who was a step behind her, ran up the stairs to get his dad.

Julia was starting to regain consciousness when Reggie lifted her in his arms. "You're going to the doctor right now!" She was too groggy and weak to protest, so she remained quiet the entire ride to Washington Hospital. Shay and Brian rode in the backseat.

The emergency room was unusually calm for a Saturday afternoon. Shay talked with the registration clerk, while Reggie accompanied Julia to yet another trip to the bathroom.

"There's nothing left to come out," she said and washed her face. Within twenty minutes, she was in an exam room, receiving IV fluids. Shay and Reggie were on each side of her, standing.

Reggie dabbed her forehead with a wet paper towel. "Relax, sweetheart. You'll feel better soon."

Dr. Kimberly Davidson, her regular physician joined them a few minutes later. "Julia, what's going on with you today?" she asked after she greeted Shay. "Is this your new husband? Sorry I couldn't make the wedding."

"Yeah," Julia answered just above a whisper.

Reggie introduced himself and quickly turned his attention back to his wife.

Dr. Davidson repeated her original question. "What's going on?"

Shay remained quiet, as Reggie gave a recap of the last three days. She then stepped out of the room while Dr. Davidson examined her mother.

Reggie stood back against the wall while Dr. Davidson worked. He took a hard look at his wife laying there on the thin white paper. For some reason her feeble demeanor reminded him of Alysse. Over the last month, he had noticed subtle changes in her body, but thought nothing of it. Changes in her breast size and the shape of her hips. He didn't complain because he liked the changes. "No," he whispered when the idea entered his mind.

As hard as he tried, he couldn't think of one time in the last three months when he'd been turned down because of Mother Nature, and there were plenty of times. Julia was always ready. Her drive was just as strong as his, if not stronger. He loved that about their relationship.

He also knew they had not used any form of birth control, not once. "No, she can't be." As the words danced in his head, his mouth parted into a grin.

Dr. Davidson completed the examination and disposed of the gloves. "Julia, I don't think you have a stomach virus. If you did there would be other symptoms besides the nausea, and that wouldn't explain the tiredness."

"Maybe you should check for pregnancy?" Reggie's words startled Julia.

"What?" Julia's voice found some strength. "Why would she want to do that?"

"Just to make sure," he answered.

"There's nothing to be made sure of, I can't have any more children." Her voice grew stronger with each word.

"Why not, Julia? You haven't reached menopause yet," Dr. Davidson interjected.

"No, but I've never ovulated on a regular basis. I haven't had a period in over a year, and I'm too old!" Her voice was full strength now.

"That doesn't mean that it's not possible. In fact, you have classic pregnancy symptoms. You're forty-one, and people still have babies at your age," Dr. Davidson explained.

"Not me! Shay is nineteen years old, what do I look like having a baby?" Julia was nearly yelling.

"Calm down, Julia. Let's take a pregnancy test first and go from there. I will say this; I think your husband is right." She handed Julia a specimen cup.

This time, Julia didn't need Reggie's help. She dismounted the table with ease and stomped to the bathroom. Reggie laughed at her when she forgot she was connected to the IV pole and had to march back to retrieve it.

They waited. Reggie paced the small room and Julia sat sideways on the exam table, fuming. Neither said a word to the other.

Ten minutes later, Dr. Davidson returned with an ultrasound machine.

"Congratulations, Reggie, on your accurate diagnosis; the test is positive. Julia, you are pregnant!"

"Great!" Reggie cheered.

The color drained from Julia's face.

Dr. Davidson continued, "I'm going to perform an informal ultrasound to see how far along you are."

Julia was speechless as Dr. Davidson squeezed the cold gel onto her abdomen. Reggie walked over and kissed her forehead. This was definitely unexpected, but wonderful news to him. For him, this was their love child. Julia was horrified.

"It's not official, but you appear to have a nine-week fetus growing inside," Dr. Davidson said excitedly.

"Oh, God, this can't be," Julia said, as the nausea returned.

"I'm afraid it already is. And everything appears to be fine," Dr. Davidson added.

Julia cried quietly as Reggie and Dr. Davidson discussed ways to control the nausea and the need for an amniocentesis, because of Julia's age.

"I can't do this," she moaned, as she got dressed.

Reggie beamed with joy when they rejoined Shay and Brian in the waiting room. His arm rested on Julia's shoulder.

Shay stepped from Brian's embrace. "Is everything all right?"

"Everything is better than all right," answered Reggie as he squeezed Julia and kissed her forehead.

Shay gave Reggie a puzzled look. "Why are you so happy?"

"Because my baby is having my baby."

Shay didn't understand his answer. "What does Brian have to do with Mama being sick?"

Brian understood completely. "Congratulations, Dad, Mama J."

Shay was still in the dark, so this time it was Brian who helped her out. "His baby," he said, pointing to Julia, "is having his baby," he said, pointing to her stomach.

"Oh. OH!" Shay said when she finally got it. "Did you plan this?"

"No, but it's good news just the same," Reggie answered.

Shay's face twisted. "Aren't you guys a little old to be making babies?"

Reggie cocked his head. "Apparently not, young lady."

"Well, as long as the two of you are happy." Shay thought for a second. "This means I won't be an only child anymore."

"That's a good thing." Brian winked at her. "You're too spoiled."

As the four of them left the emergency room, no one noticed that Julia never said a word.

* * *

Julia finished brushing her hair and placed the hairbrush on the vanity. She stared at her reflection in the mirror while she ran her hands over her flat abdomen. The unreal news she received earlier that day was now a reality to her. As she studied her form, she wondered how she had managed to miss the signs of her early pregnancy.

She thought about Reggie and how happy he was. The only time she'd seen him happier was the day he met Brian. When they returned home from the hospital, it was Reggie who spent over two hours on the phone with both their families and close friends. More than once during his conversations, he reached over and rubbed her stomach. At one point, he even kissed her stomach. She believed he didn't notice that she wasn't happy.

When she stepped from the bathroom, Reggie was busy getting his clothes for Sunday service.

He stopped ironing. "How are you feeling?"

"I'm better. The IV fluids helped, but I don't think I'll be able to make service tomorrow," she answered, sinking her bare feet into the carpet.

"I don't think that's a good idea either. That's why I asked Shay to stay here until I return from church."

She sat on the side of their king-sized bed with her back facing him. "You think of everything, don't you?"

"Sweetheart, what do you think we'll have? A boy or girl?" He didn't wait for her to answer. "I think a daughter would be nice, but I would love to have another chance with a son."

She rubbed her hands against the sheets.

He continued, "You're nine weeks now. There's a good chance the due date will be on or near your birthday in August. How do you like that?"

"Reggie, I can't do this," she finally said without looking at him.

He unplugged the iron and reached for a hanger. "You can't do what; have our baby on your birthday?"

"No, I can't." She stared straight ahead. "I can't have this baby on my birthday, or any other day."

He stopped mid-stride en route to the walk-in closet and looked at her. "Julia, what are you trying to tell me?"

She looked down at the carpet thread and swallowed hard. "I'm trying to tell you that I can't have this baby."

He shrugged. "Why not? You're in good health."

"I know, but this is not right," she answered in a tone so low, she wasn't sure she'd actually voiced the words.

"What's not right about it?" She didn't answer and he went and stood over her. "What's not right about you giving birth to our baby?"

"I just can't do it," she finally said.

"You can't, or you won't have our baby, Julia?"

She heard the anger in his voice, but remained firm. "I'm sorry you don't understand, but I can't do this." She kept looking down at the carpet.

"What's there to understand? We're married and you're pregnant. Why can't you have our child?" His jaw flexed and his chest inflated, while waiting for an answer.

"I just can't. I'm sorry." Her eyes started to water.

"And exactly what do you plan on doing to my baby?" he demanded to know.

"I don't know what I'm going to do. I just know I can't have this baby." She wiped her eyes with the back of her hand.

As Reggie stood over her, he fought hard to control his emotions and lost. He was both angry with Julia and hurt. He was stunned by her dissertation on what should have been a happy situation. How could the woman he loved more than anything, his wife, sit there and tell him she didn't want the life they had created?

Julia was in excellent shape and he didn't see any logical reason why she would refuse to have their baby. They had never discussed having children, but he didn't think she was closed to the idea.

He had to get away from this stranger and go find the loving woman he had married. He grabbed his clothes and stomped to the door. "Our marriage won't survive if you kill my child. If you don't want it, I'll raise it myself."

The sound of the door slamming shut brought down the tears she'd been holding back.

The next morning, Reggie didn't speak to her before he left for service, and after he returned home he stayed downstairs in the den. Even after Shay and Brian left to go back to school, he didn't go upstairs to check on her.

Julia didn't leave the bedroom either. Shay brought her meals upstairs and while Shay changed her linen, Julia sat in one of the lounge chairs in front of her bedroom fireplace. Every time she thought of Reggie and the baby growing inside of her, she cried. She loved Reggie so much, she felt lost without him. The broken emotional connection was too much. She'd heard his words last night and believed every one of them. Their marriage wouldn't survive if she ended the pregnancy. After losing Brian for so long, there was no way Reggie would stand back and lose another child. The irony was, Julia really wanted their baby. She just didn't believe she could have it.

Sunday evening Julia's cell phone rang. Julia cleared her throat in an attempt to make her voice sound happy. "Hello, Mama."

Ana Simone still hadn't learned how to beat around the bush. "Julia, what's wrong?"

"What do mean, Mama?"

"I mean what I said. What's wrong? I waited for you to call last night and all day today, but you never did. That tells me that something is wrong with you or with this pregnancy."

"Nothing is wrong with me, Mama. Dr. Davidson said the pregnancy appears to be normal, but I'm going to have an amniocentesis because I'm over forty."

"So why aren't you happy?" Ana asked abruptly. When Julia didn't answer she continued, "Baby, I know something is wrong. Reggie went on and on about the baby when he called yesterday, but you never said one word and that's not like you."

As always, Julia lost the battle to conceal the truth from her mother. Between sobs she explained the previous night's events to her mother.

"Why on earth did you tell him something like that?"

"Because I'm scared, Mama."

"But you love him. You let that love outweigh any fear you have. Tell him how you really feel; he'll understand."

"But, Mama, what if something happens to the baby?"

"What if nothing happens to the baby? Did it ever occur to you that this baby is destined to be here? Think about it. You hardly ever ovulate and on a fluke, your ovaries decide to produce eggs within days of you marrying your soul mate? Why do you think your body decided to wake up after your life was in order?"

Julia listened to her mother. What she said made sense and she was probably right. When her mother told her to pray about it, Julia realized not one time had she really prayed about her fear. *God forgive me*, she silently repented. She talked to her mother a while longer and actually felt better about her situation when they disconnected. She knelt beside her bed and prayed until she felt peace.

Monday evening, Reggie walked into their bedroom for the first time in two days. He'd been sleeping in the den downstairs and showering in the guestroom. He didn't know what to say to his wife, so he avoided her. He loved Julia, but couldn't stand being away from her any longer, he was determined to bridge the gap that had grown between them.

She was taking a shower and he joined her. After her initial shock, she welcomed him.

He held her close to him. "I miss you," he whispered.

"Me, too," she answered.

Later, as they lay face-to-face in their bed, he brushed her cheek with the back of his hand.

"Sweetheart, how can you love me the way you just did, so freely and completely, and not want our baby?" he asked with pleading eyes. "I don't understand."

She buried her head in his chest. "I never said I didn't want our baby. Of course, I want our baby. I just don't think I can have it."

He lifted her chin. "Why? Tell me the real reason why you think you can't have our baby. Tell me, what's the problem and I'll try to fix it."

Tears ran down her face, not because she was sad, but because she loved him so much for wanting to take care of her. She was reminded of the words her mother had spoken to her the night before.

"Because I'm scared," she finally admitted.

He pulled her to him. "I'm here. What do you have to be afraid of?"

"Honey, my last pregnancy was devastating for me. I lost more than my unborn child; I lost a part of myself. I'm afraid it might happen again and I can't handle that. You're not abusive like David was, but what if I fall, or get into an accident, or have complications because of my age and lose the baby? I can't go through that emptiness again."

"Is fear the only thing preventing you from being happy about our baby?"

She nodded her head.

"Sweetheart, God did not bless us with this baby so you can live in fear. This baby is a chance for us to enjoy the fruit of our love, and I'm not going to let you spend the next seven months living in fear.

We are going to do everything possible to ensure you have a stress-free pregnancy, the rest we'll leave in God's hands. All right?"

She stroked his cheek and for the first time since learning of her pregnancy, she gave him a smile. "All right."

His eyes darkened, indicating his renewed desire for her. He pulled her onto him and enjoyed another make-up session.

Chapter 39

The members of True Worship were thrilled for their Pastor and First Lady.

"First Lady, by the middle of August, you'll be holding that handsome baby boy in your arms," Mother Elsie said after they made the announcement. The amniocentesis confirmed it three days later. The due date was August tenth, two days before Julia's birthday. Reggie was ecstatic to learn she was carrying a boy. True to his word, he did everything possible to ensure her pregnancy was stress-free.

Instead of two days, he had the housekeeper work full time, and on Fridays, he allowed Julia to work only half days. Either he or Shay handled all household business. Outside of her light morning workouts and evening walks with Reggie, the most Julia did was cook. And every night Reggie rubbed her stomach and prayed for their baby. He also accompanied Julia to every prenatal appointment.

She used some of her free time to help Nikki plan for her summer wedding. Nikki never asked, but Julia made sure her best friend enjoyed the wedding of her dreams. Nikki was disappointed though when Julia backed out of her wedding.

"I don't care if you do look like a whale; I want you in my wedding," Nikki complained. Julia tried to pacify her by agreeing to sing Nikki's favorite song. When that didn't work, she conceded and wobbled down the aisle for her friend.

At church, the members wouldn't allow the First Lady to do anything for herself. The Pastor's Aid made sure she had everything she needed, from water to comfortable shoes. They even purchased a therapeutic pillow for her back, so she would be comfortable during service. Early in her pregnancy, Reggie allowed her to sing with Praise and Worship. Now, he only asked her to sing from time to time before he preached his sermon.

Lately, Reggie had been busy and frustrated with the renovations of the new building. Reggie wanted the project finished before the baby arrived, but the contractor was stalling. He never talked to Julia about it, but she'd overheard him on more than one occasion, arguing with the contractor. From his telephone conversations, she knew the name of the contractor and what the problems were. In fact, she'd worked with the contractor many times on Pinnacle's projects. Knowing Reggie would never ask for her help, Julia decided to use wisdom and save her husband from a heart attack.

She parked her new SUV at the building site and wobbled out of the vehicle. At seven months pregnant, her Jaguar had become too small for her. After she grabbed the picnic basket from the backseat, she searched for her husband. She found him standing outside of the office trailer talking with the project manager. Julia waited patiently while they complained about the contractor's plan to delay the project for sixty days, because of some more important project. The contractor was due back in a few minutes and Reggie was ready to lay hands on him.

"I hope you're hungry, handsome," she said when the project manager walked away.

He hadn't seen her standing there. He tried to smile. "Hey, sweetheart, I didn't expect you today."

"I know. That's what makes it a surprise." She extended her neck to meet his kiss.

His right hand sprayed her stomach. "How is my boy treating you today?"

"Wonderful."

He took the picnic basket and they went inside the portable trailer and enjoyed lunch.

After he ate, Julia tried to relieve his stress by massaging his head and shoulders. He closed his eyes and leaned back against her stomach. He moaned his appreciation as her fingers worked. She was just about to kiss his neck, when the contractor stepped inside.

"You wanted to see me, Reverend Pennington?" the contractor asked nonchalantly.

Julia removed her hands, so Reggie could stand.

"Yes." Reggie pounded his fists on the desk. "The project manager has informed me of some unnecessary delay?"

"Yes, well, something has come up…"

Julia stood next to Reggie.

"Julia Simone, what are you doing here?"

She gave Reggie an innocent look before she answered, "Hello, Frank, this is my husband." She grabbed Reggie's hand and smiled.

"I didn't know that. I knew you had recently been married, but I didn't know to whom." The contractor looked down at her stomach. "I see marriage has been good for you."

She squeezed Reggie's hand, hoping he'd get the hint and keep quiet. "It sure has. We're expecting our new addition in August." Her expression turned serious. "Which is why this addition had better be finished by July."

Frank's smile disappeared.

"I've done a lot of business with you over the years, Frank. I would hate for that to change, but if you take advantage of our church, our business relationship is over," she said firmly. "Do we understand each other, Frank? I don't care how many other projects you're working on. This one will be finished, complete with permit filings and cleared inspections, by July."

Completely aware of the influence Julia Simone carried, Frank had no other choice but to concede.

"Sorry about the misunderstanding, Reverend Pennington, I'll see to it personally that we're completely done by the original deadline." Frank put his head down and walked out.

Julia waited for Reggie to start in on her.

"Woman, you don't know how to leave stuff alone, do you?"

"Not when that stuff is stressing my baby out. I'm too old to be a single parent again. I'm not going to sit back and let that man give you a heart attack, when I can easily set him straight."

He pulled her as close to him as her extended abdomen would allow. "Thank you, baby."

"You haven't thanked me, like you're going to." She kissed him deeply.

"I could lock the door," he teased.

She swatted his arm. "You are so bad."

"No, baby, I'm so in love."

Not quite ready to return home after leaving Reggie, Julia drove to Brian's to check on the house. She was surprised to see Shay's PT Cruiser parked in the driveway. Since Brian now had a roommate, Julia knocked on the door instead of using her key. Reggie agreed to Todd staying at the house, so Brian wouldn't be alone and Brian could use the rent money for living expenses. So far, the two college freshmen had proven to be responsible. The house was reasonably clean and the yard neat.

"Hey, preggo," Shay said when she answered the door.

"Hey yourself." She hugged her daughter. "What are you doing here?"

"Waiting for fathead. We're going skating before he leaves for Arizona tonight."

"I forgot this was the weekend he's going to see Alysse." Brian usually visited his mother one weekend a month. Now that school was out for summer break, he'd planned to stay a couple of weeks.

Julia looked around and didn't see Todd. "Shay, how did you get in?"

"Brian gave me a key a while back," she said matter of factly.

Before Julia could respond, Brian stepped through the front door.

"Hey, Mama J." He kissed her on the cheek.

"Hey, son."

"Are you going skating with us?" he asked with a straight face.

"You've got jokes, huh?" She affectionately hit his arm. "I had some free time and decided to drop by, that's all."

Julia sat at the kitchen table. "Is Todd going with you guys?

"No, just me and Ms. Know It All," Brian answered.

"I wish Todd's fine self was going," Shay smirked.

Brian ignored Shay's comment and offered Julia some fruit. She attempted to refuse, but he wouldn't have it. "That's my little brother in there and we Penningtons like to eat."

Julia knew if she refused to eat, he'd be on the phone with Reggie, so she ate the banana and grapes while she chatted with them.

Brian was happy he made it through his freshman year with a 4.0 GPA. He'd gotten used to the California weather and wasn't looking forward to going back to the Arizona desert.

Shay was preparing for her junior year. By the time classes resumed, she vowed to have a major. She would never tell him, but Shay admired Brian. He was almost a year younger than her, but he knew exactly what he wanted to do with his life.

After a trip to the bathroom, Julia prepared to leave.

"Brian, you and Todd are doing a good job with the house."

"Thanks, Mama J." They walked her outside.

"Tell Alysse and Mark we said, hello."

"Sure thing."

Julia watched Brian and Shay in her rearview mirror as she drove down Campus Drive. To her, they acted like boyfriend and girlfriend, with their arms wrapped around each other's waist. Come to think of it, she'd never heard either of them refer to the other as a relative by marriage. Reggie always introduced Shay as his daughter, and Julia, Brian as her son. But with Brian and Shay, it was always "fathead" or "Ms. Know It All" and sometimes an occasional "friend."

Her cell phone distracted her thoughts. It was Chantel.

"Hey, sis, what's up?" she answered.

"Your baby shower, that's what," Chantel answered.

"I forgot to tell you, the ladies at the church are throwing me one the last Saturday in July, why don't the family join in?"

"That's a good idea, because your old behind don't need two showers." Chantel laughed.

"Remember, you're older than I am."

"But at least I know when to shut the baby factory down."

"If you had a man as fine as mine, you'd open back up for business," Julia joked.

"I know that's right. Why do you think I had four babies for Greg? That man was just too fine!" Chantel laughed.

"Seriously, girl, I'm happy for you. Reggie's a good man and he's going to be good to his baby."

Julia rubbed her stomach. "He already is."

"Have you chosen a name yet?"

"Yes, but I'm not telling until he gets here."

"You're not still afraid, are you?" Chantel asked.

"No, I just want to wait until the baby's born, that's all,"

Julia explained. She hoped that was all there was to her hesitation.

* * *

Julia was sitting up on the side of her bed, rubbing olive oil on her extended belly when Reggie arrived home that evening.

"Hey, beautiful." He kissed her lips. "Did you miss me this afternoon?"

"Of course, I did," she replied, enjoying the feel of his hands rubbing her stomach. Reggie smiled when he felt his unborn son respond to his touch. "Honey, we need to talk," Julia said.

"What's on your mind, sweetheart?"

"Our children."

"So you've noticed it, too?" he asked, standing to his feet and unbuttoning his shirt.

"What?" Julia wanted to see if he was thinking the same thing she was.

"That Brian and Shay are attracted to each other."

"Yes. Did you know he gave her a key to the house?"

"No. Did you know they have keys to each other's cars?"

"This is worse than I thought," Julia said, positioning herself against the bed pillows. "How do you feel about this? I mean, we're married, is that okay?"

"It's awkward, but I can't say that it's wrong," Reggie said, stepping out of his pants. "We're married, but technically they are not kin. They see us as husband and wife, but they don't consider themselves brother and sister. And why should they? Brian and Shay have known each other for barely a year and they have never lived as siblings. I accept Shay as a daughter and you, Brian as a son. But that's our relationship with them. That has nothing to do with the relationship between them."

Julia wasn't convinced. "Why not? Shouldn't it?"

"When Brian looks at Shay, he doesn't see a sister, he sees a young woman. Shay sees a young man. They are not children. They're young adults whose parents just happen to be married."

"I don't know, Reggie," Julia said, shaking her head. "People might not accept that."

"What is there to accept? They haven't admitted the attraction yet. They're more like buddies. And what people will accept is not important. Brian and Shay must be content with any choices they make for themselves."

"I know Shay's in denial. I watched her get mad the other day because one of her girlfriends from school gave Brian her number."

"And Brian told Todd not to pursue Shay," Reggie added.

Julia still wasn't convinced. "Won't this put us in an awkward position? This could cause problems for you and I."

"Nothing is coming between us." Reggie extended his hand to Julia and she accepted it, allowing him to lift her from the bed. He turned her so that her back was to him. Wrapping his arms around her body, he spoke seriously. "What happens or doesn't happen with Brian and Shay is between them. If anything does come of their attraction, it will happen without any interference from us. We will pray that if they do decide to have a relationship, they will do it in a Godly manner and for the right purpose, but that's all. We have our own lives to live. I plan to spend the rest of my life keeping you happy."

"I'm pretty happy right now." Julia moaned when he kissed her neck.

He stroked her body. "What about now?"

"Very happy."

Chapter 40

With six weeks left in her pregnancy, Julia and Reggie spent their Saturdays setting up the baby's room. Brian helped his dad paint and Tyrone assembled baby furniture. Nikki and Shay put the borders around and hung pictures. Julia did absolutely nothing. That's the way her husband wanted it. The only thing he allowed her to do was communicate what things she wanted and where she wanted them.

After Reggie and Tyrone brought in the last piece of furniture, Reggie took a moment to admire his wife. Her nose had spread and her feet were swollen, but for him, nothing had changed. She was beautiful, almost glowing, sitting in the new rocking chair rubbing her swollen belly. He could tell the baby's movements were making her uncomfortable.

Squatting down in front of her, he moved his hand over her stomach. The baby must have recognized his father's touch, because as soon as Reggie's hand made contact, the baby relaxed.

She smiled. "He knows your touch."

"What about his mother? Does she remember my touch?" He'd given her a full-body massage two nights prior.

"Vaguely," she flirted.

"I'll refresh your memory later." He kissed her hand, then her arm.

Shay cleared her throat to remind them that they were not alone. Brian didn't seem to mind.

Julia ignored her and continued flirting with her husband. "Why wait until later?" Her tongue brushed against her lips, sending him an invitation that he quickly accepted.

"That's nasty! I'm going to be sick!" Shay exclaimed.

Lately, Julia's tolerance level had dropped to an all-time low. If Shay didn't know, she was about to find out. Julia pushed Reggie away and maneuvered from the chair.

"LaShay Seana Hampton," she said sternly. "You are not a little girl anymore. You are a grown woman who happens to live at home with her grown mother and her mother's husband. And your grown mother enjoys doing 'grown' things. How do you think you got here? Stop behaving like a prissy spoiled brat and grow up!"

Shay's mouth fell open and wouldn't close, even after her mother left the room.

This was the first time Brian had known Shay to be speechless, so he made the most of it.

"Would you like me to help you find it?" he asked her.

She rolled her neck at him. "Find what?"

"Your face, you seem to have lost it." Brian laughed.

Reggie withheld his laughter. "Brian, that's not fair." He turned to Shay. "I'm sure your mother didn't mean to embarrass you. She's been a little irritable lately because of the pregnancy."

"Whatever." She rolled her eyes at Brian and stormed from the room.

Later that evening at dinner, Julia acted as if nothing had happened.

* * *

August 14

Frank held true to his word and had the renovations completed by the third week in July. The True Worship Community Center was ready to open for business. Reggie was happy and Julia was miserable.

She was only four days overdue, but she was sick and tired of being pregnant. She wanted her body back. She was tired of being uncomfortable and the countless trips to the bathroom. The summer heat only made matters worse. She spent most of her time indoors in the air conditioning and she fought constantly to control her temper. Every little thing seemed to bother her, including Reggie. She loved him with all her heart, but lately she didn't like him very much. The night before, she kicked him onto the floor, because he was breathing too loud.

She'd turned forty-two, two days ago, but she refused to leave the house, because in her eyes as long as she was still pregnant, there was nothing to celebrate.

"God, please help me," she prayed that morning as she dressed for church. "I can't go on like this."

Reggie said a prayer of his own, after voicing he didn't know how much longer he could tolerate her mood swings.

In church, Julia waved at her parents, sitting next to Mother Elsie. They were in town for Julia's delivery. After her daughters gave birth, Ana usually stayed with them until they recovered. Julia being forty-two didn't make a difference; Ana was still going to take care of her daughter.

Julia blushed when Papa blew her a kiss. As Reggie started his sermon, she tried to get comfortable, but was having a hard time. The baby must have agreed with what his father was saying, because from the moment Reggie started speaking, the baby moved nonstop. She adjusted herself in her chair to relieve the pressure she felt in her back.

Minister Watson, noticing she was uncomfortable, asked, "First Lady, are you all right?"

"Yes, I just need to use the restroom."

Minister Watson helped her to her feet, but before she could take a step, the warm liquid ran down her legs. Minister Watson stood behind her and walked her into Reggie's office.

Reggie was preaching, so he didn't know his wife's water had just broken. When he saw Ana, Angie and Shay stand and walk toward his office, he looked back for Julia. When he didn't see her, he quickly brought his sermon to a close and turned the service over to his ministerial staff.

He found her in the bathroom, changing her clothes. "Sweetheart, what's the matter?"

"My water broke," she answered timidly.

"How do you feel?" He helped her with her clothing.

"I'm not having contractions yet."

"Are you ready to go to the hospital?"

"Angie and Mama said I should and Shay has already called Doctor Davidson." She lowered her head.

He held her face to his. "I don't want you to worry about the delivery. Everything is going to be fine. I'll be there with you the entire time. Do you remember what you told me the night of Shay's accident?"

"I think so," she said just above a whisper.

"You told me when you didn't have any strength, that I gave you some of mine. Nothing has changed. Baby, I'm right here."

The love she felt from him was so strong; it brought tears to her eyes. She kissed him. "Sorry about last night."

"You'll pay for that later." She knew exactly what he meant.

"Yeah, in six weeks," she laughed.

Three hours later, both Julia's smile and sense of humor were long gone. For the last hour, her contractions came every five minutes and seemed to intensify with each one. She looked around the delivery room; it was filled with the women in her life.

All of her sisters, and Nikki, were there to support her, rotating turns. Sisters-in-law, Alaina and Janice, were also present in the waiting room. And, of course, Ana and Shay. She felt love all around her, especially on the right side where her man was stationed.

Always true to his word, Reggie never left her side. He coached her breathing, rubbed her back, and wiped the sweat from her forehead or whatever she needed him to do. As the contractions intensified, her grip on his hand was almost unbearable, but he never let go.

Dr. Davidson examined her again. "It won't be long now, you're fully dilated and one- hundred percent effaced. It's time to start pushing," she announced happily.

Julia asked the nurse to get Angie and Shay from the Simone-packed waiting room.

"Brian just got here," Shay informed Reggie.

He acknowledged her statement with only a nod, while he helped Julia get into the birthing position. Silently, he prayed for her.

For the next thirty minutes, Julia pushed hard with each contraction, which was now every minute. Reggie encouraged her with each contraction. Watching her suffer, he made a decision. His wife would never experience this agony again.

Angie and Shay cheered as the head peeked through.

"You're almost done, Julia," Dr. Davidson called out and guided the baby's shoulders.

"I'm tired," she responded breathlessly.

"Just a little while longer, sweetheart," Reggie encouraged.

"I can't. I'm too tired."

"You can do it, Mama."

Julia braced for one last push. She gave it everything she had until her relief came. She held her breath, then listened to the noise.

Josiah Michael Pennington came into the world with a loud scream. Dr. Davidson held him up, so Julia could see him.

"You did it, baby! Thank you. I love you." Reggie cried and showered her face with kisses.

Dr. Davidson called Reggie over and Shay videotaped him cutting the baby's umbilical cord.

"Is he all right?" Julia asked her sister.

"He's perfect," Angie answered.

Shay's camera stayed focused on her little brother while the nurses cleaned and weighed him. "Mama, no wonder you were so tired, this boy weighs eight pounds," she said with amazement.

Dr. Davidson still had work to perform on Julia. Shay took the opportunity to update the waiting room.

Angie started to follow her, but stopped after she glanced back at Julia. Her medical training took over. Julia was breathing too fast and she looked faint. Angie studied the monitors; her heart rate was much too fast.

Watching Julia's color rapidly disappear, Reggie grew scared. The look of panic on Angie's face confirmed his fears.

"OH JESUS!" Angie screamed a second before Julia stopped breathing.

Chapter 41

Inside the waiting room, Ana sat quietly, while Shay passed the camcorder around.

"Darling, what's wrong?" Carey Sr. asked.

"Papa, something's not right." Ana was certain.

Like always, Brian and Shay were getting along perfectly.

"He looks like me," Brian affirmed.

"No, he doesn't, he's cute." Shay acted like a juvenile and stuck out her tongue.

"I guess you think he resembles you, huh?"

"Of course, he looks exactly like me."

"Code Blue, Labor and Delivery Room Nine." The waiting crowd was too busy celebrating to hear the overhead announcement.

"The only thing he has of yours is that big forehead," Brain retorted back at Shay.

Shay was about to let Brian have it. "Why don't you take…"

"She's not breathing!" Angie screamed as she ran into the waiting room. What she said didn't register with the group, because they continued smiling. Everyone, except Ana.

"Who's not breathing?" Mike asked his wife.

"Julia's not breathing," she yelled.

The reality of her aunt's words overwhelmed Shay. "MAMA!" she screamed and took off running. Mike and CJ reached her just as she was about to burst into the room.

"You can't go in there, let them handle it," Mike ordered.

Shay fell into her uncle's arms and sobbed uncontrollably.

An uncomfortable quiet filled the waiting room. In a few short minutes, the smiles and laughter everyone shared were replaced with tears and prayers. Ana still sat quietly, but now she also rocked back and forth.

"Where's my dad?" Brian finally asked.

"I'll take you to him," Angie answered. "Tyrone, you may want to come."

They followed Angie, but they really didn't need her assistance. Reggie and Shay's cries filled the entire ward.

Brian found his dad on the floor opposite Shay, outside of Julia's room. With his face buried in his hands, like Shay, he cried uncontrollably.

"We should clear this space," Angie said. Mike and CJ guided Shay back to the waiting room.

Tyrone assisted Brian with his dad. Once in the waiting room, Reggie collapsed in a chair. Brian sat in the chair between Shay and his dad. Shay placed her head on his shoulder and cried some more as he tried to comfort her and support his dad.

The sudden turn of events was unreal to Reggie. One minute he'd cut his new son's umbilical cord, and the next minute the love of his life stopped breathing right in front of him. He'd never forget the look in her eyes as she slipped away from him.

A few minutes later, Dr. Davidson surveyed the waiting room. "Reggie, Lashay and Doctor Angelique Sorenson, I need to speak to you privately."

Reggie and Shay quickly stood. Brian stood behind them both.

"Doctor, whatever is wrong with my daughter you can tell all of us, we're family," Carey Sr. stated.

Reggie wiped his face and nodded his consent. He didn't know what she was about to tell him, but he wanted his family with him. Needed his family with him.

Dr. Davidson inhaled and exhaled deeply. "Julia has a pulmonary embolism, meaning she has an obstruction lodged in her lungs and it's blocking the blood supply to her lungs. She's breathing now, with assistance, but she needs surgery immediately to remove the blockage. We're prepared to perform an embolectomy right now, if you give the consent. Julia signed prior authorization for the three of you to make medical decisions for her, in the event she could not."

Angie knew what was coming next and explained the procedure to the family in layman's terms.

"The operation has become relatively common, but there's a chance something will go wrong, depending on the size and exact location of the embolus. In the event that Julia codes on the table, do you want us to resuscitate her?"

Reggie didn't hesitate; he quickly signed the documents. "You do everything medically possible to save my wife."

Dr. Davidson turned to leave.

Ana finally spoke. "We'd like a moment with her before she goes into surgery."

"All right, but make it quick, she's being prepped. Doctor Lawrence and the surgical team are ready to go."

Right before Julia left for the operating room, Ana and Carey Simone gathered their six children, who were present along with Reggie, Shay and Brian. They encircled her bed and held hands.

"God blessed me with eight children, and not a one of them will leave this earth before I do!" Ana proclaimed and went to work.

Chapter 42

A fter receiving Tyrone's call, Minister Johnson informed the members at the evening service of their Pastor and First Lady's plight. Regular service was suspended as the prayer warriors went to work. To make sure she'd heard right from the Lord the first time, Mother Elsie prayed for five minutes, then she stopped.

So many church members showed up at the hospital, they filled the main lobby downstairs and blanketed the front entrance. They were courteous though, and left the surgery waiting room for the family.

The True Worship family expressed the genuine love they held for their leaders. They prayed non-stop and the hospitality group supplied food for the family, so they wouldn't have to leave.

Tyrone tried to comfort Nikki, but he was scared for his friend. He knew if anything happened to Julia, part of Reggie would die with her. She had literally given Reggie his life back.

Tyrone stared at his friend; he seemed to have aged over the last hour. His eyes were red and sunken, his skin was ashen, and his shoulders slumped. His eyes were sad and he looked defeated. Inwardly, Tyrone prayed without ceasing.

Nikki tried to think of a time when she didn't have Julia in her life. She couldn't find one. For twenty years, they'd been part of each other's lives. Julia was the sister she never had. And she took care of her; Julia never gave up on her. She never made Nikki feel bad because she didn't have as much money as she did or that she came from alcoholic parents. Julia just loved her. "God, please keep her safe," Nikki prayed.

Tears ran down Shay's face as she watched her little brother through the nursery window. The nurse invited her in, but she refused. He was so little and precious. She'd never admit it to Brian, but little Josiah did resemble him and Reggie. The cute left dimple served as the family trademark.

Her thoughts turned to her mother. She loved and admired her mother. To her, Julia Renee Simone-Pennington was the strongest woman in the world. She'd proven to Shay that she could do anything. Shay had seen firsthand the obstacles her mother had to face and conquer in order to provide a good life for her. All she wanted was for her mother to be happy. And Julia was happy. "It can't end like this."

Brian quietly entered the nursery.

Back in the waiting room, Reggie suddenly grew uncomfortable when he finally raised his head and surveyed his surroundings. The room was filled with his family. All of Julia's married siblings were present and being comforted by their spouses. He had no one. He wanted to hold his wife. His anxiety overtook him and he left.

"Where are you going, son?" Carey Sr. called after him.

"To the nursery, Papa."

Brian wanted to comfort Shay, but he didn't know how. The only thing worse than seeing his dad all broken up, was seeing Shay fall apart. Shay was his buddy and his friend. Sure they argued all the time, but that was just their way.

"It'll all work out," he said and put his arm around her shoulder.

She sniffled. "How can you be so sure?"

"Because I know Mama J, she wouldn't go out like this. Not with all these prayers going up." He handed her some tissue.

"Brian, I don't know what I would do if anything happens to my mother. You know I never knew my father. She's all I have."

Brian pulled Shay into his arms and held her while she cried. Shay relaxed to the touch of his hands against her back. For some strange reason, his arms were calming.

Brian wanted to make her feel better and he was doing a good job. He felt her body relax and her sobs cease. "I'll never leave you, Shay. You will always have me," Brian whispered.

She lifted her head, so she could see his face. "Promise?" she asked.

"Promise," Brian answered right before their lips met. They separated just as Reggie opened the door. Shay turned and ran out the door.

"She's not handling this well," Reggie stated to Brian.

Brian exhaled deeply. "No, I don't think any of us are."

Reggie stayed in the nursery with his sons until his cell phone vibrated. He read the text, then ran outside.

"She made it!" Nikki met them at the elevator.

He rounded the corner to where his family was and listened as Dr. Davidson gave the status report.

"Julia's a strong woman. If she hadn't made that last push when she did, there's a good chance neither she nor the baby would be here. The blockage was larger than we thought, but we were able to remove it. She's not breathing completely on her own yet. We're going to slowly wean her off of the oxygen."

"When can we see her?" Everyone wanted to know.

"When she comes out of recovery, we're going to keep her there longer than normal, just to make sure she doesn't have a relapse, but after that she's going to the sixth floor."

"You might as well take her up there now and turn off the oxygen because my baby is not having a relapse! God doesn't perform relapse healings, when He does something He gets it right the first time." Reggie's strong proclamation drew "Amens" and shouts of praise.

Dr. Davidson smiled her agreement. "I hear you, Reverend, but I have to follow hospital protocol."

The waiting room sounded like Sunday morning worship service as the Simone family sent up praises of thanks to God. They hugged, kissed and cried.

Ana Simone spoke up. "Y'all don't listen to anything I say. Humph, I told you my baby wasn't leaving here before I do."

Everyone in the room wanted to remind her that she was just as worried about Julia as they were, but knew it was a lost cause.

"Whatever you say, Mama. You're the boss," the room agreed.

* * *

Reggie and Tyrone went to the main lobby to deliver the good news to the True Worship family.

Pastor Reggie addressed them. "Thank you for your prayers and acts of kindness toward my family. You are the best church a pastor could ask for." Reggie looked around and was surprised when he didn't see Mother Elsie.

By midnight, Julia was sleeping on the sixth floor. Her breathing and heart activity were still being monitored by machines, but she was breathing on her own to the surprise of the medical staff.

Before her family members left for the night, they each spent a few minutes with her. Mike and Angie were the last to leave.

"You were wonderful today, Reggie. Thank you for being there for my sister. I'll check in with you later," Angie said right before she left.

It was just after 3:00 a.m. and everyone was gone except Nikki and Shay. They were asleep in the waiting room.

Exhausted, Reggie sat next to Julia's bed. With his finger, he outlined her face. After all she'd endured, the pregnancy, labor and an emergency surgery, she was still the most beautiful woman in the world to him. If it was possible, she was more beautiful now than before. He removed the hospital cap from her head and stroked her hair. That always helped him to relax. Careful not to touch her incision, he leaned forward and kissed her lips.

Watching her sleep, he reflected on their short life together. So much had happened since the day he walked into her Emery Bay office. He remembered their first Valentine's Day and the gold cross he wore around his neck. He remembered the day she brought Brian back into his life. He remembered the day he proposed to her and how happy he was at her acceptance. Images of her singing as she walked down the aisle brought tears to his eyes. In his ears, he could hear her singing:

♪*I believe this is gonna be what you want it to be*♪

He lowered his head and tenderly mouthed the ending of the song. "Thank you, baby. Thank you, baby. I just love you, baby."

"When I lose my way, your love comes smiling on me." Julia's voice was so faint that he thought he was still daydreaming.

"I love you, baby. I just love you, baby," she continued.

Reggie lifted his head, "I love y..." Her eyes were finally open and she gave him a faint smile. "Sweetheart, my love, you're awake." He kissed her again.

"How's the baby?"

"He's fine, now that his mother is better."

She didn't understand his statement. She moved her hand and tried to massage the soreness she felt in her chest, but the bandages prevented her. Her confusion showed on her face.

"What happened to my chest?"

He held her hand and recapped the missing hours for her.

"Oh, my God, I almost died." Her tears flowed.

"But you didn't. God knew I was not ready to live without you."

"Will you ever be?"

"No. Woman, I love you forever."

"Me, too."

She inquired about the baby again. "Can I see the baby? I haven't held him yet." She was weak, but excited about holding her son.

"With your incision, you may not be able to for a few days."

"Oh." She didn't try to hide her disappointment.

"I'll be right back." He went to the nurse's station, determined to keep his wife happy. When he returned, he adjusted her bed so that she was sitting up. A few minutes later, a nurse from the nursery rolled in a basinet and parked it alongside her bed. She was happy again. Her husband picked up their son, and laid him in the arm opposite her incision. Reggie supported Josiah with his hand to keep the pressure off of Julia.

Tears ran down her cheeks once more, as she held her son for the first time. She rubbed his head, touched his ears and counted his fingers. He was the perfect combination of the two of them. Just as her husband said, he was the fruit of their love. "I see he has the Pennington trademark," she said, referring to his left dimple.

"Do you know what today's date is?" he asked.

She thought for a second. "It's August fifteenth."

"And that makes it the middle of August."

He smiled and Julia kissed her handsome baby boy. "Mother Elsie was right again," they said in unison.

Epilogue

Six-week-old baby Josiah sat wide-eyed in his carrier, watching his parents run around frantically.

"Do you have everything?" Reggie asked her again.

"I think so." Julia felt like she was packing for vacation, instead of going to church with her new son for the first time.

"Did you pack an extra blanket, just in case it gets cold?"

"Reggie, we are in the middle of an Indian summer, it is not going to get cold."

"What about his pacifier?"

"Oops. I'll get it from the nursery and meet you in the car," Julia said.

Reggie picked up his son, gave him a kiss and headed out. A minute later, he returned for the diaper bag he'd forgotten and an extra blanket.

With Josiah securely in the SUV, Julia came with not only his pacifier, but also a few of his favorite toys. "Sweetheart, he's going to church, not daycare."

Julia waved off her husband's comment and got into the vehicle. Pastor and First Lady Pennington held hands as they drove down Interstate 680. October was definitely their month. For the third consecutive first Sunday in October, something new and exciting was happening in their lives.

Julia leaned over and kissed her husband on the cheek.

"I wonder what the next October will bring."

"I don't know," he answered, "but I'm ready to collect."

"What are you talking about?"

"It's been six weeks and five days; it's time for you to pay up." He flashed her a knowing look.

She couldn't have agreed more. "Whatever you say. You're the boss."